For Alison & Erin

HUNTING
THE HANGMAN

HOWARD LINSKEY

NO EXIT PRESS

First published in 2017 by No Exit Press,
an imprint of Oldcastle Books Ltd,
PO Box 394, Harpenden, AL5 1XJ, UK
noexit.co.uk

Editor: Steven Mair

ISBN 978-1-84344-950-8 (print)
978-1-84344-951-5 (epub)

2 4 6 8 10 9 7 5 3 1

Typeset in 11.5pt Minion Pro
by Avocet Typeset, Somerton, Somerset TA11 6RT
Printed in Great Britain by Clays Ltd, St Ives plc

For more information about Crime Fiction go to @crimetimeuk

Get FREE crime books and other great offers from No Exit Press

Hitler's heir is in Prague.
He is going to kill eleven million people.
Two men have sworn to assassinate the Hangman.
Even if it costs them everything.

Introduction

I can vividly remember the moment when this book began to take shape, in my mind at least. Back in the year 2000, I came home from my day job and turned on the History Channel half way through a documentary on the assassination of Reinhard Heydrich; a man I admit I was only dimly aware of.

By the end of that programme, I was hooked on the tale of Operation Anthropoid, one of the most thrilling and extraordinary missions of the Second World War. I started devouring books on the Third Reich and the SOE, trainers of Heydrich's would-be assassins, plus anything I could get my hands on about the Nazi occupation of the Czech capital and the mission to kill the Nazi general. I was determined to recount this story in a novel.

The cast of characters features virtually every senior figure in Nazi Germany, as well as Winston Churchill, the Czech President in exile, Eduard Beneš, the head of his secret service, and the incredibly courageous members of resistance networks in Prague, who lived under constant threat of exposure, torture, and summary execution, and of course Gabčík and Kubiš, the men chosen for the mission. I flew to Prague and went to the key locations in this book, including the Church of St Cyril and St Methodius; now a shrine to the men and women involved in this story, visited by thousands from all over the world each year.

Reinhard Heydrich is perhaps not as well-known as other leading Nazis like Himmler, Göring, Hess, Bormann or

Goebbels but he was an immensely powerful, much-feared, senior figure in Hitler's inner circle and considered his eventual heir. Heydrich was Heinrich Himmler's deputy and the head of the Reich Main Security Office, which oversaw the Gestapo. He was also Reichsprotektor of Bohemia and Moravia, which made him dictator of the former Czech territories, holding the life or death of its entire Slav population in his hands, ruling over them all from Hradčany Castle and executing so many (ninety-two in his first three days and thousands were to follow) he became known as 'The Butcher of Prague' and 'The Hangman'. He is also universally acknowledged as the true architect of the Holocaust. Hitler called him 'the man with the Iron Heart'.

What struck me most about Reinhard Heydrich was his lack of compassion, empathy or need for friends of any kind. Even in the SS he was known as 'the blond beast', yet he was not without talent. Heydrich was a virtuoso violinist and an expert skier, an Olympic standard fencer and a man who flew combat missions during the early years of the war, so he did not lack courage. His obvious abilities were almost entirely devoted to his own ruthless self-advancement, however. When he was tasked with the extermination of an entire race by Adolf Hitler, it seems he never once doubted the morality of the undertaking, merely fretting about the length of time it would take him to accomplish the systematic murder of eleven million men, women and children of Jewish origin. At Wannsee, Heydrich chaired the only meeting from which minutes have survived to prove genocide was the Nazis' preferred 'final solution' to the Jewish question.

If I found Heydrich to be a fascinating, albeit almost wholly evil character, I was just as intrigued by Josef Gabčík and Jan Kubiš, the men who volunteered to kill 'the Hangman', for entirely different reasons. These two incredibly brave individuals risked everything to strike back on behalf of a defeated nation, in a move designed to preserve its very existence, and the more I learned about them, the more determined I became to tell their story.

It took me three and a half years to research then write the first draft of *Hunting the Hangman*. The book secured me a literary agent and a year or so later we were sitting down with an editor interested in publishing the book. I then became bogged down in interminable rewrites, including the creation of fictitious episodes that 'fleshed out' the story, partly at the behest of the publisher and partly because I was trying to second guess what he wanted, which is always a risky business. I ended up with a bloated, part-fact, part-fiction novel that didn't really work and, along the way, the publisher's interest waned.

Undeterred, I went on to write six more books and, when each of them in turn was published, I promised myself I would one day return to this story and finally do it justice. Prompted partly by the seventy fifth anniversary falling in 2017 and the release of not one but two Hollywood movies (*Anthropoid* and *The Man with the Iron Heart* that no matter how good, could not possibly tell the whole story), I finally put aside the time to do this. I blew the dust off *Hunting the Hangman* and rewrote it meticulously, removing every fictitious part of it and simply sticking to the core story. To the best of my knowledge, everything that happens in this book actually occurred, though I obviously had to imagine dialogue between the characters and I took one liberty, by setting a scene in Kutná Hora that likely happened elsewhere in reality. When you reach that point in the book you will realise why I found this location irresistible.

The story of the attempt by Gabčík and Kubiš to bring down one of the most powerful men in the Third Reich and its terrible aftermath needed no other embellishment from me. Thankfully I found a publisher in No Exit who agreed and shared my fascination with Operation Anthropoid, for which I am supremely grateful. So here it is; one of the most exciting, exhilarating, dramatic and devastating incidents of the Second World War and all of it true. I hope you find this story as intriguing as I do.

Howard Linskey – May 2017

Cast of Characters

Josef Gabčík & Jan Kubiš	chosen to carry out the assassination of Reinhard Heydrich for Operation Anthropoid
Reinhard Heydrich	SS OberGruppenführer, Reichsprotektor Bohemia and Moravia, Chief of the RSHA (Reich Main Security Office), Himmler's deputy, architect of the Holocaust
Anton Svoboda	originally selected for Operation Athropoid
Eduard Beneš	Exiled President of Czechoslovakia
Edward Taborsky	Private Secretary to President Beneš
František Moravec	Head of the Czechoslovak Secret Service in exile
Emil Strankmüller	Major; Moravec's deputy; recruited Kubiš and Gabčík for Operation Anthropoid
Winston Churchill	British Prime Minister
Anthony Eden	British Foreign Secretary
Ron Hockey	Flight Lieutenant, RAF; pilot of Halifax Bomber used to parachute Gabčík and Kubiš into occupied territory
Anna Malinová	girlfriend of Jan Kubiš
Liběna Fafek	girlfriend of Josef Gabčík

Paul Thümmel	'Agent 54' – German double agent who spied for Czech secret service
Silver A Team:	Lieutenant Alfréd Bartoš, Sergeant Josef Valčík & Corporal Jiří Potůček
Silver B Team	Vladimír Škacha & Jan Zemek
Outdistance Team	Lieutenant Adolf Opálka, Sergeant Karel Čurda & Corporal Ivan Kolařík
Bioscope Team	Sergeant Josef Bublík & Sergeant Jan Hrubý
Tin Team	Sergeant Jaroslav Švarc & Sergeant Ludvík Cupal
Jindra Resistance Network Prague	Ladislav Vaněk, Jan Zelenka, 'Aunt Marie' Moravec, Ata Moravec, František Šafařík, Josef Novotný
Father Vladimír Petřek	Church of St Cyril & St Methodius
Adolf Hitler	Führer, Nazi Germany
Rochus Misch	Hitler's bodyguard
Heinrich Himmler	Reichsführer SS
Walter Schellenberg	Head of the Reich's Foreign Intelligence Service
Karl Frank	State Secretary Bohemia and Moravia – Heydrich's deputy in Prague
Martin Bormann	Adolf Hitler's private secretary, head of the Reich Chancellery
Adolf Eichmann	organiser of Heydrich's Wannsee Conference
Heinz Pannwitz	Head of Anti-sabotage Section Prague Gestapo
Max Rostock	SS Hauptsturmführer tasked with destroying Lidice
Lina Heydrich	Wife of Reinhard Heydrich
Johannes Klein	Heydrich's driver

1

'The people need wholesome fear.
They want to fear something.
They want someone to frighten them
and make them shudderingly submissive'

Ernst Röhm, Head of the SA (Hitler's Brown Shirts),
Assassinated by the SS on the Night of the Long Knives

Aston Abbotts, Buckinghamshire, Autumn 1941

'So it's murder?' he asked reasonably.

'Not murder, no,' his president answered.

'An assassination then,' František Moravec held up his hands to indicate he had no objection to this, 'just so we're clear.'

'Call it what you will but never call it murder,' answered Beneš, 'an execution perhaps or you *could* name it war,' the exiled Czech leader told the head of his secret service, 'if you prefer.'

'Let's call it justice?' suggested Moravec but Beneš was already tired of this.

'Suppose we simply call it *what must be done.*'

Moravec seemed happiest with that definition for he had merely been testing his leader's resolve. 'But how to do it?' he mused, as if asking himself this and not Beneš.

'How indeed?' said Beneš. 'That part I will leave up to you.'

The President looked smaller here with everything hemmed into his office in the old abbey at Aston Abbotts. His desk was an unfeasible clutter of transcripts, memos and telegrams and he seemed reluctant to allow any of them to be filed away. Every available inch of it was covered in paper. A large bookcase was fixed to the wall behind him and it towered above his shoulders but there was no space here for books. It too had been commandeered for the papers of state. They were piled high in horizontal stacks or wedged together vertically, in such close order that their spines had warped under the pressure of the confined space they occupied.

'It won't be easy,' said Moravec.

'I understand.'

'You want to send men back to our conquered capital to kill the most senior Nazi in the country,' said Moravec, 'a man with the rank of a general who rules like a king. Heydrich isn't just a Nazi puppet. The man ranks second only to Heinrich Himmler. He is Hitler's personal favourite.'

'I would go further,' said Beneš. 'I'd say it is likely Hitler regards Heydrich as his heir.'

'The next generation,' agreed Moravec, 'of the Thousand-Year-Reich he has promised his people.'

Beneš suddenly rose from his seat and crossed the room. It was a restless movement with no specific purpose behind it. He stared out of his window at the garden of his English bolthole. The village of Aston Abbotts was not a new dwelling place; it was mentioned in the Domesday Book but you could walk its entire length in a little over five minutes. There were neat little nineteenth century houses here, tied cottages, a couple of ancient pubs and a Norman church with a stone memorial to an earlier conflict. The former abbey was as good a spot as any for the exiled President's hideaway. Guards patrolled the area discreetly or held back in the shadows provided by the dark grey stone of the house – and at least one would be in permanent occupation of the tiny, picturesque lodge, a thatched and white-washed cottage by the gate. 'Then it would be an even bigger blow,' he told Moravec purposefully, 'one they would feel in Berlin.'

'What about the British?' asked Moravec. 'Are they going to help us?'

'They will,' said Beneš firmly and Moravec realised his President had yet to ask Churchill for his blessing. 'I know this is no ordinary mission, František,' Beneš continued, 'our target will be heavily guarded.'

'An army couldn't kill Heydrich,' said Moravec and his President seemed concerned he might have already admitted defeat until he added, 'but two men might.'

'Only two?'

'With help from others.'

Beneš seemed satisfied Moravec had already been giving the mission serious thought. 'And you could find me such men?'

'There are many who wish for nothing more than the opportunity to continue the struggle against the Nazis, so yes, I can find you two men.' He spoke as if that was the easy part.

'But they must be the right men?' Beneš realised what he was getting at.

'We'll only get one chance. Fail and Heydrich won't travel anywhere again without an armoured convoy around him.'

'Thousands came to England to continue the struggle when our country fell,' Beneš reasoned, 'there must be exceptional men among them.'

'There are,' Moravec agreed.

'Get them then,' Beneš ordered and he turned back to the window to give Moravec his cue. Their meeting was over. The rain that had been threatening for hours finally came and thick droplets padded against the window outside. Moravec made as if to leave.

'František,' Beneš stopped him, 'make sure they understand.'

'That they might not be coming back?' and Beneš nodded.

'Good men would know that already,' he assured his President.

2

Josef Gabčík was playing at soldiers again. He had just leapt from an imaginary landing craft, an L-shaped jetty yards from a Scottish beach, into an admittedly very real sea and was now wading towards the shore, chest deep in the salty surf.

Using his peripheral vision, he noticed he was at the head of a dozen men who had jumped into the water. There were a few gasps from his comrades, and a number of loud curses at the initial shock of the cold ocean, but the swearing strangely cheered him, coming as it did in his native tongue. He ignored the icy chill of the water, the salt in his eyes and the burn of the pack's straps on his shoulders, and pressed on.

Gabčík held his rifle high above his head with both arms, trying not to stumble on the uneven, shifting surface of the seabed, bending forward to allow for the 40lb pack full of rocks that was strapped to his back. He advanced as quickly as the buffeting of the ocean would allow.

A few more steps and he was pulling himself free from the grip of the water, which tugged at his soaking fatigues, weighing him down, and he became instantly aware of the harsh cries of the two British NCOs waiting on the shingle.

'Move yourselves! Move yourselves!!'

'Get out of there now! This is not a fuckin' tea dance!'

Both men were with the Special Operations Executive and, with the sadistic enthusiasm to which Gabčík had become accustomed, they were hell bent on turning him into a commando. As soon as he was free from the surf, he sprinted across the cove in a stumbling run, feet sinking into the shingle, running like a child trapped in a bad dream who cannot get away fast enough. His lungs heaved under the exertion and the breath caught in his throat, before it was expelled in little clouds of vapour that were immediately left behind him as he powered forward.

Now he was almost there, he could make out the giant shadow of the cliff face in front of him, even though his head was down to avoid the pretend bullets of an imaginary machine gun they were assured was in the cliff tops.

'Diggah! Diggah! Diggah!' screamed the Glaswegian corporal. 'Yer fuckin' deed Kubiš!! Unless you get yer bastad heed doon!!'

Like Gabčík, Jan Kubiš would barely have understood a word from the Scotsman's mouth but he would have easily picked up the meaning. That's what it was like here; a few half comprehended phrases of command were all they had to cling to. That and a desperate yearning to one day return to their homeland to fight the Germans who occupied it.

Till then their world was a completely foreign place. These defeated Czech soldiers awoke each morning in a Scottish barrack block in Mallaig, to be ordered around by officers, they could just about understand. As for the NCOs, they were a grim bunch of hard soldiers, with varied and unusual communication skills. Everything was barked or yelled in a guttural holler. That was fine, it was the same the world over and Gabčík was a six year veteran of the Czech army, when it had an army, but the few words of English he and his comrades picked up were torn and tortured beyond understanding by these career soldiers. The NCOs were cursing now as some of the men made a slow and unsteady progress across the beach.

'What's wrong with you lot? Are you all pissed or something? Gabčík! You short-arsed little runt! All you've managed to prove is your legs are not long enough to get you where you need to be!'

With these inspiring words of encouragement ringing in his ears, Gabčík finally reached the cliff face at a full sprint, almost slamming into it. As always, he did not let up until he was at the very end of his task.

He leant against the rock gasping for breath, a few of the quicker, fitter men having arrived at roughly the same time. Gabčík was pleased that, at twenty-nine, he was among the first there, could still hold his own. His short frame was stocky and powerful, making him capable of feats of strength that would defeat larger men. Gabčík had a volatile temper that could cause embarrassment in civilian life but served him well during a hail of bullets or shelling. And he had already fought, and killed, Germans.

He had beaten Kubiš there by a yard and felt no less respectful of the slightly younger man for it. Jan Kubiš was still a fine soldier and theirs a good friendship, forged under the most maddening of circumstances. As the NCOs got the men together he noticed Kubiš, like him, was quickly recovering.

'That woken you up?' asked Gabčík.

Kubiš was breathless. 'There's nothing like a nice walk along the beach.'

The corporal immediately rounded on him. 'Save your breath, you're gonna need it.'

The Scottish corporal was away again. This time it was

an unrelenting rant at their inability to cover the yards of beach-head within the desired time; a limit Gabčík was savvy enough to assume would always be a few seconds quicker than their fastest man, such was training, such was the army.

'Now you are going to redeem yourselves with a nice gentle climb!'

The NCO cajoled the men into one final effort, an eighty-foot vertical ascent of a sheer rock face.

'Make it look good or we will throw you off this course. You can go and dig potatoes with the Land Army girls. I've seen a couple of them up close and they are a fucking sight scarier than you lot. Now move it!'

And so Gabčík climbed, for he knew it was his only way back into the war. With three and a half thousand other Czechs, Jan and Josef had endured a perilous sea journey to England. The Czech Brigade based itself at Leamington Spa and the two veterans had experienced the boredom of army camp life there with no imminent prospect of a return to action. After a year of frustrated inactivity, the request had gone out for volunteers to join the SOE. Neither man hesitated and they were on the move again; to Mallaig and the six week commando course that was more than two thirds through by the time Gabčík found himself stranded half way up the cliff face.

He clung perilously to the rock; red face pressed against the stone, hissing profanities to himself in Czech. He was about to fail his assignment and would likely be thrown off the course as well, and it was all down to his own stupidity. Had he listened to the instructor when he urged them all to use proper footholds and not just grip the rope with their hands like they always did? The cliff face was too high for that. Gabčík's biceps burned and the small of his back throbbed with the effort required just to stay still. He tightened his grip round the length of grey, wet rope that hung from the upper most point of the crag and rubbed the skin from the palms of his hands.

Moments ago he had admitted to himself he was stuck, unable to go back down and seemingly stranded without the footholds needed to carry him the extra forty feet to the summit. All about him lesser men than Gabčík were making steady if unspectacular progress. The humiliation was too much and it spurred him into action. Rage welled up inside him and it slowly replaced the fear and the doubt; he cast his eyes to the left and spotted an outcrop that was tantalisingly out of reach. If he could just spring from his current spot, he might get enough leverage with the rope to propel himself onto this toehold. Gabčík hesitated for a moment, closing his eyes and summoning up his anger, the storm that had always served him so well in battle. He had to make it and fear of falling must not be allowed to prevent him. If he did not make the jump he could not move higher. If he did not climb higher he would never reach the top and would not then pass out of the commando course, to join the other would-be saboteurs – his only opportunity to engage the Germans and remove the shame he felt at abandoning his country. And so, he jumped.

For a second there was nothing but air around him, then his left foot connected with the rock, his left hand scrabbling for an indent, and it held. He clung there, the rope drawing fresh blood from the base of his thumb, which he contemptuously ignored. Gabčík barely paused. Instead he hauled himself higher and propelled his other hand into the air. He could not see the ledge above him but grasped it firmly and pulled his body upward again, stretching out his right foot till he connected with a large outcrop. And so on it went; Gabčík rising, cursing and rising again, using his self-recrimination to push him on, catching up with the others.

He remembered the last thing the Scottish corporal had told them in the briefing.

'When you reach the top of the cliff I want you to give me a battle cry. Let me hear the roar from each of you. Pretend

I'm a Nazi machine gunner. I want you to scare the shit out of me!'

Gabčík took him at his word and shot over the edge of the cliff with the most bloodcurdling cry imaginable. Even Corporal Andy Donald was impressed.

Gabčík careered past him at a full sprint, only stopping at the rallying point, which was already beginning to fill up with his fellow Czechs, who sat on the ground next to, or on top of, their packs. One of them was foolish enough to let out a laugh at Gabčík's crazed countenance and they exchanged a handful of insulting words. That was it. Without pausing for a moment, Gabčík whirled on his mocking colleague and smashed a fist squarely into his chin.

Corporal Donald immediately began to shout new orders, to have Gabčík dragged away from his hapless victim. Gabčík was in one of his private worlds, all red mist and hot rage, and Donald had seen him like this before. It could start with something quite trivial, an upended mug of tea or the frustration borne of an inability to complete something; assembling a Sten gun blindfolded perhaps. Corporal Andy Donald was a hard man, scared of nobody, but even he recognised this soldier had a truly awesome temper, the kind that, if harnessed correctly, would take him through any obstacle without a second's hesitation; bullets bouncing around him would go unnoticed. It would take a lot to stop Josef Gabčík if his mind was set.

It took three of Gabčík's comrades to haul him away. That is what happens when you train men to kill but don't let them anywhere near the enemy, thought Donald.

'Alright, that's enough! Enough!!'

Had Gabčík really seen Nazis as he reached the top of the cliff? Probably, knowing him. For a second Corporal Donald almost pitied the poor bloody Germans.

3

*'All is over, silent, mournful, abandoned,
recedes into darkness'*

Winston Churchill on the invasion of
Sudeten Czechoslovakia

'One more please. Please Herr Gruppenführer, just one more, with the big smile, and so! Now perhaps we have Frau Heydrich with little Heider is it? Heider yes! Heider and Klaus, and of course the little Princess Silke. We haven't forgotten you, have we?'

The photographer cooed absurdly at Reinhard Heydrich's baby daughter, shaking his head. 'No, we haven't, no!' – she sensibly chose to ignore him.

Hauptsturmführer Zentner belonged to Goebbels' propaganda division and his mission today was to capture the Heydrichs at home – on film at least. Reinhard had agreed to the photo call weeks ago, aware of the need to project a positive image at all times, and to every section of German society. It was part of his strategy to reach the very top. He had even consented to be photographed out of uniform, in a ridiculous pair of shorts and shirt sleeves, in order to contrast the man at home with the man of state, as Captain Zentner put it.

First, it was full silver/grey SS dress uniform, complete with ceremonial sword, at the foot of the staircase; then behind his desk, again in uniform, black this time, pretending to peruse a blank sheet of paper as his pen hovered above it motionlessly, until the click of the shutter and the flash of the bulb melted him from the frozen image he had assumed.

Now the whole family was made to cavort ridiculously on the lawns to the rear of the Panenské Břežany mansion. But the photo shoot was taking too long, as these things always did, and Heydrich's mind was elsewhere. He had postponed a liaison with his mistress for this and began to long for the delicious friction of her even as he posed, with his children all around him, smiling inanely at the lens. Today, though, he had weightier matters to consider and he wondered what had happened to his driver. Klein had been sent back to Hradčany three hours ago to collect a batch of urgent signals. He had been told not to pause even for a cup of coffee but to return as soon as he had the papers and hand them personally to Heydrich. What on earth could be keeping the man?

Heydrich's irritability found a target in the photographer. Zentner was a small, thin streak of nothingness with a lispy, effeminate manner, who danced round them enthusiastically as he sought the perfect picture of the Heydrichs. Too enthusiastically for Reinhard, who eyed the man contemptuously. He was convinced he was a bum boy, like that scrawny drag queen he once had the misfortune to witness in a Berlin nightclub, at a time before the Nazis had shipped out all of the fags along with the gypsies, the communists and the Jews. But hadn't Lina already established that he had a wife? While he was setting up his tripod and cameras on the grass, and bossing his two silent and anonymous young assistants, she had trilled in a nervous, eager to please manner.

'And is there a Mrs Zentner?'

Did she actually hold this photographer in some form of awe?

'Back in Koblenz, yes, Frau Heydrich!' He had called back familiarly, as if she were the wife of a sergeant.

No children though I'll bet, thought Heydrich, probably a show marriage, to take suspicion away from his unnatural, nocturnal activities. What was Goebbels thinking, employing degenerates like this fellow? Heydrich had been told they were sending one of the best men from the propaganda division and the photos would be seen all over the Reich. There was another SS man close by with a cinematograph machine, so the ideal Nazi family unit could be displayed across a thousand film screens as well. Lina was loving every minute of it, which was perhaps why she was so uncharacteristically civil to the captain.

He remembered how she had been in a fury the day they had seen the first, sanitised newsreel footage of the Goebbels family, a prelude to the feature attraction of some Berlin cinema. There was Magda, the archetypal Aryan matriarch, seated and flanked by no fewer than six children. Her adoring husband Joseph stood at her shoulder, beaming down at her, while a rousing commentary extolled the virtues of maternity, motherhood and the glorious provision of young Nazis to serve the greater German Reich. Cut to shots of sexless young women doing exercises in a field somewhere in Bavaria. Dressed in identical white blouses and dark shorts, fine figures of Germanic girlhood one and all, they danced in synchronicity and on the spot, while the commentator told them how healthy bodies produced healthy babies and urged them to marry the right Aryan boy, and immediately begin gestating for the fatherland.

This little insight into Nazi thinking ended with a final shot of the beaming Magda, provider of life, champion producer of children. Of course, at the time of the film Joseph, the perfect family man, had been screwing Lída Baarová, the famous Czech film star, whose career he had extravagantly promised to advance. But no one was going to put that in a newsreel.

Lina proclaimed Magda to be a vain and common bitch parading herself in this manner. She had obviously forgotten this heartfelt opinion now, for she scooped all three of the Heydrich brood to her arms at once and clasped them to a more than ample bosom, as she tried to persuade them to smile for the camera. Heydrich thought it an impossible exercise as Silke was entirely uninterested and Klaus appeared to be choking on her breasts. Lina was unlikely to spot his distress, however, so entranced was she by the adoring camera.

'Lina, you're suffocating the boy.'

He wandered away from the scene as Frau Heydrich flushed, before trying to turn the whole thing into a joke, desperate to stifle Klaus' already welling tears. Heydrich lost interest in this charade the moment he noticed Klein. His chauffeur was literally running towards him across the manicured carpet of lawn that divided them. The two men met a few yards from the cameras.

Klein saluted, 'Apologies, Reichsprotektor, the signals arrived late and I had to wait for the dispatches to be decrypted.' Klein knew Heydrich cared little for excuses but was determined to prove the delay was most certainly none of his doing.

He handed over a sealed folder containing several sheets of paper. Receiving no further instruction from Heydrich, who simply wandered away wordlessly as he scrutinised the information.

Avoiding the distractions of Lina's wittering and the unchecked hollering of his children, Heydrich read the eastern front dispatches. It took only a moment's perusal to realise operations were not moving quickly enough, not by a long way.

The memos contained a detailed report on the *Einsatzgruppen* and their daily ratios, and they were letting him down. The *Einsatzgruppen* were Heydrich's personal responsibility; along with controlling the entire secret service of the Reich and running the 'Protectorate' of Bohemia and Moravia as the Czech territory was now known, he had volunteered for one more assignment, a pet project very close to the Führer's heart. Only by achieving success in all three arenas could he be assured of further advancement. The top job in France was his next target, for he had noted with satisfaction how the current administration had the country far from under control. It would take the SS to subdue the French and Paris would prove the perfect stepping stone. Then, one day, the longed for call to Hitler's bedside, when an ailing leader would publicly name Heydrich as his successor and leader of the German people. Nothing would stop Heydrich from reaching his goal but the *Einsatzgruppen* would have to improve, and quickly.

The majority of the three thousand men of the *Einsatz-gruppen* were of a civilian background, often from the professional classes; disgruntled doctors, lawyers, government officials and clerks, all sharing one trait, a fanatical belief in the semi-Darwinian theory of Nazism. Their three weeks training at Pretzsch Police School in Silesia was an indoctrination period, reinforcing the mantra of eugenics, not a lesson in tactical combat. Let the strongest survive, eliminate the weak and, of course, it is the Germans who are the strongest, the Jews occupying the lowest rung on the human evolutionary ladder. The men of the *Einsatzgruppen* were not being trained to fight, they were being taught to kill. These 'Action Groups' would go in after the first wave of German soldiers. Once the *Wehrmacht* had broken enemy lines and secured the area, the work of the *Einsatzgruppen* could begin in earnest. Under their mandate to carry out 'Executive Measures', they would rid the land behind the lines of undesirables, subhumans and, of course, the insidious plague that was Jewry.

And so it began; the firing squads, the hangings and the officially encouraged pogroms, carried out by non-Jewish locals under the watchful, indulgent eye of the all-conquering Germans. As the *Wehrmacht* swept through Soviet territory, the area behind them was being cleansed for future occupation by German settlers, who would find nothing there to disrupt their utopian *lebensraum*. Heydrich assured Hitler his trademark ruthlessness would be put to good use marshalling the four Action Groups that would prepare the land, and he had received the Führer's blessing to command operations, but how long would he remain a favourite if progress was too slow? Had he not used the same argument to oust his predecessor Von Neurath from the seat of power in Prague? How easy it had been to convince the Führer a new man was required to get the job done, that all it took was a change of personnel to fulfil his grand vision. Heydrich knew he was on dangerous ground; having promised stunning success he could hardly deliver anything less.

The noise from the photo shoot became like the buzzing of so many distant insects as he scrutinised the numbers Klein had provided. One of the memos took the form of a table, with meticulously logged figures ascribed to particular dates and locations. Along the top ran the words: Men, Women, Children, and Total. From this chart Heydrich could see, for example, that nine hundred and sixty Jews had been executed by the men of the *Einsatzgruppen* on such and such a day in September, outside some unpronounceable village in Lithuania; that of these, four hundred and ninety two were men, three hundred and fifty seven women and one hundred and eleven children. Heydrich skipped the majority of these specific incidents and went straight to the tables at the foot of the memo. In total forty three thousand Jews had been eliminated in that same month across the whole region, an improvement of almost twelve thousand on the previous month.

It wasn't enough, not nearly enough!

'Leave papa alone, Silke. He is trying to work.'

Silke typically ignored her mother and blundered on her unsteady infant legs straight into her father's shoes, tripping over them in the process. He looked down at the bemused figure of his infant daughter blinking back up at him. Silke seemed perplexed as to why she was now sitting on her backside in front of him, so he scooped her up into his arms and he clasped the gurgling, blonde child to his chest with one arm while he continued to read the papers, now held outstretched in his free hand.

'Who's papa's girl then?' he trilled.

He was never comfortable with baby talk but Silke was the sole creature on the planet capable of reducing him to that level.

'Who's daddy's favourite little girl?' He checked another figure at the bottom of the page. Was the ratio of executed Jewish men disproportionately higher than that of the women? One would have expected almost an even spread but, judging by the quick sum he had done in his head, the women made up under forty per cent of the total number of adults killed. Were some of these *Einsatzgruppen* formations trying to dupe him? Allowing the women to flee while more comfortable killing off their menfolk. He was sure of it, and far from certain the men entrusted to carry out this most important work were hard enough to fulfil their mission.

Silke gurgled and a trail of dribble fell from her mouth onto the breast pocket of his shirt, staining it dark.

'Thank you, Silke, thank you so much, you messy little girl,' he chided but his voice was not harsh, never departing from the sing song pitch of a nursery rhyme. He would hardly have to clean it himself and had been given the perfect excuse to call a halt to Zentner's little farce. Besides, he could never stay annoyed at Silke, his pretty little blonde princess. Heaven help the man who wanted to take her away from him when she was older.

Returning to the report he now examined the number of children eliminated. This surely was far too low. Some of these Jews bred like rats and had sizeable broods tagging on behind them. Was he really to believe the majority of the men and women killed were childless? Eleven per cent was an improbable figure. He would have it immediately questioned and investigated. The men in charge of the region were shirking their duty, letting children escape the necessary purging of Jewry. If they could not be relied upon to carry out the task he would replace them and find others who were stronger willed, without such ridiculous scruples. How often had they been told that to spare a child is only to assure Germany of a future enemy? Worse, it could allow cross breeding and the very real chance that polluted blood would be admitted into the Reich. Would they never learn? He felt he had hit upon the essential paradox that confronted these partial executioners. Even they would have to admit the folly of their acts of mercy when they thought about it closely.

Heydrich kissed his unreceptive baby daughter on the forehead before handing her back to a beaming Lina. The photo shoot was apparently over after all and Frau Heydrich appeared delighted with proceedings.

Heydrich, however, could not dismiss his anxiety over the partial failure in the east. The figures did not lie. In four months, the *Einsatzgruppen* had managed to dispose of just half a million Jews, by hangings, firing squads and other sundry methods of dispatch, and there were ten and a half million more to eliminate if Europe was to be entirely cleansed of Jewry. At this rate, it would take them approximately seven years to complete the job, a timescale Hitler simply would not countenance. No, this was very bad news indeed.

And there was a further complication. Two days earlier

Heydrich had been alarmed to receive Himmler's secret memo, wordily entitled *Observations concerning the psychological effects of the campaign in the east*. The Reichsführer SS went on to list an array of negative symptoms, associated with the trauma of such wide scale killing, on the SS men tasked with the destruction of the Jews.

While many SS men are comfortably shouldering the burdens placed on them, and a significant number relishes the accomplishment of this most important task, there has been a marked increase of late in the numbers requesting transfer to traditional, frontline combat duties, where they wrongly perceive they are facing a more equal and direct enemy. Suicide is not entirely uncommon and there have even been cases where SS men have turned murderously against their own comrades and have had to be eliminated for the protection of others. Naturally these cases have never, nor will ever, be made public. I have personally witnessed the special work being carried out and confess that it has the capacity to disturb even the strongest of wills. In conclusion, it would seem a solution is required to alleviate the psychological burden on our men. Please advise your earliest thoughts on this matter most urgently. Signed Heinrich Himmler – Reichsführer SS

Heydrich had burned the memo instantly before returning to his desk to ponder its implications.

Now, days later, he was still wrestling with the great logistical problem of processing eleven million Jews expeditiously and with the minimum of fuss. There must be an easier method than this he reasoned. A great administrative brain like Heydrich's could surely come up with a more efficient system than the random lynching or ad hoc firing parties. Something more humane was required. That is, more humane to the killers.

It had to be done to safeguard Heydrich's future. He was running the east like a corporation, crossing Jews off the balance sheet, but not quickly enough. Not nearly quickly enough.

Lina set Silke down and watched as she scampered after her brothers. Frau Heydrich walked adjacent to her husband, slipping her arm between his, and he noticed the bulge of her pregnancy was beginning to become visible now. Previously it had been hard to tell where the matronly figure of a woman in lower middle age ended and the early signs of maternity began.

Lina rubbed her stomach joyfully. 'I think that it is a boy.'

They strolled slowly back to the house, the older children running ahead of them to keep up with the photographer and his assistants. The sun was beginning to reach its highest point of the day and the servants would be preparing lunch.

Heydrich watched as Zentner bent to show little Klaus a camera, pausing to lower its strap over his head, looking for all the world as if he was awarding the little boy a medal. Klaus bent forward, his tiny head forced down by the weight of the camera, but he was entranced by its expensive, highly engineered, mystery.

Heydrich and Lina were still some way from them, walking at little Silke's unhurried pace.

'Zentner?' Heydrich asked sourly of his wife. 'Does that not sound like a Jewish name to you?'

4

'The Czechs may squeal but we will have our hands on their throats before they can shout. And anyway who will come to help them?'

Adolf Hitler

'I hope you don't mind my insistence on alcohol with every meal, Eduard,' said Churchill. 'I cannot abide it myself but I am afraid I am on strict doctor's orders'.

Eden let out a slight chuckle, not in the manner of the sycophant but with the tone of an equal who has heard the joke many times before but still finds it amusing nonetheless. Churchill wrinkled up his forehead in a mock frown, screwed up his eyes in feigned concentration and embarked upon his tale.

'While visiting America some years ago, I had the distinct misfortune to be run over by an automobile,' the Prime Minister informed Beneš, 'I had failed to predict its speed and the driver was unable to anticipate my... erm... lack of it. Mercifully the damage was slight and, save for a few dents, it appeared both the car and I would make a complete recovery. However, while being treated for a concussion, I was fortunate enough to be attended by a somewhat unorthodox physician, a Dr Otto Pickhardt. I told him there was nothing at all wrong that a stiff drop of brandy could not immediately cure. I firmly declared that a glass or two would banish my rather foul humour. I have to concede I was not the most tolerant of patients nor he, in turn, an overly indulgent physician. The good doctor had spent a lifetime treating more worthy patients, with far greater ills and much lesser notions of their own importance, than I. He looked me up and down before proclaiming with an undisguised loathing, "If that be the case I prescribe large quantities of alcoholic spirits at each and every meal time" and damned if he didn't write out a prescription to go with those very words.' Churchill let out a great snort.

Beneš was charmed by a man of Churchill's stature making fun of himself so easily.

'I hear he carried that blessed piece of paper on him for years,' Eden told Beneš.

'Of course I did!' confirmed the Prime Minister with a delighted snort. 'How else could I convince Clementine? Every time I wanted a tipple she'd protest and I'd say "Look, look, doctor's orders!" Used to infuriate her. In the end she'd mutter "You do what you want, you always do." Doctor Pickhardt knows not the size of the favour he did me!'

Their meal in Downing Street was indeed topped and tailed by first rate and carefully chosen wines; the men now completed their dining with a large measure of Hine and a fine Camacho and Romeo y Julieta. Beneš let the cigar last, puffing on it languorously between sips of Churchill's brandy. Only after the cigars had almost been smoked did the talk finally turn to the specific matters on Beneš' mind.

'In the spirit of our joint campaign against the Nazis, I would like to repay your faith in us with a gesture from the Czech nation that will severely damage the German war effort.'

'Any gesture of that nature would be sorely welcome,' affirmed the Prime Minister.

'For some time now my capital has been under the

increasingly oppressive rule of the SS. There have been executions, detentions without trial, most cruel tortures and the elimination of the population's few remaining liberties. I would place most of these vile acts at the hands of one man; the so called Reichsprotektor, Reinhard Heydrich.'

'Agh yes, we know of him don't we, Anthony? A most disagreeable Nazi, even among that godless bunch.'

'We have files that will surely hang him after the war is over, even before we take into account what he is currently doing in Prague,' agreed the Foreign Secretary.

'I have a proposition to put to you that may eliminate the need for such files.'

Churchill was watching him intently now. Was that a frown of disapproval?

'I propose to send men into Prague to carry out the assassination of Heydrich. I seek your endorsement of this mission as an act of defiance against the Germans.'

'I see,' said Churchill in a tone that betrayed his surprise.

He took a deep puff from the cigar, smacking his lips together audibly to coax out the precious smoke he had long ago become addicted to. Churchill's ruddy complexion became obscured for an instant by a billowing grey veil, which finally dispersed as he began his answer and Beneš realised he was literally holding his own breath.

'Just before the Battle of Waterloo, a conflict which decided the fate of Europe then as this one will now, the Duke of Wellington looked out at the fields in front of him, where one hundred and thirty thousand men stood ready to do battle, and he knew, inevitably, that a good number of those would lose their lives that day.

'At that moment a young officer by his side pointed out a horse-backed figure in the middle distance, riding from one point of the French ranks to the next. It was clearly Napoleon, the Duke's arch nemesis and the man to whom all of the coming carnage could justly be prescribed. Realising he had wandered within range, and in his eagerness to please the Duke and make history in the bargain, our youthful soldier offered to take a pot shot at the Froggy Emperor and eliminate all of England's problems in one dread swoop. Wellington was outraged and admonished the officer for a gross act of ungentlemanly conduct and I don't doubt that it was.'

Beneš realised he was in for a lecture. Lord save me from the English and their outmoded sense of fairness, he thought. This is 1941, where Germans shoot hundreds every day, giving them a far less sporting chance than Napoleon of dodging the bullet. Beneš was just about to politely remind Churchill that it was no longer 1815 when the great man laughed.

'But then Wellington didn't have to contend with the Nazis, did he? If I'd have been astride his horse on that day, I'd have ordered every sharpshooter I had to open up on the bloated Frenchy and the battle would have been won in ten seconds not ten hours. Fifteen thousand British troops would have most probably been spared into the bargain.'

Relief flooded through Beneš. Churchill was looking at his Foreign Secretary for confirmation, 'We have looked at assassinations, even went so far as to put together some plans on how to dispose of the Nazi bigwigs, didn't we? Poisoning, shootings and the like.'

'We had SOE examine the vulnerability of targets like Göring, Goebbels, Himmler and, of course, Hitler himself at one stage; nothing ever really came of it. The file is still open but not active,' Eden concluded reasonably.

Churchill was addressing Beneš again. 'Some of my compatriots dislike assassination attempts on moral grounds. I'm afraid I don't share their view. How can we compete with the Nazis if we are only half as ruthless? Hitler wouldn't flinch at having you or I hanged so I think it only fair to keep things mutual. No, I tend to be against it more because it's messy and has little guarantee of success. So, the question is, do you really think this mission can be achieved?'

'Our most recent intelligence reports indicate Heydrich has a distaste for normal security arrangements. He does not appear to believe we have the nerve to come after him.'

Churchill harrumphed 'Doesn't he though? More fool he.'

Eden was privately amused at his leader's disdain; a hypocritical reaction considering the ulcers Churchill was undoubtedly causing Inspector Thompson, his earnest but harassed looking protection officer. The Scotland Yard Detective was continually hampered in his duties by Churchill's cavalier attitude to the Blitz. At one point he had taken half the cabinet on to the roof of a tall building during the middle of an air raid to '*watch the fireworks*'.

'According to my head of intelligence, he travels with one driver only for much of the time.'

'It would certainly give Hitler a bloody nose and that's no bad thing.'

He was quiet again for a time and both Beneš and Eden found themselves waiting patiently for his next proclamation. 'Of course, if you sent a force into occupied territory to despatch this criminal they would find it extremely difficult to get away afterwards, wouldn't they – what with hundreds of aggrieved Germans hunting for them?

'We think two well-chosen men could handle it.'

Beneš was deflecting. He knew where the PM's train of thought was leading.

'Sounds a bit like a suicide mission to me.' He pronounced it without emotion but Winston was looking directly into Beneš' eyes now, leaving the President with the feeling he was being tested, that the Prime Minister wanted to see just how unflinching he could be.

Beneš took a sip of brandy. When he spoke, it was in a dead voice. 'Regrettably, I think that it is.'

Churchill would not let the matter conclude. 'There is also the issue of retaliation against the civilian population. It would be harsh.'

Eden added. 'In France, they execute ten for every German private soldier killed during occupation. An SS general would exact a far bigger penalty.'

'It is a regrettable fact the Nazis will leave a great many Czech orphans and widows before the end of this war whether we act now or not. There is no guarantee the figure will be any lower if we stand idly by.'

His tone was more sullen than Beneš intended and it clearly meant *this is my business not yours*. But it had the desired effect.

There was a moment's silence while Churchill pondered the implications of the request, until finally he said, 'Well then, there we have it. You have clearly thought matters through, Eduard, and we will be happy to grant you as much operational assistance as we are able.'

'Thank you once again, Prime Minister.'

'Assuming, of course, you can find the men to take on such a mission.'

5

'A highly gifted yet also very dangerous man whose gifts the movement has to retain... extremely useful'

Adolf Hitler on Reinhard Heydrich

Schellenberg felt every bump as the Mercedes trundled along the cobbles. He had always found Prague to be an agreeably pretty place but today it held no interest. As the state car sped past the Gothic and Baroque residences of the old town, a tangible sense of dread hung over the new head of AMT VI, the Reich's Foreign Intelligence Service.

Schellenberg glanced out of the window, barely registering the morning bustle of activity, as the Czechs went about their day-to-day business, providing evidence that life still continued here, despite the presence of an occupying German army. He wound down the window of the Mercedes then flicked his spent cigarette into the cold air. The car had reached a *Pekarna* and the unmistakably sweet aroma of fresh pastry found him through its open window. The metropolitan streets were filled with people. Some stopped to pick up packets of *Jubilejní* cigarettes from the tobacconists or a copy of *Národní Politika,* turning up their collars against a drizzle that piggybacked in on a sharp eastern breeze, sending it almost horizontally into squinting eyes. The summer was long over and the heat of the city had given way to a stubborn, muggy rain that coated Prague's buildings in a transparent grey shroud.

All of this Walter Schellenberg barely comprehended. He had survived numerous difficult and life threatening situations, regularly sat down with Heinrich Himmler, endured more than one audience with the Führer himself, steeling his nerves as Hitler ranted against the Jews, the Bolsheviks, his own generals. None of those meetings produced the symptoms he was now experiencing as his car crossed the River Vltava at the Manesuv Bridge, trundled inexorably up the precipitous hill beyond it and inched ever closer to Hradčany Castle – official residency of Reinhard Heydrich, surely the most dangerous man in the Fatherland.

Schellenberg's palms were moist against the leather of the car seat, his stomach turning over, an acid sting in the pit of his belly that, for once, was not caused by the over indulgence of one of his senior Nazi hosts. They liked to gorge in Hitler's hierarchy; too much beer and wine, more than enough food. Perhaps this explained the insatiable appetite for conquest; collecting countries into one huge, corpulent empire.

The Mercedes swept beneath the twin statues of the Battling Giants and into the courtyard of Hradčany, allowing a serious looking sentry to complete the formality of a challenge. Schellenberg preferred to address the man, a Waffen SS Oberschütze, personally. He wound down the window and held out identification for the senior private to examine. The guard took the papers in his gloved hand and scrutinised them carefully before admitting them.

The car moved off through the Matthias Gate and passed the Church of the Holy Rood. Then it pulled up crisply outside the presidential offices. The driver was out of the car and opening the rear door in an instant. Schellenberg alighted slowly, a thin and slight figure, looking somewhat older than his 31 years, largely, he felt, because of the long hours and stresses of his position. Even in SS uniform, with its death's head cap, he still managed to resemble the amiable lawyer he once was and his face, with its long nose and cautious, languid eyes, could never hope to be described as threatening no matter what he wore.

A sharp-eyed major was already advancing across the courtyard to meet them. Once again, he wore the familiar uniform. Schellenberg realised he had barely seen a soldier since the airfield not sporting the regalia of the *Schutzstaffeln*. Prague was undergoing a second coup; first the *Wehrmacht* took it and now the SS was stamping its authority all over the city.

'Welcome Colonel, I am Major Kreuzer. General Heydrich awaits you in the banqueting hall of the Lobkowicz Palace.'

Hitler on a bad day, rudely awakened from one of his famous afternoon naps; Himmler at his most absurdly mystic, contemplating aloud ways to preserve the souls of deceased SS men; Göring's swagger; Bormann's obsequious plotting at the Führer's side; all of this he would have happily stomached in the same afternoon if he could just turn the car around and leave now. Heydrich was a man so without pity even senior SS men routinely referred to him as the Blond Beast. He was also Schellenberg's boss and, unless Walter's every instinct was incorrect, was now gunning for his former protégé.

That was it with Heydrich – no one was entirely safe from him. He did not have friends, was incapable of understanding the concept. Lately Schellenberg had begun to think of him as a cold, dead planet, drawing others towards it with an irrepressible gravitational pull. If you fell into Heydrich's orbit you revolved around it for a while, entirely at his control, and hoped you would somehow emerge again without being dashed to pieces.

Schellenberg trailed a yard or two behind Kreuzer as they

crossed a courtyard with the dark Gothic backdrop of St Vitus Cathedral. On a better day he would have marvelled longer at the architecture but now he began to wonder, irrationally, if he would ever leave Prague.

Hard to recall it now but there were still those who envied Schellenberg's position, at the right hand of the man who controlled the RSHA, the National Security organisation of Nazi Germany, not understanding that loyalty to Heydrich meant *you are with me only as long as you are of use to me.*

Perhaps that would prove to be his undoing. Schellenberg now had the job he had always wanted, heading the Foreign Intelligence section. But did Heydrich, the man who had appointed him, perversely now see him as a threat? It seemed likely and why not, for the general had used a similar position, under Himmler, to ingratiate himself with the Führer. Heydrich would now expect plotting from Schellenberg, would view it as normal behaviour in fact. For now, though, Heydrich had the rank and position he coveted, General and Reichsprotektor of the former Czech held territories. Here he was ruler – an Emperor of sorts.

They finally reached their destination and Schellenberg followed Kreuzer into the banqueting hall where he was immediately greeted with a great cry of disappointment. At first Schellenberg wondered what he had done to prompt such an outcry. Peering into the brighter lights of the hall he realised no one was paying him the slightest attention. Instead the crowd of twenty or so onlookers was gathered in an uneven circle around two athletic figures, clad all in white.

The action had stopped for a moment, following the shout of disappointment, and one of the fencers had removed his face protector and turned away. He grasped a towel from an aide's hands, wiped sweat from his forehead and turned back to face his opponent. As he dropped the towel and strutted back to resume the contest, Schellenberg realised it was Heydrich, his short cropped crown of blond hair, parted neatly down the left side and matted slightly with sweat. He wore the traditional fencing garb, all white, apart from the black buttons that fastened from the shoulder up to his neck, and the SS flash on his left arm. His athletic figure was offset by an unusual broadening of the hips that made him look a little off balance. That and his slightly high voice lent him a decidedly androgynous quality, which, if anything, made him an even more disquieting presence at close quarters. He did not acknowledge Schellenberg as he replaced his mask.

Around Heydrich was a curious assortment of cronies; uniformed officers from his personal staff, of course, that was a prerequisite when Heydrich performed, but here and there were women also – well-heeled ladies dressed in an opulent day fashion so at odds with the dowdy normalcy of the civilian population. Were they wives of senior SS men or some of Heydrich's mistresses, or both? It was not inconceivable. Schellenberg recognised one from a visit to the theatre Heydrich had insisted they make on his previous visit. She ought to be familiar to his trained eye, as she had played the lead role in the production. Now it seemed she was involved in a much more dangerous performance with Heydrich.

The women were even more abrasive and unchecked than the men. Their brash cries of support or alarm intruded in this sedate ballroom, where every sound, however slight, echoed across the wide, polished wooden floors.

Heydrich resumed his opening stance, against an opponent that, judging by the earlier, strained look on his now covered face, and the reaction of this bunch of sycophants, had just displayed the great bad taste to score a hit against the Reichsprotektor. That would never do and the captain of the SS fencing team was looking to immediately redress the balance. In any competition Schellenberg had witnessed,

Heydrich could never bear the thought of losing. It was one of the qualities that made him the man he was, always to finish first, always to be the top dog.

Schellenberg was not aware of the intricacies of fencing and he found himself almost bored as the two men thrust and parried their way around the matting, in short, sharp attacking movements, each one probing for an opening. How often had he seen this before, Heydrich the Germanic Emperor, holding court? Sometimes it was Reinhard the virtuoso violinist, classically trained as a child, who could bring a room to weeping with his exquisite playing, or Reinhard the renowned skier, who had to be the fastest and most accomplished athlete on the slopes. This time it was Reinhard the fencer, a sport that suited him; here he could be agile, graceful and devious, using his innate cunning to outfox an opponent.

Then a great cry of triumph rang out from one of the fencers and the contest was over. Amidst the cheers and applause as the masks came off, it was absolutely no surprise to Schellenberg that the victorious gladiator was Heydrich. He stood there, arms outspread, acknowledging the excited reaction of his subjects, then clasped a fraternal arm around his opponent, who had bowed gracefully in defeat. Schellenberg heard later he was a young SS captain, a talented fencer who had the good sense to lose the contest narrowly, whether by accident or design.

Presently the gathering broke up and Heydrich marched briskly to the door where he finally acknowledged his protégé.

'Walter! I didn't see you arrive.'

The first lie of the day so soon, thought Schellenberg. Heydrich noticed everything, particularly who was in the room with him at any one time.

'I have something very important to discuss with you.' Was that a gleam in the eye of the Reichsprotektor? 'Let's go to my office.'

Half an hour later, Heydrich had changed into his silver-grey uniform and was seated opposite Schellenberg behind a desk in his office, addressing him without looking up from the day's correspondence, two dozen reports that he balanced in a pile on the very edge of the desk. He always had the ability to focus on two things at once, without detracting from either. It was a quality that impressed and irritated Schellenberg in equal measure.

As he spoke he read each one in turn and left short comments after a paragraph or at the foot of the page. The most lethal weapon in the Third Reich was not a knife or a gun but a file, with initials in the margin, thought Schellenberg. That was how they did for you in the Fatherland. It was enough to get you a train ride to a concentration camp, an appointment with the interrogators down on Prinz Albrechtstrasse, or simply a bullet in the back of the neck. Schellenberg wondered how many men had their fates sealed during that one hour in Heydrich's office.

'So how is your new wife?' Still face down in the files and matter of fact. Schellenberg had been married for a second time and for just nine months.

'Good, on the rare occasions I see her these days.'

'Mmm, indeed.' He chewed the edge of his pencil in contemplation.

'And Frau Heydrich?'

'In her element as a matter of fact. You should see the work she is putting in at the Panenské Břežany.' Heydrich was warming to the subject.

'Really?'

The Reichsprotektor was intensely proud of the sprawling estate that came with his position. The land and manor house were taken from a Jewish entrepreneur who had made his fortune trading in sugar. Now Frau Heydrich was adding a woman's touch to the renovation of the building.

'Yes, we have forty Jews out there working their arses off thanks to Lina. Building a swimming pool at the moment. She's got them moving at quite a rate I can tell you.'

'She's very conscientious,' Schellenberg assented.

Heydrich frowned at one of the reports, giving it his uncharacteristic full attention. He left Schellenberg alone with his thoughts and the sense of dread began to return. Now Heydrich was speaking quietly into the phone, issuing instructions to an unknown subordinate. He had an air of studied calm about him but it did not fool Schellenberg for a moment. He had been in situations like this before. Heydrich would sometimes even announce no work would be discussed at all and lure his subordinates into a false sense of well-being, before suddenly ruining their evening with an accusation or a heart stopping assignment.

Behind Heydrich's desk was a huge mahogany unit. Row upon row of enormous, brass handled drawers were set into the biggest personal filing cabinet the Head of AMT VI had ever seen. This was Heydrich's power base and the reason he was both loathed and feared by most of the key figures in the Reich. He stored hundreds of files here and always kept the keys on his person, far from the prying eyes of even the most trusted of his staff. If you had a vice or a weakness it was here: Göring's morphine addiction and art thefts from the occupied territories, Himmler's quasi-religious experiments on Aryan SS men, even Hitler's turbulent mental condition, based on purloined medical files from the Führer's personal physician Dr Brandt. It was all here. The files would stay locked away until the day when one would be needed. Then an important member of the Fatherland would find out who had the real power to make things happen in Germany. It would be hard to resist Heydrich when he had information that could consign you or your family to Dachau.

Schellenberg was becoming restless now and he decided to force the issue, however risky. He waited until Heydrich had completed yet another phone call.

'There was a matter you said you wished to discuss, Reichsprotektor. You mentioned it was of some importance.'

'Oh yes,' he answered absentmindedly, but Schellenberg was not taken in for an instance, 'I think you may wish to read this.'

Heydrich leant down to a desk drawer on his right hand side, opened it and withdrew another file. He handed it across the table to Schellenberg and resumed the trawl through his papers. Seeing he was not going to receive any further guidance or explanation, Walter transferred his full attention to the brown file in his hands. It was marked *Geheime Reichssache*, the highest rate of secrecy the Reich could afford a document. Since the vast majority of the paperwork that passed through Schellenberg's hands was similarly labelled, this in itself was no reason for alarm. He opened up the manila folder to survey its contents and his blood immediately went cold.

There in bold lettering at the top of the first page was written *SS Standartenführer Walter Schellenberg*. The file had been prepared under his previous rank some weeks before but, judging by the weight of the papers within, it had been updated since and often. His eyes went straight to the word etched below his name – *Ahnenpapiere*, the documents that proved the racial purity of their subject and his family. Contained here were the papers Schellenberg had been forced to submit when he had first become engaged to his 'new wife', as Heydrich had referred to her just a few minutes earlier.

All SS men were compelled to apply directly to Reichsführer Himmler himself if they wished to marry. Then an extensive check was undertaken on the Aryan credentials of their future wives. This would go back several generations and, for Schellenberg, it had not been a simple process. His betrothed's mother was Polish. Walter's future mother-in-law came from a country that was taking the full brunt of the racial policies of Germany. Heydrich had promised to intercede in the case personally but Schellenberg was still surprised when he eventually received permission to marry from Himmler, via the office of the *Rasse und Siedlungshauptamt*. The Race and Settlement office was not normally as compliant, so perhaps he really did have Heydrich to thank, or so he thought at the time.

He turned over the first leaf of the file. Underneath the covering letter was a crisp new memo on expensive paper with a Nazi watermark. It was a letter to his nemesis Heinrich Müller, from a Gestapo operative who had conducted a follow up report into his application to marry. This surveillance initiative had concentrated on the branch of his wife's family based in Poland. There at the foot of the page was a paragraph that would have far reaching consequences if it ever became more public. According to the investigation Schellenberg's mother-in-law had a sister. That sister had a husband, and the husband was a Jew.

Schellenberg knew the implications instantly. His wife's mother had a Jewish mill owner for a brother-in-law. The man could be picked up and sent to a concentration camp instantly. The wife, corrupted by her interracial marriage, would surely follow him, and the rest of his wife's family would be guilty by association. In short, Heydrich had finally got him.

He glanced up to find the Reichsprotektor watching him.

'Obviously Müller realised the importance of this information immediately and had the file sent for my personal attention by secure courier. No one else has seen the surveillance report yet.'

The last word hung in the air for a moment. 'I am aware of the devastating effect this could have on your wife's family and the inevitable repercussions for your own position in the Reich.'

Heydrich's face took on a look of forced seriousness, as if he was about to make an announcement of monumental proportions. 'That is why I have decided not to forward the file to Berlin. Instead I will keep it here for the time being.'

Schellenberg knew at once he had lost. 'The Reichsprotektor is most generous. I am of course extremely grateful for his discretion.'

'Good.' Heydrich rose from the leather chair, took the letter from Schellenberg and walked to the back of the room. He had the key to the filing cabinet in the pocket of his *feldbluse* and he opened up one of the large drawers, selected a bulky file, presumably containing other choice observations on Schellenberg's life and career, inserted the damaging information and closed, then locked, the drawer. He placed the key back in his pocket and turned to face Schellenberg with a smile.

'It's remarkable what can be revealed by a routine follow up report, don't you think? We really had no idea.'

'Indeed.'

Yes, and who had authorised the follow up surveillance in the first place but Heydrich? More likely the information had been readily available before the report went in to Himmler and had been suppressed by the Reichsprotektor, who had waited more than six months to casually slip it into an afternoon conversation over coffee. That was his way, always to know more than others.

Heydrich sat back down again, made an elaborate show of draining the cooling dregs from his cup, and fixed Schellenberg with an earnest look.

'Don't concern yourself from this point on, Walter.' He soothed his new creature while the document that could bury Schellenberg was entombed behind them. 'I really don't want you to worry about a thing.'

Schellenberg nodded weakly. He was an accomplished

marksman, capable of hitting a target at ease and from distance, but he knew his hand would shake uncontrollably if he ever had to point a Luger in Heydrich's face.

6

'Get me good men; brave, patriotic and true'

Eduard Beneš, at the beginning of Operation Anthropoid

Strankmüller's head fell forward.

'Emil? EMIL!'

The words came from miles away and they jolted him back to life. His head shot upwards, as if snatched by an unseen hand, and he was at his desk once more, dragged back from exhausted sleep.

'You were snoring. Well, you snored once to be exact.'

The words were not expressed unkindly. Major Johnson, one of three liaison officers assigned by the British SIS, knew Strankmüller had barely slept in three days; not since his emergency crash meeting with Moravec.

'I knew you wouldn't want to miss the lieutenant colonel. He'll be here in twenty minutes. Time for a quick wash and brush up, don't you think? And I'll organise us a brew.'

Johnson was speaking to him as one does to the recently bereaved, excusing all unusual displays of behaviour. In another, previous incarnation Major Emil Strankmüller would have been embarrassed at his unkempt appearance and the nodding off at his desk, but most of all by the claxon call of his solitary snore. He found now, to his surprise, none of it mattered. There were far more important considerations.

'Thank you, Ralph. I'm sorry I disturbed you.' He said it by rote not conviction and the reply was equally matter of fact.

'Not a bit of it.'

Johnson left the room in search of water for brewing and Strankmüller blinked at the files in front of him, willing his gummy eyes to widen and stay that way, at least until Moravec had come and gone once more. It had been seventy two hours since the lieutenant colonel gave Strankmüller his orders – the most important he'd received since they had escaped Prague together eighteen months ago, when they flew out of the capital in a violent snowstorm on the eve of the German occupation. Soon he would be expecting to see evidence of Emil's labours.

They had spoken privately in the Porchester Gate hotel, whose rear offices doubled as the temporary headquarters of the Czech secret service. Since that day, Strankmüller had remained in the little office. When he was not behind his desk, chain smoking his way through the hundreds of files stacked on and around it, he dozed fitfully on a metal cot in the far corner – three, four hours at a time. Food was brought in on a tray and he had taken to punctuating his days with cups of Camp coffee, the better to keep track of them.

The grooves under Strankmüller's eyes were darkening and his hair becoming unruly through lack of attention. Where it had once been oiled and slicked to the point where he could be mistaken, in this country which mistrusted male grooming, for a spiv, or at best a professional ladies man, Strankmüller's locks now sulkily rebelled. He was more conscious of his stubble, but only because it itched and irritated him.

He was a man on a mission.

What that mission was nobody, but Moravec who'd assigned him it, was permitted to know. But even a casual observer would realise Strankmüller was looking for personnel. If you were in the Czech army, you'd escaped the invasion of France and you could shoot straight, Strankmüller had read your file, for a second or two at least. Most likely he had discarded your particulars instantly, with a muttered Czech curse at you for delaying him in his search for the perfect Joe; as all agents with SOE were commonly called. And you would never know you had been considered, however briefly, for Operation Anthropoid.

He had started with those already on, or graduated from, the SOE course, but broadened his search in case there were undiscovered talents hiding anonymously in the wings, like understudies waiting for the leading man to fall from the stage and give them their chance.

Gradually, the heap of rejected files grew larger until they were stacked high against the outer panel of Emil's desk, three piles wide. Only when they threatened to topple did he allow Johnson to remove them, and the Englishman would stagger out into the corridors under the weight of unwieldy armfuls of manila.

Dominating the desk itself, so that scarcely an inch of the cushioned leather inlay could be made out, were the possibles and the probables. Several piles of well-thumbed folders Strankmüller had read again and again; explosives experts, wireless operators, machine gunners, athletes, linguists, saboteurs; the assembled expertise of the common man that lies fallow in years of peace but becomes the much cherished currency of war time.

Strankmüller's obsession, for such it seemed, was born of two urgent, conflicting notions. He was choosing men who must succeed. And he was choosing men who would most likely die. By discarding someone's file, removing them from the stack of would-be assassins, he was ensuring they would not be killed, on this operation at any rate, and he felt a strange euphoria in the act. He told himself he was only sending two men to their deaths not two hundred and, as the pile of rejected files grew, he gained great comfort from glancing over it. How could he explain why he first snapped at Johnson when the fellow quite sensibly suggested they be moved out of the way? How could he make the man understand it was this stack that kept him going into the night and well into the next morning? That the only cheer he had these days was a cup of coffee, a distracted cigarette, and the knowledge that the mother of Platovský, Private, DR; would not be made to mourn him on Strankmüller's watch; that the wife of Kopecký, Corporal, FS, would avoid the tragic certainty of widowhood until another mission at least. He was playing God, saving lives. Men who would have no idea they were even considered for the mission would live to fight another day and it was all down to him.

Some were patently unsuitable for the task and he weeded them out early, using the comments of their commanding officers as an unquestioned guide to these souls he could never hope to find the time to meet. This one was too left wing and this one too much to the right. This one questioned things; still another lacked the imagination to function effectively on his own initiative. This one drank and this one had a weakness for skirt.

But as the time grew close and the files had been slowly whittled down to a handful, the pressure began to tighten round Strankmüller like a noose. Almost all of the remaining men had an equal level of ability, guts and nationalistic credentials. He could recommend any one of them to Moravec with equal conviction and he would have to become more subjective to choose the final two, following instinct and that intangible gut reaction honed by years of running his own agents.

Then he convinced himself they might achieve their mission, and escape safely after all, if he were just to choose the right two men; providing the perfect combination, a partnership that would work so flawlessly these impeccable Joes could achieve the unachievable, then fly right back to base again like homing pigeons. So perhaps he really was playing God now.

And all the while the words of the President stayed with him. The single, simple brief Moravec had passed to him. Strankmüller had asked what kind of man he was looking for, expecting a precise breakdown of the skills required. Instead he was given barely a sentence, 'Get me good men; brave, patriotic and true.'

There was one stipulation, however; a little less noble but designed to ignite the dampened flame of nationalist fervour in occupied Czechoslovakia; one of the men had to be a Czech and the other a Slovak. Thus, the two former halves of the republic would strike back in unison at the evil forces of occupation.

Now a decision had to be reached in a little over a quarter of an hour. Two men needed and three remaining files in front of him, set aside from the pack, an aura of doom about them. After all his searching, he had decided on men from the same intake of volunteers at the SOE sabotage course – Gabčík, Svoboda and Kubiš.

He had put it off right to the end. As long as there were three in the running, he was still not sending two specific men to their deaths. Any one of them could survive his selection procedure, be entirely ignorant of it in fact.

He picked up Gabčík's file first. A brown folder, well worn, its contents memorised by the major till he could recite them during his snatched moments of sleep. Gabčík, Sergeant, J; born in the Slovak district of Žilina, twenty-nine years of age. Currently on operational secondment to SOE, training course almost over, expected destination RAF Brickendonbury, to be trained as a saboteur, most likely to be deployed behind the lines in rural Czechoslovakia. Aim, to link up with what remains of the resistance. From there Sergeant Gabčík is expected to think on his feet and act on his initiative, to instigate a campaign of terror against the less obvious targets of military action; factories, arms plants, bridges, railway tracks. Gabčík is loyal, unquestioning and patriotic, it says here, with unquestioned abilities as a soldier and is already the proud recipient of medals for gallantry. He is expected to be a fine exponent of the art of subterfuge and will doubtless lead the thousands of occupying enemy soldiers a merry dance as he blows up factory after factory along his terrible way. That is the gist of his superior's comments at any rate. He is short in stature but evidently strong with, if the dog-eared photograph clipped precariously to his folder is to be believed, a fierce and determined demeanour. He is of course unmarried, as are all three of the men Strankmüller has selected.

Svoboda, Sergeant, A. Has a remarkably similar military record to Gabčík's, except Anton is a Czech and could suitably partner Gabčík if required, thus fulfilling the political brief Strankmüller has been set by his president. He is another short-arse, if you pardon the expression, and Emil does indeed excuse himself with his fogged inner voice, but hardy, rugged and unstinting in the determination to rid his homeland of the Nazis.

Finally, there is Kubiš, just as *brave, patriotic and true* as the others. A Czech also, from Třebíč in Moravia, so it is to be one of either Kubiš or Svoboda it seems, unless Strankmüller feels so strongly about the qualities of the latter men that he consigns Gabčík to the pile of also-rans and insists on them. But he does not. There is nothing to choose between them and no grounds except spite to ruin the unnecessary synchronicity of Beneš' little scheme. Kubiš' picture disturbs him though. The face, so youthful he had the man's age independently checked more than once. Surely he could not be twenty eight years of age? He looked barely eighteen in his picture; like a boy playing at soldiers, standing to attention in his father's oversized, old uniform before marching up and down in a game of make believe. But no, he has reached the rank of sergeant, an impossibility for a teenager, and been presented with the Czech War Cross by none other than Beneš himself. He may yet get the opportunity to meet his president again before this episode is through, thinks Strankmüller.

Still he has not reached his decision and the hour will soon be upon him. He has just enough time to leave his desk for a few moments, for the wash and shave Johnson urged on him, and he may even get to finish the cup of tea that will await his return, before making a final choice.

But there is no more time. Implausibly, a shadow crosses his desk, cast by the remaining light outside yet, broken by the broad rampart of his shoulder blades, it disappears almost instantly. Strankmüller does not have to look behind him. It is the almost imperceptible sign that Moravec is early. For all the years he has known his superior he has failed to grasp the lieutenant colonel's anxiety at this most auspicious of assignments. Unable to perceive that the fastidiously punctual Moravec may choose, wraith like, to ascend the rear stairwell, an entrance specifically designed for his clandestine use alone, a good fifteen minutes earlier than they had agreed.

And the decision not yet made.

A surge of hurt ran through Strankmüller – all his work, his tireless effort, so close to a decision, and now Moravec here early to spoil it all. How could he let his superior see a final choice has not been taken? Refusing to leave himself open to charges of weakness or procrastination, he reaches out with his right hand, as instinctive a decision as he has ever made, sweeps up one of the files and flips it lightly to the far corner of the desk. There it refuses to hide from his gaze and instead flaps open, billowing for an instant before landing heavily, like a bird with a broken back. The photograph of its subject stares accusingly up at him as a second shadow crosses it, indicating that his commander has come silently through the rear door and is finally at his side.

'Emil, have you found me good men?'

There are never any pleasantries when Moravec is experiencing the burdens of operational pressure.

'Yes,' rasps his subordinate, becoming peculiarly aware that he has lost his voice along with his other senses, every one of them drained by lack of sleep. Before he can correct himself and start again, this time to include a more formal greeting, his CO continues.

'One Czech and one Slovak?'

'Of course, sir.'

What an idiot he feels, as his words break once more under the burden of his heavy throat. It is all he can do to stop himself from wailing at the unfairness of it all. This is not how he has foreseen the briefing. Days before, when the pile of potential assassins was waist deep from the floor upwards, he had rehearsed in his mind the gravity of his tone, as he firmly but respectfully outlined the career highlights of the chosen Joes. Moravec would throw in the occasional taxing question for which Emil would have the perfect considered response. Instead, it is his destiny to reply to his commander's earnest entreaties in the comical rasp of an old man.

'Very good. Hand me the files and I'll read them while you get a wash up. Then we will eat downstairs in the hotel and you will get a good night's sleep before waking early tomorrow.'

'Tomorrow?'

'Yes, you will need to travel personally, to collect the men from wherever they are currently training.'

'Of course, sir,' Emil croaked.

Moravec frowned at him, picking up Strankmüller's almost empty cigarette packet and peering suspiciously into it as if searching for clues.

'Smoke many of these do you?'

The major nodded unhappily.

'Mmm, thought so. Suggest you cut down a bit.'

Could there be a more inglorious beginning to a mission, thought Strankmüller. Moravec nodded at the two files that lay in front of his deputy.

'So, what are their names?'

Strankmüller cleared the back of his throat with a racking cough and when he spoke he was thankfully able to enunciate more clearly. 'The first is Gabčík. Sergeant Josef Gabčík. A good man, seen action, decorated, almost through training.' Emil knew his CO liked a short, to-the-point briefing.

Moravec nodded in seeming satisfaction. 'And the second?'

For a fraction of a moment Strankmüller's stomach churned. Which file had he discarded and which remained? In truth, he knew the answer but the prospect of getting the name wrong, and disgracing himself further, was more than he could have borne in his dishevelled condition. Composing himself he took a breath, then let out the name purposefully.

'Svoboda. Sergeant Anton Svoboda. Very competent, fearless in fact, according to the instructors.'

'He'll need to be,' asserted Moravec, and he scooped up the two men's files, walked over to Johnson's vacant desk, sat down and began to read. Without looking up from his task he called out to his deputy.

'Right go and get a wash and shave, Emil. I'm not dining with you looking like that.' He tried to sound stern but was unable to stifle a slight smirk of amusement at Strankmüller's wholly evident dedication to the task he had been set.

'Sir,' mumbled his subordinate glumly.

Strankmüller stumbled from the chair and wandered distractedly out into the corridor, leaving behind a bare patch of wood on his desk for the first time in three days. The rest of its surface was still littered with folders. All were fastened and piled anonymously on top of one another in a number of messy heaps. Save for one, which lay open. In the top left hand corner of this rebellious document the impish face of Jan Kubiš peered determinedly out at the world, showing no outward sign of disappointment at being passed over for the mission.

7

'The Slavs are to work for us. In so far as we do not need them, they may die. Slav fertility is not desirable'

Martin Bormann

George Watson's tuneless whistling interrupted the tranquillity of a late English afternoon. The rain had decided against its expected visit and the sky was just light enough to venture out into a back garden that required his constant attention.

From here he attempted a barely recognisable version of Anne Shelton's *Let the Curtain Come Down* that was frequently punctuated by a phlegmy cough or asthmatic wheeze. That morning he had pronounced himself secretly in love with the eighteen-year-old, though he had never seen her face. Little Anne, as he called her, had become the latest 'forces' sweetheart', serenading British troops in North Africa from their radio sets, to the accompanying sounds of the Bert Ambrose band.

George maintained that hearing her voice would bring him closer to his only son David, a member of the Desert Army whose morale was temporarily lifted each week by *Introducing Anne* on the BBC. Kubiš suspected his motives were not entirely paternal, however. 'They say she still sings in her school uniform,' George confided to Jan.

From the garden, the whistling would occasionally peter out, replaced by a breathy gasp of exertion that could mean only one thing – George was digging for victory. He grunted as his spade turned over yet another sod from the lawn that had once been his pride and joy, before the need to turn every piece of trivial garden into working land. England was now a patchwork of arable plots, every lawn an allotment, and middle-aged men the land over were taking an obsessive pride in vegetable patches and compost heaps.

There was silence for a moment. Perhaps George was allowing his not inconsiderable bulk to rest against the handle of the shovel for a while. Now he would be quietly surveying his handiwork, with the assurance of an Englishman who knows he is doing his bit to combat the U-boat threat. The North Atlantic convoys might be decimated by Hitler's cowardly, torpedo launching assassins but there would still be potato pie on George's plate. Then he would know the pride of the farmer at harvest time.

George let out a racking cough, caused by more than twenty years' consumption of cigarettes, and sent another shovelful of earth against the side of the Anderson shelter. Kubiš could easily picture George, though unable to see him from his prone position on the hard little bed. He would be sweating now, visible droplets of moisture clinging to a forehead entirely unencumbered by hair. His receding pate would glow red, as it always did during physical exercise, shining like the copper-bottomed pans that were the pride of Victoria Watson's spotless kitchen.

On a different day Jan would have jumped to his feet and gone downstairs to help George with his labours, mindful of the debt of gratitude he owed for the shelter of the Watsons' neat, little home. He had been staying with them for longer than expected while he was on the parachute course because it had been delayed for some reason no one had bothered to explain to him. That was the army for you; soldiers were always either rushing somewhere frantically or hanging about for hours waiting for someone to tell them what to do next. The parachute course was the next stage of their training following their successful completion of the commando course at Mallaig. The delay meant much of the recent work in the garden was a joint effort – with Jan providing some youthful muscle to augment the middle-aged man's hours of careful, strategic planning. Together they had dug up flower beds and planted vegetable plots, tied saplings with second hand string and nurtured the fruits of their labour assiduously, taking tips on horticulture from slim government manuals.

The project occupied George's mind, keeping it from brooding concern for his son. For Jan there was a chance to make recompense for the fact that he now occupied young David's bed, for a while at least. When he was able to put his commando-trained physique into physical labour, he would be encouraged with hearty cries of, 'That's it, Jan, give it the old heave ho. Good man!' and he would feel less the interloper.

But, even though they had volunteered to take him in, exhibiting great pride in this small contribution to the war effort, he would still feel the, almost subconscious, resentment of David's mother. He instinctively knew her occasionally sharp, maternal utterances of 'Make sure you take your boots off, Jan' or 'Don't go letting your meal get cold now, Jan, there's many would be grateful for a plate of something hot tonight', were her way of exercising frustration at the stranger in her house, occupying her son's bed while young David was risking life and limb on a different continent. Meanwhile Jan merely spent interminable months 'training', risking nothing more serious than splintered fingers in George's garden. Mrs Watson viewed him suspiciously, this artful cuckoo, dropped suddenly into her ordered, red-brick, gable-end world.

Even if she did not think that way, Jan felt she surely ought to, which amounted to the same thing. He burned with shame as he walked the streets of this small Cheshire town – while all the local men his age were away doing their bit – the longing to see action fast becoming obsession.

Today though, things were different. As he lay on the bed he was gripped by an overwhelming lethargy that precluded even the removal of his boots. They may have been scrupulously clean, sporting a reflective shine, but he would never have kept them on normally while he lay on top of the eiderdown on David's bed. If Victoria Watson, named appropriately after the long dead, humourless monarch, saw him like this, even an Anderson Shelter would not have been enough to save him. Her fastidiousness was legendary and George Watson, fearless in defiance of the Nazis, spent his days in a state of cowed submission he seemed only partially aware of. Victoria swept up around him, cleared the newspaper away as soon as it left his fingers, and perpetually shooed him out of the door with a dismissive 'Why don't you do something useful instead of getting under my feet all the time?'

'Right-ho Jan, let's take the dog for a walk, eh?' George would say with a forced cheerfulness, and he would wink exaggeratedly, as if to imply he was still the master in his own house, his wife's manner just a little feminine eccentricity that did not concern him – though Jan could sense his mild humiliation. Once outside they would walk away along the cobbled streets together, with George always cracking the very same joke.

'Come on Rover, keep up boy,' he'd say jovially to the invisible dog that he did not own as they walked instead to the pub. He had used the same weak gag on so many occasions Jan could practically see the damned animal. He'd be a black and white, droop-eared mongrel, like the pet Kubiš had when he was a small boy in Třebíč – a profoundly disobedient creature that showed no interest in chasing after sticks, sitting on command, or playing dead for the amusement of his childhood friends. Jan loved the lazy animal nonetheless.

And so it became a regular practice for George, Jan and the invisible dog to saunter the few streets to the Dun Cow, for three pints of the dark mild Kubiš was almost developing a taste for.

Not tonight though. If George asked Jan to go out and walk the dog he would make an excuse. He was not feeling well, he had an early start the next day, he had damaged an ankle in parachute training that very afternoon. Jan had no real idea what he would say but no longer cared if he sounded convincing. His totally consuming depression left him apathetic to all concerns, even the importance of keeping on the right side of the Watsons. So, his boots stayed on the eiderdown and his head remained rooted to the pillow, even as George continued to toil alone outside. For Kubiš had lost a friend.

The day had seemed full of possibilities when he reported, in good order, to the Tatton Park mansion that housed the parachute course. This was Jan's third jump and he had almost overcome the sheer mind-rushing terror of throwing himself out of an aircraft at eight hundred feet. The first time had been by far the worst. Only fear of failing the course had been stronger than all his instincts as they screamed at him not to launch himself from the plane.

By now he was beginning to get used to the jumps. As the fields rushed up to meet him Jan even remembered to keep his feet together, then bend the knees sharply at the point of impact. As soon as he hit the ground his body pitched forward hard and he tumbled onto his left side, in a shuddering collision that knocked the wind from his body. He lay motionless for a second before catching his breath, then realised that, aside from a little light bruising, he was in all other respects unharmed. That was all it took for the euphoria of adrenalin to kick in. He had done it. Jan had forced himself from a speeding aircraft, not once but three times now, throwing himself at the ground in an irrational dive that defied the gods. And he had lived.

The fourth jump, later that same morning, was even less traumatic. He took great care to concentrate on the mechanics of the act, checking his chute, securing the helmet a second time, and listening hard to any advice or word of warning from the NCO who travelled with them. Then he hurled himself into the air.

Even the landing was smoother, and he managed to touch the ground more than once with his feet, before stumbling head first again and scraping his face as the chute dragged him along the terrain, powered by a crosswind.

Jan climbed to his feet, folded the chute, draping it clumsily across an arm, and walked slowly back to the muster point. His smile was broad and his mood that of the invincible. If four parachute jumps from eight hundred feet could not kill him, what could?

When Kubiš reached the truck that would return them to the debriefing, he was aware of a preoccupation among the little band of men who had made the jump. He had expected smiles and congratulatory slaps on the back, while everyone spoke breathlessly of their own specific and personal adventure among the clouds. Instead there was quiet and, surprisingly, the soldiers were allowed a moment's breather. They slouched on the ground around the truck, sharing cigarettes no less – unheard of until they were dismissed for the day. What could have prompted this suspension of formality? Not an accident – please God.

Kubiš looked beyond the truck for a clue and his eyes came to rest on a second vehicle – a regimental staff car parked a short distance away. There was an officer to one side of it, a young major, with slicked back, dark hair and a no nonsense demeanour, and he was earnestly addressing two of Kubiš' comrades. As Jan drew nearer he recognised one as Svoboda and the other as his good friend Gabčík.

Moments later, while Jan puffed distractedly at a cigarette, his two comrades left separately and without a word of farewell, leaving no clue to their destination. Everyone behaved as if this were entirely normal.

By the time Kubiš called at Gabčík's billet that evening, the house of a sour, silver haired widow named Mary Bramley, he already knew his friend would be long gone.

'He's been called away,' it was enunciated suspiciously, as if Jan were a known German spy. 'I don't know where, I'm sure,' Mary concluded primly and she eyed Jan dubiously, despite having seen him in Gabčík's company on several occasions. In response, he turned his back on her without comment and trudged gloomily away before she had time to close the door in his face.

So Jan has lost his best friend Gabčík, who may as well be dead with his location secret and his mission even more so. Kubiš scolded himself – to think a so-called soldier could become forlorn because he was unable to say goodbye to a comrade, in a world where hundreds were dying every day.

Then he reproached himself further – for not being selected. What had Josef and Anton shown his instructors that he was unable to? Had he not tried hard enough? He was a good soldier, decorated in combat, so that was all it could be. Jan had missed his chance, the opportunity to go back to his homeland, fight the Germans and, of course, see Anna once more.

Anna Malinová – possessor of the sweetest smile; Anna, whose tender nature left him entirely selfless in her company, so that all he craved was *her* happiness, *her* wellbeing. Only

Anna could leave him feeling like a tongue-tied, nervous young boy again. Anna whom he missed to the point of physical pain – an ache somewhere deep in his stomach that returned every time he thought of her. God preserve her until they could be together once more. But perhaps that day would never come, he ruminated sulkily, alternately blaming himself, his instructors and the two chosen men whom he couldn't help but envy even though they were his friends.

This was no use. He would have to pull himself out of his listless state. He could not blame everyone else, and should not blame himself. Perhaps it just came down to luck. Somewhere deep within him he knew he was as good a man as Josef, as fine a soldier as Anton. Yet he could not rid himself of the black mood that engulfed him, and he was unable to climb to his feet just yet. So he remained motionless on the bed, staring up at the ceiling, remembering the soft yielding of Anna's kiss and trying to ignore George as he now whistled *The Band Played On* entirely without harmony.

And Jan did endeavour not to think of her that afternoon, expelling sentimental remembrances of Anna from his mind as soon as they appeared but, in these quieter, reflective moments, the thoughts he has tried so hard to banish return to him.

8

*'Whether other nations live in prosperity or perish
through hunger only interests me in so far as we can
use them as slaves for our civilisation'*

SS Reichsführer Heinrich Himmler

Gabčík sat in the back of the battered American jeep,
gripping its open sides tightly as it sped over the grass.
The jeep was part of a recently arrived consignment of
equipment from Roosevelt that had survived the treacherous
Atlantic crossing. Churchill was going through his 'Give us
the tools and we will finish the job' phase. Day by day he'd
lobby, beg and cajole the Americans for more support. More
ships, more gold and more guns – enough to wage a war on
Hitler, enough to save his beloved empire from the Nazis.
If the Americans could not yet actually fight the Germans
themselves they could do so by proxy, with sizeable grants,
loans and the use of second-generation equipment that would
otherwise be consigned to their breakers' yards. And so it was
that this Czech soldier found himself careering across the
English countryside in a neutral American jeep.

Gabčík was the only passenger, for Svoboda had gone
missing. There was little cause for alarm. The British sergeant
overseeing the night drops had previously explained there
were crosswinds. So Gabčík was despatched back to the

requisitioned stately home that served as a temporary HQ while the British soldiers continued to look for the unfortunate Svoboda. Gabčík smiled to himself in the back of the jeep. Poor Anton, he's probably stuck up a tree – dangling helplessly from his parachute, wondering if they will ever find him. It shouldn't be too long now though. They would be aided considerably by the dawn beginning to break all around them, and Svoboda would be thankful the second night jump had been delayed and they had finally parachuted down during the last remaining moments of pitch darkness. Even now Anton was probably slowly trudging across the damp grass, lugging the unwieldy folds of parachute silk in his arms and cursing his misfortune.

Now the sky was lightening, turning the fields around them into a silver grey landscape, and they could begin to pick out individual landmarks where earlier there had been an impenetrable black mass.

There had been little time for reflection since Gabčík had been chosen for Operation Anthropoid, whatever that was. Strankmüller promised all would be revealed as soon as they had completed the hastily arranged night drops that were to be an integral part of the mission. Gabčík contented himself with the thought that he could at last consider himself of use. He was in a far better state than his former comrades, who restlessly endured the endless wait for an assignment.

Gabčík's training with the SOE usually left him exhausted each evening, with little time to question things. But lately, just lately, he has begun to wonder. Gabčík is twenty-nine, single and, until recently, proud of the fact, particularly when he has watched the lovelorn Jan, as he disappears within himself at the very mention of the girl he left behind in Prague. But Josef has survived combat, with its near misses and arbitrary destruction of friend and foe alike, and it has affected him. He asks himself if he will survive the war and who would mourn him if he did not? There are no wife and children waiting by his fireside that's for sure and perhaps, if he is lucky enough to get out of this unholy mess unscathed, he will turn his sights towards a nice, young Czech girl who will make him feel welcome when he returns home each night.

When they arrived back at the stately home Gabčík was surprised to see Strankmüller waiting for them. He climbed out of the jeep, which immediately sped away, and walked towards the major.

'Sergeant Carter just radioed in. They found Svoboda.' And something in his tone made Gabčík fear the worst. 'He's alive but landed heavily. Anton took quite a bang on the head. Apparently he's "spark out" according to Carter.' And he laughed grimly before mimicking the British sergeant further. '*Of course, I'm no doctor but he won't be jumping out of any more planes for a good while.*' And Strankmüller said it with such ill will that Gabčík felt the unconscious Svoboda was being blamed for his own misfortune.

Strankmüller launched his cigarette butt into the roses. 'Looks like we are going to need another man, Josef, and quickly.'

9

'It is not the job of the party leadership to appoint leaders…
if you are stronger than your enemies then you'll win…
if you aren't and you lose, then that's simply
the way it should be'

Max Amann, Editor of Nazi newspaper *Völkischer
Beobachter*, writing on behalf of Hitler

Heydrich sat opposite the unsmiling, lightly pockmarked
face of Rochus Misch, Hitler's bodyguard. Misch
stared straight ahead into the middle distance as he
stood gravely to attention, guarding the door that kept the
outside world from his beloved Führer.

Heydrich had seen the man before, of course, during
the regular briefings from Hitler or the hastily summoned
meetings the leader called with Reichsführer Himmler,
Reichsmarschall Göring or, his favourite little lapdog, the
revolting Martin Bormann. Usually Heydrich would not have
given the fellow a moment's thought but he had been waiting
in the anteroom at Hitler's Rastenburg bunker for hours now
and had little else to occupy his mind.

The East Prussian retreat was a simple, functional HQ.
Hitler adored *The Wolf's Lair* and its secret location amid
the woodlands. The Wolf's Lair? That had to be Hitler's very
own idea. He had a seemingly endless enthusiasm for such

childish monikers. So it was that German submarines went
to sea in Wolf Packs, men who distinguished themselves in
the Reich had the hearts of Lions or Tigers, and the Führer's
den was always an Eagle's Nest or a Wolf's Lair. Heydrich
thought these immature fancies quite ridiculous but it would,
of course, have been madness to say so. Even his position was
not so strong that he could afford to pour scorn upon the
great leader.

What would Misch do, Heydrich contemplated idly, if he
were suddenly to pull out his Luger and bear down on the
door Misch guarded? If Heydrich said *out of my way Misch, I
am going to kill the Führer.* Undoubtedly young Rochus would
put up a fierce fight – more than ready to lay down his own
life for his leader. He probably fantasised such scenarios in
his bed at night. What more glorious death for a soldier than
to lie mortally wounded in his adoring Führer's arms, tears
of gratitude falling on his face as he gently passes away, safe
in the knowledge he has thwarted an attempt on the great
leader's life? It was pathetic really, one could expect equal
intelligence and self-sacrifice from a well-trained Alsatian
dog.

Heydrich was secretly amused at Misch's silent and
unquestioning devotion and made note of it. When he
finally assumed the leadership of the nation, as was surely
his destiny, all German soldiers would swear a personal oath
of allegiance to Heydrich, as they had previously done to
Hitler. That was the way to guarantee unswerving loyalty
from Germans.

But now he was bored with Misch. How much longer must
he wait for Hitler? What crisis could be detaining him so long?
He had witnessed the leader walking purposefully down the
corridor hours earlier, with the insufferable Bormann at his
side – the latter sporting a look of fierce protection. Nobody
got near the Führer these days without going through

Bormann and he was fast becoming the most hated man in the Reich – perhaps more so even than Heydrich.

At first the Reichsprotektor had been secretly glad of the delay. It gave him an opportunity to review the facts of his briefing once more, before he presented it to Hitler personally. Did the figures match his conclusions in the precise manner he desired? Had his subalterns remembered to have the documents prepared with print three times the normal size, so that Hitler's appalling eyesight could cope with them? Everything had to be right. Heydrich was sensible enough to realise these periodic appointments with the most important force in Germany were his catalyst for advancement. True, it is important to do a good job in the fatherland but, much more vital, is the Führer's perception that you do a good job. That was what really mattered – and Heydrich was a master of presentation.

And so, not being unduly concerned at the briefing and having fully prepared for it, Heydrich simply became bored at the unexpected delay. Just as he was wondering whether it was worth unfastening the leather document pouch for one last unnecessary examination of the munitions production figures for the Sudetenland, the door behind Rochus Misch finally opened.

Misch almost leapt out of the way in his haste to allow the Führer access but Heydrich merely rose to his feet with a practised calm, as the unmistakeable figure of Adolf Hitler strode magisterially towards him. Heydrich gave the Nazi salute and was about to greet his leader when he stopped in his tracks. Hitler was staring straight at him, sporting a furious countenance Heydrich found instantly alarming. There was a look of absolute mania in the Nazi leader's eyes. Heydrich had seen this look before but never been on the receiving end of it until now. What could he have done to prompt such anger? Hitler's stare was unflinching and even the fearless Heydrich wanted to look away and stare down at the floor in shame, like a naughty schoolboy too frightened to admit some misdemeanour. Instead he merely continued to stare into eyes that were a mirror of hate, seeking some clue to his fall from grace. He wanted to ask what misunderstanding had led to this but he had seen enough of Hitler's rages to know that no reason or argument would be brooked once the leader's mind was made up.

Heydrich awaited the onslaught now; the catalogue of crimes that would be thrown at him; the charge sheet that would see his medals and titles stripped from him, his lands confiscated, his wife and children sent to separate concentration camps, while he ended his life ingloriously hanging by piano wire suspended from a butcher's hook. Heydrich knew the next exchange could be the most important of his life and he steeled himself.

But the Führer did not speak; instead he did something far more terrible. He gave Heydrich a look of singular disgust – then simply walked away from him. In that moment he felt truly doomed. What could have prompted this reaction? How had he been reduced from favoured acolyte to despised pariah in the space of days? Then Heydrich received his answer. Standing in front of him was the podgy figure of Martin Bormann. From his smug countenance and oh so timely appearance, Heydrich instantly realised he was the victim of intrigue. By God, he was supposed to be the master of this game and he has allowed a chubby faced secretary to defeat him.

Bormann's eyes were hooded by dark brows and a steep, shelving forehead that set them further back into his face than seemed natural. It was entirely in keeping with his Machiavellian personality. Even here he seemed to be hiding something. What he could not shield, as his jowly face tensed in an effort to control his emotions, was the glee he was deriving from Heydrich's predicament.

'The Führer does not wish to see your report,' he said simply.

With a look of complete victory, Bormann left Heydrich standing alone in the corridor, as he sauntered calmly after his master and the staunch, ever-present figure of Rochus Misch.

10

'If you have sacrificed my nation to preserve the peace of the world, I will be the first to applaud you. But if not, gentlemen, God help your souls'

Czechoslovakian Foreign Minister, Jan Masaryk, to British Foreign Secretary Lord Halifax – Munich conference 1938

Strankmüller lolled like a badly made wooden puppet every time the train rounded a bend. His chin gently bumped against a uniformed chest before his head fell back once more, causing his mouth to gape open silently like a cadaver's. Kubiš could not have slept now if he had wanted to.

The Manchester Piccadilly train was making steady progress to London, yet Kubiš was increasingly impatient to reach their destination, for he was the recipient of an astonishing turn of good fortune. What else could explain his liberation from the training programme and a fateful, surely predestined pairing with Gabčík for Operation Anthropoid?

Certainly poor Anton Svoboda had been cruelly unlucky, but it was not as if he was dead or even severely injured. He simply had a major concussion – so what was that but a very bad headache? In a couple of weeks he would be fit to return to his unit and they would find some other mission for him to undertake.

Kubiš is alone in the carriage, save for the sleeping figure of Strankmüller. He tries to distract himself with the view from the train window – a kaleidoscopic blur of amber and dark green that passes him at such a rate he can barely distinguish where individual trees and bushes start and end – but it is no use, his mind is racing.

This time it was his turn to be called out of a training exercise – on silent killing – before the lesson was complete. Now it was Jan who spoke with Strankmüller, as the other men stood to one side while he had been singled out for a special assignment. Svoboda was injured, he had been told, nothing serious but he was unable to continue with his mission. Would Kubiš possibly be willing to take his place and work alongside his comrade Josef Gabčík on this most secret and dangerous undertaking? Of course he would. And this eager consent was all it took for him to be released from the training programme and to leave his instructors behind.

His belongings were swiftly cleared from David Watson's tiny little room, while George and Victoria received a short lecture in their front parlour from Strankmüller, regarding the destination of their lodger – most secret – and the fact that they could not know the nature of his mission – top secret. However, the true government of Czechoslovakia thanked them for the kindness of their hospitality and their selfless contribution to the war effort. They were then warned never to speak of Jan's premature departure, except to say, if asked, that he had returned to Scotland for further training.

The look of pride on George Watson's face, as Jan said his hurried goodbyes, was almost as sweet as the obvious realisation from Victoria Watson that she had not been housing a shirker after all, but a true and committed allied agent, destined for some daring and heroic mission heaven knows where.

Jan had been selected above others. He will strike back at the hated Germans, regain his sense of purpose and fulfil the promise he made to return to his country before the war is over. And – unimaginable good fortune – the destination is Prague, which means his prayer for Anna Malinová has been answered, and he will soon be with her once more. Now he can permit himself to think of his girl and enjoy the contrast in emotion. Instead of maddening despair, he experiences the uncontained optimism of one who is convinced fate itself has favourably intervened. The realisation he was back in the war again gave Kubiš a tangible burst of energy. *I have been asleep for months but now I am awake.*

As the train rolled south, he tried to recall Strankmüller's words, yet only fragments come back to him now. The rest was lost in a rush of emotion and adrenalin caused by the prospect of impending action. *You have been selected because you are a proven soldier... loyal, patriotic and true... this mission is considered extremely hazardous, you are not expected to survive its completion... we will not order you to take part... you can return to your unit without a blemish on your files... you must be sure that you wish to volunteer for this operation...*

And so forth, but he is a soldier and what else is he going to do? Stay behind and sweep the parade ground? Where does he have to sign?

Kubiš envied Strankmüller the gift of sleep. If only he could snore his way along the main line, not waking until the train has come to a stop, nudging itself gently against the buffers at Euston station.

The JU52 parted the clouds, turning them into thin wisps of vapour that clung longingly to the plane's wings, until it dropped through the white canopy and emerged into a bright blue expanse of sky above the airport. As the Junkers began its unhurried descent into Ruzyně, Heydrich's nerves finally began to calm.

He had begun the flight in the blackest of moods – he was doomed and knew it. The Reich's greatest strength was also its most obvious weakness – everything centred on the Führer. If Hitler appreciated you, nothing could prevent a spectacular rise; not social snobbery, a humble past or criminal record. Alternately, if you fell foul of the leader, no one could help and few would mourn – they would be too busy scheming to lay claim to your vacant job, rank and privileges.

How often he had witnessed a once favoured, Nazi Gauleiter, broken, chained and pleading, covered in blood and his own excrement as he cowered on the floor of a cell at Prinz Albrechtstrasse. Heydrich had practically invented the system, and certainly had honed the methods by which confession, to crimes real or imagined, was seen as a merciful release. Men would say anything once you had pulled out their teeth with pliers, bent their fingers back one by one until they snapped, or crushed one of their testicles. He had viewed it all so dispassionately but now he shuddered involuntarily at the thought of spending hours, possibly days, screaming in a torture chamber of his own imaginative devising.

And all because of Bormann.

It was the thought of the fat, smug face of Hitler's secretary that moved his thoughts gradually from fear to anger then defiance. Bormann – Bormann the bastard – that jumped up sergeant major's son, that note-taking, fetcher-and-carrier, provider of coffee and glasses of water, mopper of the Führer's brow. How could he let himself be outmanoeuvred by this coarse vulgarian, whose only official title was head of the *Parteikanzlei* – Hitler's Chancellery? What did he have that Hitler valued so? How could he be destroyed? Heydrich determined to answer both questions – then they would see who came out on top.

First thing in the morning he would open up Bormann's slim and inconsequential file at Hradčany, devouring every speck of intelligence on his rival. There was not much there he was sure, and he had to admit he'd entirely underestimated this scheming spider, who only emerged in a position of influence after his boss – that unhinged victim of astrology Rudolf Hess – parachuted into Scotland six months before on a mad scheme for peace doomed to failure from the outset. But Heydrich would add to what he knew – utilising every man in the intelligence service if need be. For his enemy had shown his face – so the day had not been an entire waste.

Bormann's file would soon be vast and compendious, listing every act of corruption, moment of sexual deviancy or treasonable utterance he had ever so much as considered. A few cases of liberated Jewish booty in a Swiss bank account, a young boy in his bed one night, a solitary bad word publicly declaimed against the Führer was all it would take. Put that together and present it, with the necessary portrayal of reluctance – *Mein Führer I am sure this will be as big a shock to you as it was to me but I regret to inform you that...* and Bormann would be lying in his own shit on a Gestapo cell floor, pleading for a mercy that would not, could not, come – for his would be an interrogation Heydrich would personally oversee.

Meanwhile the Reichsprotektor would double his efforts to squeeze every last piece of production out of the Czechs – showing Hitler the iron hand he approved of – and win back his favoured status with the Führer. There was also the Jewish project, to which he had lent serious thought. He was almost ready to begin, and even a disgruntled and poorly advised leader like Hitler could not ignore the results of this masterly scheme.

The thought cheered him greatly and, by the time the plane taxied to a standstill, with a reassuring purr from its propellers, his attention had already turned towards the evening's entertainment. There was no problem on this earth that could not seem at least half cured after a few cold beers, a hearty meal and an hour between a woman's thighs.

That evening Kubiš was reunited with his friend Gabčík, who greeted him with joyful, outstretched arms as his disbelieving head shook repeatedly from side to side. He clasps those arms around Kubiš and hoists him gleefully into the air for a second before letting him drop heavily back onto his feet once more.

'I liked Anton, sure,' he told his friend moments later, 'but this? This is even better, Jan. It is fitting. We go into battle together!'

'It's fate,' answered Kubiš.

'You can call it fate if you want, Jan, or God, or luck, or our guardian angels watching over us. Whatever it is, I am happy for it.'

Gabčík had been disarmingly honest about Kubiš' selection as replacement. 'They asked me what I thought about you, sure Jan, and I said I could think of nobody finer to have at my side, but they had already chosen. It wasn't as if I had to say "What about Jan Kubiš – he's a good man?" They knew all about you for sure. Major Strankmüller had a thick file on you, knew everything from the off.'

And Kubiš felt the pride of a man whose faith in himself has been completely restored at a stroke.

11

*'Whoever is not with us is against us
And whoever is against us will be ground to pieces'*

SS Brigadeführer Karl Frank, State Secretary of the
Protectorate of Bohemia and Moravia

Moravec strode into the room at the Porchester Gate hotel without fanfare. Gabčík clicked smartly to attention as soon as he caught the flash of gold on the Lieutenant Colonel's shoulder and Kubiš copied his movement. Moravec did not even look at them. He took the coming to attention as his right and walked round the desk in his own time, slowly removing his cap and placing it carefully on the blotter as he took his seat.

'At ease,' he said.

The room was thick with the musk of old wood and pipe smoke, lending it a scholarly and ancient feel. The overwarm air and odour of tobacco instantly reminded Gabčík of his school days. Somehow he could not rid himself of the feeling of going before the headmaster.

'Gentlemen, Major Strankmüller has explained you have been chosen for a most special undertaking. You have both been trained to return to the occupied homeland and carry out operations of sabotage. That training is ideal preparation for a new and very different mission of far greater importance to your country. The sanction for this operation comes directly from the President himself. Your task will be the single greatest act of defiance to the Nazis since the conflict began.'

Gabčík could be fairly accused of cynicism on occasion, but even he did not possess complete immunity from the chest swelling pride of the trusted man, chosen above others. Though unbidden, he felt compelled to respond.

'We are both prepared to do everything necessary, sir.'

'Good, I am sure you are both equal to the task. In a few days you will be parachuted back into Czechoslovakia as planned, but you will not make contact with the local resistance. Your mission is of such importance we cannot afford to have it compromised by any lapse of security, and our networks there are simply too fragile to trust against infiltration. Instead you will make your own way to Prague. There you will mount a surveillance operation on the commander of the German occupying forces, SS General Reinhard Heydrich.'

'You will have heard many stories regarding the brutality of Heydrich's regime; and I am in a position to confirm these reports are in no manner exaggerated.' Moravec did not have to rely on Czech sources for this information. His most prized asset in the occupied territories was a double agent in the Abwehr, Germany's military intelligence organisation. Agent 54, as he had been christened, confirmed everything the resistance network had told him about the brutality of Heydrich's regime. 'Heydrich is personally responsible for the torture and imprisonment of innocent civilians, for the relentless suppression of our resistance networks and for the literally hundreds of summary executions in the capital. He is a criminal who has lost the right to be treated as a soldier. Your mission is to analyse Heydrich's movements and plan an assault on his person that will result in his death. This will send the message to Hitler that our nation will never be a satellite of Germany and resistance will continue.'

Moravec halted for a moment and looked at each man in turn, searching for a reaction.

'Before you enter into a final commitment, I need to understand if you have any doubts about the nature of the task. This is an assassination, pure and simple, with no room for sentiment or old-fashioned notions of military honour. Are you both prepared to do what is required?'

Kubiš was familiar with Heydrich's name through the extensive rumour mill among the Czechs training with the SOE. Each new arrival had his own tale of cruelty involving a relative, neighbour or friend.

'The way you describe the situation in Prague, Heydrich has made himself a legitimate target,' said Kubiš.

Gabčík nodded. 'He is a criminal, a murderer. Murderers are executed.'

'It is important you have no misgivings. Once in the capital it will be too late for second thoughts and I can only send men who are truly dedicated to success. I need agents who will fulfil this mission come what may. It really is that vital.'

When no other observations were forthcoming, Moravec moved on. 'I assume you have questions.'

'Is Heydrich well-guarded?' asked Gabčík, keen to get as much detail from his superior as possible.

'He is not surrounded by bodyguards for the majority of the time, preferring for the most part to travel with just one driver-escort. However, you must always remember you are in a city wholly controlled by the Nazis, with large detachments of SS troops, minutes from all major locations. You can expect an extensive network of spies and, regrettably, paid informers from the civilian population. Remember, not everyone is sad to see the Germans. There are always people who prosper – even from occupation. You must proceed with extreme caution at all times. My advice would be to act as if you were in Berlin.'

'So it may be possible to get close to Heydrich,' reasoned Gabčík, 'but how do we get away afterwards, with no help from the resistance, if the whole city is crawling with SS?'

Moravec took a moment to formulate an answer. He stared down at the blotter in front of him as if the words he needed were etched on it, then straightened and caught Gabčík's eye.

'That will be part of your plan of action. We will offer advice and assistance but you will be on the ground, so only you can make a judgement on how to kill Heydrich and then make an escape.' Gabčík and Kubiš remained silent. 'I will not lie to you about your chances. We have contemplated this mission for some time now and have reached the conclusion that it may be possible to kill Heydrich; difficult but possible. However, we have also concluded that the likelihood of escape following the assassination is slim.'

There was a silence for a moment that seemed to stretch out before them while each man waited for the other to speak. It was finally broken when Gabčík began to feel a twinge of defiance. Moravec's uncharacteristic honesty demanded a positive response or they may as well both return to normal duties there and then.

'Slim,' he said quietly, 'but not impossible.'

Was that a half smile from Moravec?

'Prague is a big city,' added Kubiš, 'two men could easily lose themselves there.'

'Excellent, then I can assume you are both committed to the mission?'

'You can count on us, sir,' and Gabčík meant it.

Even Moravec seemed a little moved at their simple haste to serve the nation.

'I will speak with you again soon. For now, you will report to Major Strankmüller. He will oversee the completion of your training. It is vital we get you both through more night jumps. That will be all for now. Dismissed.'

'Sir!' they replied in unison, saluting together, before turning on their heels and marching smartly from the room.

Moravec was left alone to ponder the suitability of Strankmüller's Joes. They both seemed resolute but did they entirely appreciate the risks involved? He had deliberately tried to expose them to the cold reality of the mission, sparing them nothing, but perhaps they had failed to take his words seriously enough. Did they both fully grasp the notion that attacking Heydrich was very likely to be their last act? For a moment Moravec was assailed by doubts. What right did he have to send these men to their sure and certain deaths? Then he reminded himself he too had made sacrifices for his country. Had he not flown out of Prague in a blinding snowstorm, taking eleven of his finest operatives with him, the very night before German tanks rolled in? Had he not placed the well-being of his country before even his family? How could he forget the tender, unsuspecting face of his wife, as he kissed her on the cheek that morning, knowing he would not be returning to her? His mind went back to the moment more than a year ago, when he had walked to the back of the plane, pretending to do a final head count of his men, before selecting a seat in the furthest part of a commandeered KLM flight. There, alone for the first time in days, he dropped his head into his hands and silently wept as he left Prague and his uncomprehending wife behind him.

With the memory of her gentle face, and the bitterness of tears he would never admit to shedding now fresh in his mind, he told himself he had earned the right to ask these men to risk their lives. *That is what I did* he challenged the departed soldiers silently – *what are you prepared to do?*

12

TEN WEEKS LATER

'I am particularly anxious for a successful operation or two'

Hugh Dalton, Minister of Economic Warfare,
responsible for the SOE

Gabčík was about to explode. Kubiš could sense it. He knew the symptoms well enough. First the pacing, a restless movement that took him from one end of the safe house to the other and back again as if he was trying to find something but it was eluding him. Then the sighing, the head shaking and the grim face combined with the exaggerated frustration when an everyday occurrence served to confound his friend; a mug upended by accident or a tin can that refused to open, which would quickly lead to an eruption of temper. Kubiš knew the true cause of Gabčík's anger and it wasn't tin cans that refused to obey orders.

'Ten weeks!' Gabčík would incredulously remind him. 'Ten weeks, Jan, and we are no closer to our mission!'

Actually, it had been two months, two weeks and four days since Kubiš had taken the train to London to team up with Gabčík. He was just as aware of the inexplicable delay as his friend. They had trained until there seemed little point in training further; with all kinds of weapons under every envisaged scenario. Then, once they had peaked, when they reached a level of operational effectiveness that simply could not be exceeded, when they were ready to go and go soon... nothing.

Jan and Josef were forced to wait in growing frustration until a plane could be found to drop them over Prague.

'I am telling you, Jan, this mission is never going to happen! Never! They can't even get us over there!' It was a familiar rant by now. 'You remember what Moravec said to us in one of the Prague briefings, you remember?' Kubiš assured Gabčík that he did indeed recall those hopelessly naive words.

'We will get you on a plane in the next few days!' and his face was a picture of incredulity. 'We were supposed to go in days not ten weeks!!'

'We've been through this. It's not Moravec it's the RAF, they won't give us a plane.'

Kubiš was beginning to tire of the same rant from Gabčík about the inability of the Czech Secret Service, or the British SOE, to prise a plane from the Royal Air Force. Josef would invariably conclude that all involved were failing to do enough, and their mission to Czechoslovakia should naturally take precedence over all other concerns, such was its vital nature.

'The British, they don't see it like that. They've been fighting the war all this time, virtually by themselves, and they think they can win it their way.'

'What, by bombing the hell out of Germany? That's not going to win the war.'

'Maybe, Josef,' he conceded, 'but try telling the British that, when the RAF is sending hundreds of bombers over every night and losing a good number.'

Gabčík waved his hands in frustration. 'If they are losing so many they can surely spare us one!'

It was a ridiculous argument and they knew it. Kubiš didn't even understand why they were bickering but Gabčík needed to vent his frustration somehow and he did have a point. Without a plane from the British there would be no Operation Anthropoid. Both men, if they were to admit it, had begun to doubt they would ever be sent on the mission.

Flight Lieutenant Ron Hockey walked briskly across a runway stained white by a sharp morning frost. A bitterly cold wind cut through the unequal RAF tunic he wore, chilling his torso, and he picked up the tempo in an effort to warm himself. Drawing closer to the aircraft he began to make out the muffled voices of his crew, as they went about the pre-flight checks to their new and untried aeroplane.

The Handley Page Halifax stood in patient expectation before an enormous hangar, set to one side of the runway at RAF Northolt – where it had undergone recent adaptation. The work was designed to convert it from a bomber plane to an aircraft capable of transporting groups of parachutists hundreds of miles before dropping them behind enemy lines.

The process had caused a frustrating delay. First Hockey was told the Halifax was ready, then it was not – then it *was* ready but in need of further alteration, and Hockey lost another day – while they removed the bomb bay doors and replaced them with a plywood hatch, which would open up on command, so he could send another fearless Joe spiralling down into the ether. Finally, there was a problem with the winching gear needed to bring in the static lines and Hockey's frustration turned to anger, as more precious hours were lost.

The equally impatient airmen in his crew had been waiting a period of time variously described as *an eternity, a purgatory* and *till hell freezes over,* depending on which member of the crew was offering his opinion. Conventional wisdom even began to suggest that the maintenance unit worked for a new and secret section of the RAF known as Flight Prevention.

The postponement led to hours idling in the dispersal hut

at Northolt, which served as an impromptu mess area for crews in transit. Here they played cards, brewed up for the umpteenth time, read every word from the day's newspapers and ate endless pieces of toast. Occasionally, bulletins filtered back on the progress of their aircraft like news of an overdue baby. And still they waited.

Finally, late one afternoon, Hockey heard from the ground-crew grapevine that his aircraft was approaching completion and he wasted no time in pressing for its release.

'My plane ready yet at all?' He had been foolish enough to enquire with no preamble.

'It's not your plane, Hockey,' answered the officer in charge of the maintenance crew. 'I think you'll find it belongs to His Majesty King George. If and when you do get a brand new Halifax from me, it will be strictly on loan.'

With that, the precious paperwork that would see the Halifax released into his paternal care was finally produced. Hockey gratefully received RAF Form 700 – the aircraft log book – for serial number NF-V L9613 – and realised that implausibly his long wait was finally over. Back at the hut he had insisted on an early start the following morning.

'You can all get some sleep in the afternoon. The quicker you complete the pre-flight checks the quicker your heads will hit the pillows.'

This statement did not entirely satisfy the six men from 138 Special Duties Squadron who made up Hockey's regular crew. Their body clocks had failed to fully adapt to rising at dawn after weeks of night flights in their old aircraft, and they were further aggrieved when Hockey let an immense draught in through the opened hut door as he left.

All of that was forgotten once the crew was finally allowed to fuss purposefully round the new plane the next morning. When Hockey drew nearer to it the bomber's dark grey silhouette grew ever lighter as the sun slowly rose above it.

Pilot Officer Wilkin, his second in command, grinned at him as he reached the plane.

'Got us a nice new *Halibag* there, sir?' he said approvingly.

'We'll see, looks alright but we'll know for sure when we're at 12,000 feet.'

'Better than a bloody Whitley, sir, that's all I'm saying.'

There was a murmur of agreement from the men. Wilkin had flown in a 'Flying Coffin' before and had no desire to ever again experience a channel crossing in the carthorse slow, cigar shaped bomber.

Sergeant Holden appeared, cheerfully handing each man a steaming mug of tea. Hockey thanked his navigator and wrapped frozen hands around the mug's comforting heat. He let its warmth pass through him before lifting it to his chapped lips with both hands and sipping its contents.

Hockey took a step back and surveyed his new bird. It didn't look at all half bad at that and he felt an impatience to get into the air after the long wait for a serviceable new plane. He was also conscious of repeated delays to his Czech mission. It was theoretically possible he could drop the entire party tonight. The whole thing would depend on the Met office, of course – there were less than half a dozen days a month when a flight could be undertaken into Czech territory. The weather had to be favourable at both ends of the journey and they must avoid the vast banks of cloud that covered most of Central Europe if they were to find their way at all. But, if the run of luck he was having held out, he could give it a shot.

If Hockey did receive a favourable weather report they could conceivably assemble everyone at short notice if he could get the Halifax to the right location. He was contemplating the solution to this as he strode deliberately away from the Halifax, glancing back at it from time to time, enjoying the effect of the newly risen sun glistening against its freshly painted roundels.

'Tangmere,' he said to himself absentmindedly as he walked off through the hangar amid the faint, familiar smell of petrol, sawdust and engine oil. 'That ought to do it'.

What was Tangmere? A man's name, a place, a code word? Moravec pondered the answer to his own silent question as he watched Strankmüller.

The Lieutenant Colonel's deputy was holding the phone to his ear in rapt attention, and something in his manner told Moravec to close the reports he was analysing and place them back in his desk drawer. Perhaps it was the look of complete absorption on Emil's face as he listened so intently, with the minimum of interruption, save for the occasional *Yes, that's right*, or *I understand* or emphatic *certainly* that had Moravec convinced something momentous was afoot. He had waited impatiently as Strankmüller grabbed for a pencil, tore a piece of paper from his notebook then jotted down a brief note.

'Tangmere,' he had heard Strankmüller say the word aloud as he wrote, and been none the wiser.

Strankmüller finally concluded and hung up the phone. The head of Czech intelligence understood his deputy's moods and mannerisms, could read him as easily as the files he had just discarded, and he knew exactly what Strankmüller was going to tell him even before he turned to utter the words.

'It's on,' he said.

On 28 December, Jan Kubiš and Josef Gabčík were informed by a call to Stanhope Terrace that they would be vacating the safe house which had been their home for weeks that very night. Kubiš answered, took a brief message from Strankmüller then beamed at his disbelieving comrade. Gabčík had been wrong and so had he – this mission *was* going to happen. Their long wait was finally over.

13

*'I have been chosen for a mission.
I will carry it out come what may'*

Diary entry of Jan Kubiš

Moravec stood to one side of the Humber staff car, detached from the spectacle he was witnessing. President Beneš walked the grounds of his headquarters – Gabčík and Kubiš either side of him, the three men in private conversation together. The Lieutenant Colonel felt oddly superfluous.

Hearing the mission was finally underway, Beneš had insisted on speaking to his volunteers personally. They were met by the President; a bundle of nervous energy who guided them from the building almost as soon as they had entered it. Moravec was surprised to be told, 'František, if you wouldn't mind I would like a few moments alone with the men.' So he had elected to wait for them by the car. Moravec lit up a smoke, puffing at his cigarette self-consciously through a gloved hand and waited for his president's private briefing to conclude.

He correctly forecast Beneš would be keen to reinforce the importance of the mission. The President would understandably assume resolve would need to be strengthened – and some form of justification required for the appalling risks the men would soon be taking. Moravec smiled to himself at the thought, for he had spent not a little time with Gabčík and Kubiš of late, and knew the response Beneš would receive. There would be no need for further encouragement. At first Moravec had been slightly distrusting of his agents' unfettered enthusiasm. Was it some form of front, designed to fool a senior officer? And, if so, what did they really think of the mission? Were they more cynical in private? But no, after a time the Lieutenant Colonel realised they were simply two honest and determined men who believed wholeheartedly in this fight against the Nazis and he reprimanded himself for his own cynicism. There were good men left after all, it seemed.

As Moravec watched, the President stopped and turned to look at Kubiš who was responding to his entreaties. Moravec could not hear the men but it didn't matter. When Jan had completed his piece, Beneš opened his mouth to say something but no answer was forthcoming. It was the first time Moravec had ever seen his President lost for words. He had been similarly struck by the desire of the two soldiers to do what was required even at the cost of their own lives. There would be no lengthy philosophical debate about it with these two. You've given us the job and we will carry it out.

When Beneš finally returned, he walked ahead of the two soldiers and Moravec noticed his eyes were red and slightly puffy. The President realised his emotion was there for all to see and, like all good politicians, he attempted to make a strength out of weakness. Turning to face Jan and Josef, he unashamedly declaimed, 'These men make me proud of our country, František, and they give me hope – hope for the future. May God watch over you both tonight. Good luck, I know you will succeed!' He shook the hands of both men firmly and, with that final blessing, walked on into the old abbey, leaving Moravec alone with his men.

Witnessing Beneš in such an emotional state made Moravec resolve to keep the latest news from Prague to himself, for a day or two more at least. Why ruin the optimism of the moment by revealing the dreadful secret he was nursing? For Agent 54, scourge of the Abwehr, the one source of information Moravec could call upon from within the enemy's own ranks, the sole prize catch of the Czech Secret Intelligence Service, had suddenly, inexplicably, gone off the airwaves.

The President's secretary, Taborsky, met Beneš at the doorway, expecting the usual raft of instructions concerning the business of the day.

Instead Beneš said, 'Leave me alone this morning, Taborsky. I need some time…' and the sentence remained unfinished.

'Of course, sir.'

The secretary could see Beneš was emotional and as he returned to his desk he automatically wondered what hellish task had been assigned to the two young men he had seen walking with his President.

Barely a quarter of an hour later, the phone on Taborsky's desk rang shrilly. It was Beneš.

Something had changed in the moments since the President had last spoken to him. His voice was different now, unwavering and free of emotion.

'That last appointment,' and Taborsky would remember the words clearly years later for they were spoken with such firmness, 'don't make any record of it in the official diary.'

So it was as bad as that.

'No sir,' he replied and the phone clicked in Taborsky's ear as the line went dead at the other end. There was such an aura of cold finality about the President's instruction that his secretary experienced nothing less than a deep sense of foreboding. Despite this, he reached for the leather-bound diary, opened it and carefully tore out a single, lined page.

'God help them both,' he said to himself as he went about his President's bidding.

14

'Orders came for sailing
Somewhere over there
All confined to barracks
Was more than I could bear;
I knew you were waiting in the street
I heard your feet
But could not meet
My Lili of the lamplight
My own Lili Marlene'

Lili Marlene – a favourite song for both German
and Allied troops in WW2

28 December 1941

The three ton Bedford took the bend into RAF Tangmere
at speed and the lorry rattled on its axles as it bounced
out of a bump in the road, finally dislodging a covering
of snow that clung stubbornly to a bumper throughout the
journey. At the last moment, the brakes were applied and it
pulled up smartly alongside a sentry. He held a torch in front
of him and shone it down at the truck's number plate, then
up into the driver's face, before waving it speedily through
into the RAF's fighter base. The lorry and its cargo were both
expected.

Hidden beneath the dark green canvas stretched over the frame of the truck were seven men. They knew each other well but were prevented from acknowledging the fact beyond an introductory nod, a self-conscious smile or a mumbled grunt of greeting. All of the passengers were Czechs or Slovaks, had passed through the SOE course and were now part of their own individual, highly secret operations. As a result they were expressly forbidden to communicate with each other – about their missions or anything else. It was a ridiculous arrangement. The men felt like children forced to sit in silence by a strict schoolmaster. Occasionally they would exchange smiles of acknowledgement or raise eyebrows, to show their understanding of the absurdity of this position, but they continued to obey orders.

Kubiš was restless, drunk with the heady mixture of anxiety and excitement that characterised the beginning of a mission. He found himself impatient to get underway but retained a deep, nagging concern he might somehow let everyone down. The sum of their training, the hours of planning and the weeks of waiting would all come to nought if he suddenly found he was not up to the task. Right now, his dread at this eventuality was more potent than the fear of injury, capture, even death. How insignificant was his own life by comparison to the mission they had been assigned?

The men climbed down from the truck and walked wordlessly into the main building. The base was selected by Hockey for its proximity to the south coast, and its relative closeness to London where many of the agents currently resided. Its three squadrons of Hurricanes and Spitfires still formed the vanguard of the country's air defences and the building usually swarmed with pilots and aircrew alike. There was a strong likelihood the presence of a few Czech irregulars was barely worthy of comment even at this hour.

The men were separated to undergo final pre-flight checks.

Strankmüller was there to meet them and he attended to Gabčík and Kubiš personally. They were made to empty their packs for the umpteenth time, laying their equipment out for one final inspection, leaving nothing to chance.

Amid the more mundane items, the pairs of socks, the shaving razor, the carefully authenticated civilian clothing each man carried, was a Sten gun, disassembled into three pieces and a Colt Automatic pistol. There were spare magazines for both weapons and three specially adapted Mills hand grenades, green tape wrapped around them. As Strankmüller slowly inspected the array of equipment it was the smallest item in the kit that drew his eye – the article each man would keep with him at all times yet prayed he would never have to use – a single capsule of fast acting cyanide.

Strankmüller carried out a final standing search of the men, checking every pocket, scrutinising papers and examining the lining of wallets.

'We don't want you to betray yourself with an English bus ticket or a stub from the local cinema,' he explained and both men were glad of his thoroughness.

'Although I'm more likely to find a beer mat on you two,' he muttered with a mock gruffness.

That very afternoon an SOE expert had issued new clothes specially adapted to look as if they had been made and purchased in the Protectorate. Even the distinguishing marks on the zipper of Kubiš' English made trousers had been carefully erased with the deft use of an adapted dentist's drill.

Above their civilian clothes they donned heavy cotton flying suits with mottled camouflage patches of brown and dark green. Jan put on the khaki skullcap but kept the chinstraps loose until he was ready to jump. They then rejoined their comrades, filing outside into a threatened downpour of fresh snow.

Strankmüller's arrangements meant they spent their last

hour in England clustered together in a dispersal hut at the furthest edge of the airfield, two hundred yards short of the runway. There was an inevitable delay before boarding the plane.

The men waited quietly for the Halifax to taxi out, a nauseating tension spreading among them as they anticipated the burr of the plane's engines. Some huddled together, chain smoking silently like expectant fathers. Jo Valčík, a handsome sergeant, popular with girls wherever he was billeted, handed cigarettes to the two men on his team, codenamed Silver A; Corporal Jiří Potůček and his officer, Lieutenant Alfréd Bartoš. Silver A had been up in RAF planes before, with three failed attempts to get over Prague behind them – their new mission, assigned at the eleventh hour by Moravec, was to urgently re-establish contact with Agent 54. Bartoš struck Kubiš as an ambitious leader in a hurry. He was trying hard not to show nervousness but betrayed his tension as he puffed urgently at the cigarette, wearing it down to a stub in moments. The final group was Silver B. Two sergeants, Vladimír Škacha and Jan Zemek, would deliver a transmitter and much needed equipment to the resistance.

Even if conversation had not already been barred it would have been unforgivable to drown out the approaching sounds of the plane with mere chatter. Instead the apprehensive Joes stood in silence in the freezing hut, with steam rising off their damp flying suits and clouds of hot breath pouring from their mouths like cigarette smoke.

Then Kubiš heard a sound; a beautiful, throaty purr that changed everything and made them all start in expectation. The plane was taxiing towards them outside and the men were immediately energised, hastily lifting bags of equipment and stowing parachutes on shoulders, as if the plane were an infrequent village bus that might suddenly leave without them. They shuffled to the door together, adjusting their strides to avoid knocking into each other as they bottlenecked through it.

There was no time for further instruction as the men filed out silently. The only sound was the crunch of the top layer of frozen snow as seven pairs of shoes traversed the runway. Seconds later even that was drowned out by the approaching plane.

As Jan and Josef drew alongside the Halifax, Strankmüller was struck by how small and insignificant they looked next to the bomber. He wished he were going with them too, to guide, encourage and cajole them through the hostile streets of Prague. Instead he was left standing helplessly in the snow as he called out a final farewell.

'Good luck to you both and may God go with you!'

'You can rely on us. We will fulfil our mission as ordered!' shouted Gabčík.

Any further words he may have been saving for that historic moment were lost in the din of the plane's four Rolls-Royce Merlin engines. Instead they merely waved an acknowledgement before climbing up the ladder, one after the other, then disappearing into the body of the plane.

Kubiš occupied a space in the furthest corner of the Halifax as the plane began to move. He could feel every bump as it trundled along a runway liberally dusted with fresh snow. Who would have thought the weather might decide the future of a nation? Well, at least they would know nothing about it if they piled into the hedgerows.

Kubiš was pressed gently backwards as the plane picked up speed, vibrations from the metal frame numbing his limbs and torso. Then he experienced a slight lurch deep in the pit of his stomach as it finally left the ground. He could feel the craft being pushed up underneath him and he knew this was the most dangerous time. Kubiš said a quick and automatic prayer and waited helplessly. A moment passed then another and the plane continued to climb. Finally it levelled off and there was a tangible easing of tension. He knew the critical moments of take-off had passed without incident and the Halifax was making swift progress through the dark air around them.

The journey over the channel was pleasantly uneventful and, when they crossed into occupied France at Le Crotoy, Hockey breathed a small sigh of relief. The crew knew that, once spotted by the Luftwaffe, the chance of escape was slim and the possibility of rescue from a night-time parachute drop into the darkened sea virtually non-existent. All of the men dreaded the prospect of baling out into cold and choppy waters on a filthy winter night like this one.

They left the Channel behind them and crossed the hostile fields of France thousands of feet below – and still their luck held, but Hockey knew it was unlikely they would have an entirely trouble free flight. Finally, at a little after midnight, over German soil near Darmstadt, Holden picked out the first of the enemy night fighters. His voice, sounding calmer than it ought, indicated the presence of two ME 109s flying hard, hundreds of feet below the Halifax, clearly visible through a parting in the clouds. Barely had he finished noting their appearance when one of the fighters dramatically altered course.

'I think he's seen us, sir.'

Hockey needed no further prompting and he flew the virgin aircraft hard away, pushing it to its limits. The Halifax veered, pitched then rose, answering its pilot's call. He altered its trajectory repeatedly – attempting to lose the Messerschmitts in the dense banks of welcoming cloud around them. But each time they returned with the persistence of angry hornets.

Hockey tried not to think of the frozen ground below. Instead, as he wrestled with the controls of the aircraft, his subconscious mind was occupied with random images of home. As the plane pitched out of a steep climb he found himself remembering the pretty girl who delivered it; a young ferry pilot, no older than twenty two, who had calmly conveyed the Halifax for adaptation.

'This one for you, Flight Lieutenant?'

'Mmm, yes,' was all he could manage.

'Well, she's a good 'un,' she assured him, with just the trace of a West Country accent, as she strode closer, 'try not to scratch her.'

Try not to scratch her. Christ, he thought, I hope that wasn't a premonition. Don't think about it now, got to keep a firm grip on the kite. And his manoeuvres continued, above the hostile German territory. Still the Messerschmitts did not give up the search. Until finally, gloriously, Holden's voice came over the radio.

'Flare, sir. Below us at five o'clock.'

Sure enough, the pilot of one of the night fighters was betraying his frustration at the fruitlessness of the hunt by harmlessly scattering a flare into a corner of the sky they had long since departed. They had lost him.

'I see her,' replied Hockey.

He dipped his wings in the opposite direction then rose, as swiftly as the plane would allow, climbing up and away from the reddish tinge of light far below them.

Kubiš enjoyed a few moments of calm. The plane had ceased its frantic evasive action, particularly unnerving for passengers who could not tell the difference between a deliberate tactical manoeuvre and an irreversible nose-dive. Jan allowed himself to hope the worst was over and that before too long he would be gently descending onto Czech soil. His optimism was ended an hour later by a hollow sound that seemed to be coming from outside the plane.

Belatedly, he realised they were under attack. Hundreds of feet below them, German anti-aircraft batteries were opening up on the Halifax with everything they had. The sound he could hear was the dull and distant *crump, crump* as flak exploded outside the bomber and he exchanged nervous glances with Gabčík. They had little choice but to sit there and accept the random detonation of the ack-ack as it exploded all around them.

The volume increased steadily until Kubiš was convinced the flak was about to find its mark. Then slowly, so very slowly, the sound began to diminish until presently it faded away all together. The last obstacle to the landing zone had been cleared. Hockey would later recall in his flight log that flak had been experienced over Plzeň at 02.12, but was merely sporadic.

Jan felt a hand clamp firmly on his shoulder and he looked up into an urgent face.

'Get ready. You two go first. About ten minutes.'

Kubiš nodded his understanding.

The ten minutes seemed like an hour as Kubiš waited for the signal to jump. Would the chutes open? How ironic and terrible if the parachutes let them down after all this. And he wondered how many elite paratroopers had trained for months, and waited all of their lives, merely to crash into the ground before they had fired a shot, because someone had been careless packing their chute. And what would happen if they landed slap bang in the middle of a German patrol?

Even above the noise of the plane's engines Kubiš became aware of the animated conversation between Holden and the Czech intelligence officer accompanying them, Captain Šustr.

'I can't make out a single landmark for the drop zone!' shouted Šustr. 'Every river, railway, hilltop or bridge around the capital is covered by snow!' Captain Šustr's shame and agitation were understandable, thought Kubiš. He had come all this way, at great personal risk, for nothing. Following a brief consultation with Hockey, Šustr made a decision.

'We must trust in God and compass and drop the men immediately. Hopefully they will all be within a mile or so of their drop zones. We don't know when we will be able to attempt a journey like this one again. Anthropoid will go first!'

Gabčík and Kubiš climbed to their feet, shuffling forward under the weight of their packs. Jan tightened his chinstrap and watched as Sergeant Walton released the specially adapted hatch. As the pitch black hole opened up before them the men were struck by an icy blast of winter air and the noise level in the Halifax rose as the wind whistled by beneath them. Kubiš' first instinct, as ever, was to place himself away from the proximity of danger and he had to fight the urge to sit back down again. He had been dreading this moment but knew it was the only way. He had to endure.

Kubiš walked to the edge of the hatch, took a last glance at the concerned faces around him and, before fear gripped him entirely, launched himself out through the hatch.

Gabčík followed immediately, striding determinedly up to the opening. He turned to Šustr and roared over the din of the wind.

'Remember, you will be hearing from us – we will do everything possible!' And with that he too was gone.

15

'Now they'll work for they know we are pitiless and cruel'

Adolf Hitler on the Czechs

So far, so good – the static line had done its job, the chute opened almost as soon as he had cleared the plane and Kubiš was falling at a manageable rate of knots. Now he realised he would soon have a new problem to contend with. Despite the pristine layer of snow, a moon shrouded in cloud hindered his visibility, and he could barely make out the ground below. He found he had to trust his instincts as well as his eyes if he was to land right. As it was, the terrain still rushed up to meet him far too quickly and he had to squeeze his legs together hard and bend his knees as he landed.

The impact sent a shockwave up through his knees, jarring his spine. His body careered forward and he let out an involuntary gasp as he fell face first into the icy ground. Powdery snow shot into his eyes and the wind was knocked from him. Kubiš lay still for a moment as pain ebbed through his body and he struggled to regain the breath that had been forced from it. At first he was not sure how badly he had been hurt but gradually the soreness began to subside and, to his intense relief, he realised there was no lasting damage.

Kubiš stayed on his stomach, letting his eyes and ears adjust to his new surroundings. There were no barking dogs, cocked rifles or shrieked German commands and that was a fine start to the operation as far as he was concerned. The only sound was the occasional stirring of leaves from trees that marked the perimeter of the field he had landed in. He placed his hands on the ground to push himself to his feet and told himself this was Czech soil he was touching. Kubiš was home.

He tugged at the strings of his parachute and slowly dragged the canopy towards him. By now his vision had adjusted to the night and he could, with the help of the reflective snow, make out much of the area around him. Worryingly there was no sign of Gabčík.

Gradually Kubiš climbed to his feet, wincing a little at the bruising on his ribs, then set off instinctively towards the next field.

Kubiš heard his friend before he saw him. The voice was unmistakeable and the cursing entirely in character but unwise now if they were to avoid discovery. Kubiš had grown weary of wandering the fields looking for Gabčík so it was almost a relief to hear the man, even if he was putting their security at risk with his volatile temperament.

As Kubiš grew closer he realised his friend was in some distress. The first image Jan had of Gabčík on home soil was of a man desperately trying to half walk, half stumble across the frozen ground. No sooner had he witnessed this peculiar spectacle than Gabčík crashed to the snow with a wretched moan. Kubiš ran towards him.

'Josef, it's me, it's okay.'

His prone comrade's face tightened into a grimace as he rolled on the ground. This did not look good.

'What's happened?'

'This mission is cursed,' hissed Gabčík.

'What is it, Josef?'

'I have broken my ankle,' came the desperate, anguished reply.

It took Kubiš half an hour to find a spot sufficiently isolated to bury the parachutes, in snow deep enough to ensure they would remain undiscovered following the first light thaw. He then set about a recce of the nearby terrain, and was disturbed to discover they appeared to have landed literally miles from anywhere. Small wonder there were no Germans – there was nothing here at all – not even a village.

Eventually he chanced upon the edge of an ancient quarry and a series of caves created from blasting; as good a spot as any for them to hide up in while contemplating a solution to this crisis. He returned to collect Gabčík, who was seated at the edge of the field, propped up against a drystone wall. Gabčík wrapped an arm round his comrade's shoulders and the two men hobbled to the cave. Their progress was ludicrously slow and each step was punctuated by little gasps of agony and yet more muffled curses from the injured man. Kubiš was aware of his friend's normally high pain threshold and his alarm began to grow. Was the mission over before it had even started? How would he ever get Gabčík to Prague now? He did not even know the way to the capital.

By the time he had returned to the landing spot for a second time, collected both sacks of equipment and heaved them back to the cave, one on each shoulder, the sky was lightening above him and Jan began to feel complete physical exhaustion. At least the caves were isolated, hidden and dry. Too drained to fret over their circumstances further both men slept lightly against their packs for a couple of hours in the darkest recesses of the cave.

Kubiš drew the commando knife from his belt, its blade greased black to eliminate shine. He held it low by his hip –

out of sight but close enough to be used in haste if need be. He noticed Gabčík had instinctively reached for a pistol.

They both watched intently as the mysterious figure shuffled towards their hiding place; an indistinct silhouette with an imposing bulk and awkward gait. Jan half expected the man to scratch his belly and yawn. Instead he took both of them by surprise, advancing right into the mouth of the cave then speaking clearly and without fear.

'This is no hotel. This is my farm. Who are you and what is your business here?'

Kubiš started slightly, astonished the farmer could see them in the relative darkness of the cave. It was as if he had read Kubiš' mind. 'I know you are in there, you left a trail of footsteps in the snow. What do you want here?'

Gabčík turned on a torch and shone it into a face deeply lined from years of working outdoors in all weathers. The farmer raised his hand against its beam.

'Are you a patriot?' Gabčík challenged him.

The farmer screwed up his eyes against the light.

'I am a loyal Czech.'

He moved closer.

'Stay there,' said Gabčík with authority and the man halted immediately.

'You are on the run from the Germans?' he asked, his tone gentler this time. 'I am not going to hand you in, if that's what you think.'

Receiving no immediate answer the farmer advanced once more. He was more tentative this time and Gabčík permitted him to continue until they could make out his features more clearly. He possessed a small, slightly bulbous nose that hung disjointedly above a tight, mirthless mouth and his stomach pushed forward impatiently ahead of his chest, like a sprinter trying to win a race at the tape. As his eyes grew accustomed to the light he caught a glimpse of the equipment that lay haphazardly on the ground around them and immediately understood.

'Parachutists,' he muttered to himself in satisfaction. 'I knew I heard a plane last night. You are a little light on numbers for an invasion force.' He let out something between a laugh and a snort at this. 'So what are you then? Spies? Resistance fighters?'

This time Kubiš answered. 'Our mission is secret. We cannot tell you why we are here. My comrade has an injured ankle from the drop and we wish to rest here for a while until he is well enough to travel. Now, where exactly are we?'

'The nearest village is Nehvizdy. It's lucky you landed here, and not the next farm along. That old wolf would sell you to the Nazis as soon as he set eyes on you. What is your destination?'

The two men exchanged glances before Kubiš reluctantly confirmed. 'Prague.'

The farmer whistled, telling them all they needed to know about the proximity of their drop zone. He thought for a moment before eventually deciding. 'Wait here then. I can get a message to a friend. He knows some people. They are still active against the Germans, if you understand me. They could move the equipment and your friend to the capital.'

'You'll forgive me if I say we have no way of knowing you won't immediately turn us in,' countered Gabčík.

'And you'll forgive me for saying you could just as easily be German spies trying to tempt me into helping you, so you can have me shot then give my farm away to some collaborator.'

Kubiš answered. 'We could but it would be a hell of a lot of trouble to go to, wouldn't it?'

The farmer nodded, hawked up a sizeable dollop of spit, looked them both in the eye then spat it expertly onto the ground.

'Fuck Adolf Hitler!' he exclaimed with relish. 'There, does

that make you feel better? Now do you want me to contact the resistance for you or not?'

'What do you think?' asked Kubiš.

'I don't know – we were distinctly told not to go that way.'

'And we were also told to think for ourselves once we landed. How else are we going to get you out of here in this state?'

The farmer stepped closer still and, when he interrupted them, he spoke in a dry, sardonic tone.

'You are twenty miles from your destination, with heavy equipment you cannot possibly carry alone. You are dressed like renegades and have three good legs between you. What choice do you have?'

And both men realised he was right.

Sergeant Karel Čurda was entirely alone – his mission abandoned and all thoughts of a glorious return to his homeland exposed as fantasy. The day before he was forced to spend the night in a barn.

Now he stood among the trees, blowing air onto his frozen hands, nervously watching the large stone house at the far end of the village that lay in the valley below. Čurda looked for signs of life that should not be there; men in grey uniforms, unusual visitors, black marketeers perhaps, who would surely sell him as easily as a consignment of razor blades or booze, and found none, save for a slow trail of black smoke which rose lazily from the chimney.

He was bitterly cold and longed for hot food and coffee by a warm fire. The terror of the previous forty eight hours was still strong in Čurda, however, and it prevented him from knocking on the door even though it promised sanctuary. Ladislav, the man who had sheltered them when their mission went awry, had assured him the blacksmith in the next village was no friend of the Germans, that if anything went wrong he could get Čurda and his friends safely to Prague, where they could lose themselves in the city's anonymous bustle. But what did Ladislav know? He was dead already.

Čurda's three-man team, Out Distance, had parachuted in twelve days before Gabčík and Kubiš. They hoped to plant a beacon that would lead the RAF right over the Skoda plant, so it could have the hell bombed out of it one winter's night and the armaments production there would cease. It was meant to be so simple but from the outset everything had gone disastrously wrong.

First their officer, Lieutenant Opálka, injured himself right at the start landing on rocky ground. He was incapable of leaving the scene unaided, so Čurda and his good friend Kolařík had hidden the beacon then helped their officer to the nearest village, knocking on the first door they reached. How dangerously naive they had been Čurda realised now.

Old Ladislav, no member of the resistance himself, had gingerly pulled back the door and peered at them through frightened eyes. At first he was shocked by the three apparitions on his doorstep but managed to compose himself long enough to usher them in.

The next day an inquisitive farmer discovered the beacon and the disloyal fellow immediately reported the fact to the Germans. Ladislav hid Kolařík and Čurda in his loft while he arranged to get the luckless Lieutenant Opálka out of the village – an injured man being far more conspicuous than able-bodied guests, who might be explained away as visiting family members.

All was well at first and Čurda, lulled by the next few days of inactivity, decided to venture out and stretch his legs with a walk in the hills. Kolařík declined such a dangerous diversion but waved his friend off with a warning that he at least be careful.

When Čurda returned that evening, he stopped dead

at the sight that greeted him. As soon as he made out the unmistakeable shape of the armoured car outside Ladislav's house, he stepped straight back out of sight and flattened himself against the stone wall of the nearest building. German soldiers milled around the vehicle and their officers sat in a staff car parked close by. There was a body on the pavement and, even though Čurda could not see it clearly in the darkness, he realised it could only be Ladislav; shot through the head on his own doorstep and left there as a warning to others against harbouring the resistance.

Čurda watched as Kolařík was manhandled out through the doorway. They would not have taken long to find him if they already knew he was inside, thought Čurda. So they had been betrayed, but by whom he would never know. Kolařík struggled but it was hopeless and he was quickly bundled into the staff car and driven away. Terrified, Čurda slid back into the shadows, grateful of the darkness, which cloaked him. He had almost walked into the Gestapo and that could never be allowed to happen again.

Truth be told, he was no less petrified of capture now than he had been then but Čurda realised he could not hope to stay out in the open much longer. The cold was beginning to be all he could think about and tonight there would not even be the minimal shelter of the barn. How long before his comrade cracked under prolonged torture and revealed the existence of other parachutists? Čurda had to keep moving and clearly could not do this on his own steam any more. The blacksmith was surely his only chance of salvation. Čurda took a deep breath then started out down the hill towards the house and its welcoming fire.

16

'Slavs cannot be educated as one educates a Germanic people.
One must either break them or humble them constantly'

Propaganda Minister, Joseph Goebbels, February 1942

It was three days before Kubiš finally met Zelenka; a period
during which he was subjected to the careful scrutiny of a
steady stream of intermediaries, each one more suspicious
than the last. While the limping Gabčík was separately
transported to Prague with their equipment, hidden in the
back of a lorry, Jan stood before his understandably cautious
new associates in the Jindra resistance network.

He answered their questions as best he could but there
was one point he remained adamant on, as he was shuffled
between safe houses on the outskirts of Prague, onwards and
upwards until he began to meet men who held positions of
some influence in the resistance; he would never reveal the
true purpose of his mission.

There were some among the Jindra volunteers who
were disconcerted by this and others who felt it proved his
authenticity for, if Kubiš really was a turncoat, it would
surely be easier to buy their trust with some fabricated tale.
The second group won the argument, so he eventually found
himself face to face with Jan Zelenka, in a dark corner of a side
street coffee house. Here was the man who could help Gabčík

and Kubiš become entirely integrated into the occupied capital. His journey of acceptance was almost complete.

Zelenka was a slight, nondescript looking individual with hair shorn almost to the scalp. Kubiš guessed he was an educated man, judging by the softness of his hand when he shook Jan's in greeting.

'I am sorry it has taken so long before we could meet. I hope you understand the reason. The Germans are becoming adept at sending traitors among us. Czechs who feel more loyalty to Berlin than Beneš.'

'I understand, but I will not tell you my mission. I have made that repeatedly clear.'

'So you have and it is not necessary. We believe you are who you claim to be. If we did not you would be dead by now,' and he smiled disarmingly. 'I am in a position to offer you the assistance you need, whatever your mission.'

'Thank you,' said Kubiš with some feeling and his thoughts immediately turned to Gabčík. 'Where is my friend?'

'In another safe house, with a family I know – a strictly temporary arrangement while I finalise places for you both to stay on a more permanent basis. I organise a number of our friends here who help to move people round the city. In my former life I was a teacher, now I run around Prague playing at spies. However, it is a game none of us can afford to lose. Don't worry – Josef will be fine. I am told the ankle is not broken and will heel in time. You will see him again this evening when I take you both to see Hlinka.'

Hlinka the forger was an earnest looking little man with tiny, wire-framed glasses, perched on the end of a nose too small for the rest of his face. His body was equally out of proportion, with small podgy arms that barely reached his midriff, but his hands were deft and quick.

Gabčík wondered if he had always been a forger. Was he a

criminal before the war whose skills were now a prized tool of the resistance, or had he been a law-abiding clerk somewhere, in a bank perhaps, before discovering a talent for this kind of work? It mattered little to Josef, who instinctively knew he was dealing with a professional. When Hlinka peered down through his eyeglasses at the papers Gabčík had given him, he was like a dentist scrutinising a row of teeth for imperfections.

Of course, they looked realistic enough to Gabčík but then he had never actually seen the genuine articles. By the time the Nazis had issued papers to the reluctant citizens of Prague he was a soldier clambering over French fields attempting to repel the *Wehrmacht*.

First, Hlinka examined the identity card, a red bordered, double page document, which opened out into two halves; one side of which contained a photographic likeness of Josef. It was intended to look as if it had been taken at the Černín Palace and not Porchester Gate. At the top of the opposite page the words *Deutsches Reich Protektorat Böhmen und Mähren* were written, opposite their equivalent words in Czech. The information *vorname – zurname –* both equally false, were then added below. They had given him little yellow ration coupons for meat, dairy products, clothes, everything he could possibly need, including soap and coal. There was even a photographic pass, which permitted him to take the city's trams.

'It's as well you came here,' Hlinka announced matter-of-factly. 'Try and use these in Prague and you will be arrested before the day is over.'

He showed the fake identity cards to Zelenka, while Gabčík and Kubiš, reunited for the first time since leaving the cave, exchanged disconcerted glances.

'The watermark is all wrong, the inks are not close enough to the ones our German friends are currently using and the paper is of an inferior quality,' he shrugged. 'I could go on.'

Evidently deciding not to, he instead spoke to Gabčík and Kubiš. 'I'll need two, possibly three days, you understand, to make new papers of the necessary quality. You will need to stay out of trouble till then.'

'That means not going out – literally,' added Zelenka. 'I have arranged rooms for you with sympathetic friends. Jan, you will stay first with Aunt Marie in Žižkov. She is not my aunt but everybody calls her that. Marie is a remarkable woman with contacts all over the city. She will make you very welcome.'

'And me?'

'You, Josef, will stay with Fafek, a good friend of mine.'

'And remember you must stay inside until I have completed your papers,' cautioned Hlinka. 'Aside from arrest there is another danger. The Nazis are rounding up able-bodied young men and shipping them back to Germany as forced labour. I will need to get you medical exemptions. It's okay, we have friendly doctors who are not afraid to write certificates for patriots. You, my friend,' he was addressing Gabčík, 'are really not looking well. I'm no physician but I suspect you could have a duodenal ulcer.'

Gabčík smiled at Hlinka. 'You can tell that just by looking at me?'

'Oh yes, and you, sir, I feel may be about to become the victim of an inflamed gall bladder.'

'How unfortunate,' answered Kubiš.

'I recommend you refrain from heavy work for some time.'

'I'll be sure to take your advice.'

'Come on then both of you,' said Zelenka, 'we need to get you away from here now. There is no curfew currently but I don't want you out on the streets too long after dark without proper papers.'

Before Gabčík left he scooped up the banknotes Strankmüller had given them. Thankfully they proved to be entirely genuine. It seemed like a particularly generous bundle of crowns, and he had been reassured by the familiar presence of landmarks like the King Charles Bridge and Hradčany Castle on the notes. It was only when he had examined the money more closely that he realised they now contained German words as well as Czech. Even the currency had been tarnished.

17

'If Hitler were to say shoot my mother
I would do it and be proud of his confidence'

SS Reichsführer Heinrich Himmler

Fafek was a short man with a labourer's rough hands and a physique formed from a combination of hard work and the diligent intake of beer. The man was muscular yet rotund. As soon as Zelenka left his house he led Gabčík into a gloomy front parlour and introduced him to a young woman.

'This is my daughter, Liběna. She will show you where you will sleep.'

Gabčík turned to see a striking, dark eyed young woman, of 19 or so, watching him with a slightly guarded curiosity. She wore her dark hair long, cascading down over the shoulders, and her face was undeniably beautiful, with the healthy shine of youthfulness. Her eyes, which never left his, hinted heavily at intelligence.

'You have a room upstairs at the back of the house.' She spoke up now and her clear voice had a pleasing, melodic ring. Gabčík liked Liběna almost instantly. 'There is fresh linen on the bed and clean water for you in a wash bowl.'

'Thank you, I am sure it will be perfect.' Oh God, could he not think of anything better to say than that? She smiled slightly and seemed eager to continue their dialogue.

'If you are hungry I will bring you a plate of cold meats and black bread later.'

'You are very kind.' And extremely pretty, he thought.

Liběna seemed embarrassed at the praise. 'It's no trouble.' She said it dismissively and looked down at the floor for a moment before remembering she was a young woman now, old enough to be married and no longer expected to hold her tongue like a child. Before she could speak again her father intervened.

'Enough talk, the man is tired, show him his room.'

Gabčík realised Fafek immediately sensed the possibility of an attraction between this soldier and his daughter and had not taken too kindly to the idea. Josef knew it was a combustible notion, particularly while he was living under the man's roof. The sensible thing would be to stay out of Liběna's way, speaking only when spoken to, avoiding trouble but when was he ever noted to possess any sense?

'It's through here,' mumbled Liběna, motioning to a door, and Gabčík felt a spark of something in her shyness. He wandered after her dumbly, feeling a strange contentment from her presence.

No distractions – he told himself wryly as he limped heavily up the staircase after her.

Kubiš spent a depressing first day at large. Everywhere the streets were festooned with swastikas set in blood red flags. These banners were suspended from windows or balconies owned by genuine Nazi sympathisers or those who merely wished to avoid trouble.

Somehow he had convinced himself that just by being back in Prague his spirits would be lifted, and as soon as he was in possession of Hlinka's remarkably authentic looking papers he had gone out to explore the city. Now he was experiencing the grim reality of a homeland occupied by Nazis.

As he entered the Old Town Square his mood darkened further. Here the Germans had retaliated against a subversive resistance plan, encouraged by the western allies, to etch defiant letter Vs on buildings all over the city. To combat this propaganda they merely hijacked the symbol, using it as part of a V for Victory campaign – an outward sign of the capital's supposed support for the Nazi war effort. After claiming it as their own they took the scheme a stage further. Huge letter Vs were painted in town squares, and planted into every flowerbed. Now the symbol was everywhere, on trams and buses and depicted on huge banners, which hung the entire length of tall buildings.

It was a humiliation, and a degradation of the Czech nationalism so evident on the creation of this fledgling country twenty years before. And now, from the evidence of Jan's own eyes, they were even making everyone drive on the right. A Czech policeman directing traffic the wrong way around the square, under the watchful eye of an armed German sentry, was such a disconcerting sight that Jan was reminded of the first morning of the occupation. He vividly recalled the profound sense of shock when the capital awoke to find the nation had been sold down the river. Some wept openly on the streets. Others wretchedly yet loudly proclaimed the national anthem of their dead country, as they stood in small, defiant groups in Wenceslas Square. They had deliberately chosen the statue of the country's appropriately heroic, yet betrayed and martyred king as their rallying point.

As German soldiers patrolled the streets of the capital the first curfew was imposed on the stunned citizens of the city. By 8 pm the streets had been deserted except for the armed sentries outside requisitioned hotels filled with German officers, and military vehicles that arrived unopposed but often became lost in side streets with strange-sounding names. In the afternoons at least they had been able to ask Czech policemen for directions. If you looked out of your window at night, Jan remembered, you could watch them as they drove up and down the silent streets petulantly searching for a landmark, until they chanced upon the river or caught a glimpse of the Castle in the moonlight.

It was witnessing these alien vehicles in his homeland that finally spurred Kubiš to rebel, escape from the city and continue the fight. Now he once again felt the sense of violation that had driven him to take up arms in the first place.

Kubiš traversed the Old Town Square then cut through a side street, where the displays of Nazi support were less ostentatious, and continued his journey. He moved swiftly over the cobbles for he was both cold and eager to reach his destination.

Kubiš would not imperil his immediate family by visiting them – at least until his mission was over. There were too many friends and neighbours – all witnesses to his unexpected return and their questions and concerns would be an unwelcome distraction. He would stay focused until the operation was done. But Jan had to visit Anna because he simply could not stay away from her.

When he finally reached her parents' tiny home he caught a first glimpse of her through the rear kitchen window. She appeared to be reading and he paused for a moment to take in the gentle features of her face. Here was the girl he had thought of constantly during his long separation from her – no less beautiful now for the absence of makeup or a pretty dress. He smiled to himself as he knocked and waited for her.

Anna's eyes widened with ecstatic shock as she opened the back door and the long dark hair fell forward into her face as she almost stumbled on the back door step.

'Jan! Is it really you?' she demanded disbelievingly, her arms outstretched.

'Surely you have not forgotten my face already, Anna, have you?' he teased, as he pulled the delirious young girl towards him.

They made love in Anna's room, grateful for the absence of a household distracted by long factory shifts or the need to find food for the evening meal.

'You know I can't keep visiting you here like this, Anna,' he said when it was over.

Anna wrapped herself around him. 'You must. I won't let you leave me again.'

'It's too dangerous for you if I do. Today okay, we can get away with it once maybe but sooner or later I will be seen by somebody.'

Anna laughed. 'You think you visited me here today without being seen? Are you serious? Have you forgotten old Sissi Kitlova – guardian of virginity for every girl in these streets? She sees all with her widow's eyes. Even as we talk she knows you are in here corrupting me.'

'Really? And what about your mother?' He tried hard not to sound concerned.

'I told you she would not be back until much later. If I was not entirely sure of it, you can bet I would never let you into my bed like this.'

'I meant what if widow Kitlova tells her?'

'Mother would tell her to mind her own business and not dare to go gossiping about her daughter or there'll be trouble. Besides, she knows what goes on in days like these. All the old conventions seem ridiculous to the young now. We do not have the luxury our parents had. They could afford to wait.'

She laid her head against his chest. 'I was going to wait before, remember, until I knew you would be taken away from me. My mother is no fool. She merely says "Make sure you are careful Anna, that's all".'

She kissed his forehead.

'My father, he is different. He would, of course, kill you.'

'Of course.'

'But we are careful. We stop before the very end and finish outside, so there are no babies and everyone thinks Anna Malinová is a nice virgin girl instead of the terrible woman she has become, totally corrupted by her soldier lover,' she turned her head and looked up at him then, 'and he is so much older than she is!'

Kubiš tickled her in revenge until she laughed and gasped and begged him for mercy. When he stopped, he held her tightly to him.

'We should be careful in other ways, Anna. It is too dangerous for you to be seen with me. I have a mission you can know nothing about but the Germans will arrest you just the same if it comes to it.'

'Then I will have to learn to live with the danger, Jan, because I never did learn how to live without you.'

She kissed him full on the lips then and trailed her hand very slowly down his torso.

'So, you really have no choice, you see.'

She bent to kiss him again and Kubiš murmured his agreement as the hunger for her returned.

'Young love is supposed to be reckless, Jan. Come to me carefully if you must, come to me cautiously, but make sure you do come to me.'

18

The next day Kubiš met Gabčík at the Union Café – a renowned gathering place for intellectuals and would-be future statesmen, a room filled with wood panelling and ancient, gloomy oil paintings. They were there to recruit a contact to assist with surveillance on the Reichsprotektor. The man, chosen by Zelenka, was Šafařík, a joiner on the Hradčany Castle staff, who had reluctantly agreed to meet Gabčík but, when Kubiš arrived, there was no sign of this unlikely spy.

Instead he joined his friend at a quiet corner table. All around them cigarette smoke hung like incense, obscuring already clandestine gatherings further and adding to the illusion that the café was a somehow sacred place – a chapel for atheists. But who was a spy and who an informer? Who was committed to the resistance and who working for the Gestapo?

'Perhaps this was not the best place to meet,' pronounced Kubiš.

'Why?'

'Well, for a start, everyone in here looks suspicious.' Gabčík let a smile escape that suggested his friend had a point. At the next table an earnest bunch of philosophers was being addressed by a bespectacled youth with a face the colour of whitewash. 'If I was the Gestapo I'd just arrest all of them, right now.'

'Tell me,' said Gabčík, 'how are things where you are staying?'

'Good,' replied Kubiš grinning. 'The lady has a son of about twenty who thinks I am a total hero, come to singlehandedly rid Prague of the Germans.'

'He has not guessed why you are here?'

'No, but he keeps asking me.'

'And what do you say?'

'I tell him, "Ata, don't let anyone know will you, but I am on a secret mission to count the ducks on the River Vltava." An answer he does not seem too happy with.'

'As long as he doesn't tell his friends about you.'

'He won't – his mother has threatened him with bread and water for a month if he breathes a word and she is formidable, believe me.'

'Sounds like a good woman. And how is Aunt Marie's cooking?'

'Excellent. I have not eaten so well in years. What about your young girl?'

'Oh, she's a pretty good cook too.'

'I am more interested in how she looks than how she cooks.'

'She's okay – you know?'

'Okay? Josef, that *is* praise coming from you. She must be a rare beauty.'

Gabčík seemed eager to change the subject. 'And what about the lovely Anna – how is she?'

Kubiš beamed. 'Very pleased to see me, Josef, very pleased to see me.'

'I thought you had an air of contentment.'

'You should try it. It brings out the best in you.'

Suddenly Gabčík's expression changed. 'I think this is our man, Jan.'

Šafařík walked uneasily into the Union Café – a small figure, he peered apprehensively around the room before recognising Gabčík from the description he had been given and quickly joining the two men at their table. The first thing Kubiš noticed about the man was his greying beard. The hairs were long, harsh and unkempt like the bristles on a broom. When he leant in close to talk to them his breath smelt of liver sausage. Šafařík betrayed nervousness with his first words.

'This man is with you?' he asked.

'This is Jan and, yes, he is with me. You can tell him everything you wish to say to me.'

Šafařík still seemed unsure of himself but he conquered his fears long enough to nod an introduction at Kubiš before addressing them both in an under-confident ramble.

'President Hácha was at Hradčany today. He has prepared a birthday gift for the Führer from our nation. A hospital train for German wounded. The man is a total traitor.'

Hácha had been swept to power immediately after Beneš' exile. This weak and malleable little fellow found himself in the presidential chair. Heydrich tolerated his continued presence because Hácha was entirely compliant to German wishes.

Šafařík continued. 'He took Heydrich down to the bones of St Wenceslas and gave him the keys to the crown jewels. I was one of many to witness the ceremony. The Nazi even held the skull of Wenceslas in his own hands. Obviously, he is unaware of the curse.'

Kubiš grunted his understanding but Gabčík was no child of the capital.

'What curse?' he asked.

It was Kubiš who answered him. 'It is said that anyone who dares touch the bones of Wenceslas directly will meet a violent death.'

'Really?' asked Gabčík, genuinely impressed and willing to embrace any omen.

'Yes, and I am sure Hácha knew that,' added his friend.

Gabčík turned back to Šafařík. 'How often does Hácha visit Heydrich?'

The joiner looked doubtful, reluctant to continue.

'What is it?' probed Gabčík.

Šafařík glowered at him and when he continued it was in a resentful whisper.

'I told Zelenka from the start that I don't like this. I have no idea what you are up to but it smells of the grave to me. I do not want to get involved but Zelenka tells me you are good men and must have information on Hradčany; where everyone goes and when, who sees who and for how long. What the plans are for the days and weeks ahead.'

'That is correct,' confirmed Gabčík.

'I tell him okay but it is too dangerous for me to keep meeting you in public like this. They would shoot me if they found out. So he says to give this information to two girls he has set up in rooms across the way from the castle. He will give you the address later.'

'Thank you.'

'Don't thank me. I don't know you. I do this for Zelenka who is a good friend and if he says you are okay then you are okay, but I do not want to hear from you anymore. You cannot contact me or try to meet me after today because, if you do, it will finish and I will stop helping you. Is that understood?'

'Completely,' confirmed Gabčík while Kubiš stayed silently in the background not wishing to unnerve Šafařík any further.

'Good. I only came today so I could be sure you know my position. I wish you luck with whatever you are doing here but I want nothing more to do with it beyond the agreement I have outlined to you. Do you both understand?'

'We do,' Gabčík confirmed.

He was already beginning to get up. 'I will deliver the first note to the apartment tomorrow, as long as I feel it is safe. Now I must go.'

Šafařík, true to his word, rose from the table, almost knocking over a waiter who had appeared to take his order. The joiner stammered an apology then mumbled he had forgotten an appointment and was so sorry for the inconvenience. He then left the building at a pace brisk enough to arouse the suspicions of every man in the room.

'Lord,' exclaimed Kubiš when he had gone, 'that is a nervous individual. Do you think he will be able to do this?'

'I hope so, Jan,' answered Gabčík. 'I do hope so.'

Lieutenant Alfréd Bartoš counted himself a lucky man. He parachuted safely from the same plane that transported Gabčík and Kubiš to their homeland. Then he managed to evade the clutches of the Gestapo, who had searched his hometown of Pardubice following a tip-off that the resistance was active there.

What's more, he had successfully fulfilled his mission, establishing contact with Agent 54, in the agreed manner. To his initial amazement, Agent 54 asked to have his first meeting with Bartoš in the double agent's own home on the outskirts of Prague. Perhaps Bartoš had expected more clandestine meetings on park benches or in darkened restaurants, where classified documents would be passed under tables. Instead he found himself taking tea delivered by a houseboy, in a town house that befitted the status of its resident Paul Thümmel, the Abwehr's top man in the capital.

'I am surprised you chose to invite me here,' Bartoš commented once the boy had departed.

'You used the necessary access words to call a meeting and knew your predecessor. I had no reason to doubt your authenticity.' Thümmel was a stout, middle-aged man with an outward appearance of studied calm but the dark grooves under his eyes betrayed the incredible stress he was under. Bartoš could scarcely imagine what it must be like to every day play the double agent against the most brutal regime on the planet.

'I meant your choice of location.'

Thümmel smiled. 'This is the safest place I can think of. If I met you in public we could be watched. I see you here and you are just another Czech turncoat who has come to report to me on the enemies of the Reich. What's the matter, Bartoš, does that make you uneasy?' and he laughed grimly. 'You don't think I am going to take all of the risk, do you? Just make sure you watch your back when you leave here. Don't want you to end up with a knife in it; a gift from one of your patriotic countrymen.'

Bartoš did find this prospect alarming but deliberately chose to ignore Thümmel's black humour. He reminded himself the man was a hero and heroes must occasionally be indulged. 'I will, of course, meet you here regularly if that is how you would prefer things.'

'It is,' said Thümmel. 'Actually, I insist on it.'

'I understand you have been unable to communicate with us for some time now. Were you being watched?'

'Everyone is being watched, all of the time but I think your predecessor was careless. He was caught with documents that could only have come from a senior source in the intelligence community. Lucky for me they were removed from his lifeless body; he was shot while trying to escape a raid. Otherwise I have no doubt he would have given me up like that,' and Thümmel snapped his fingers, 'and I wouldn't have blamed him for a moment. We are the finest torturers in the world, you know?' He smiled with mock pride as he acknowledged German excellence in this field.

'There are not that many of us, a handful perhaps, with

access to those kind of secrets. It's a short list and I think Heydrich now has strong suspicions about me. He has let it be known they are searching for a senior double agent, now why would he do that unless he wanted to see how his suspects reacted? I think he is trying to force someone to run.'

'And is that what you want to do? Run?'

'Where would I go? There is nowhere I could possibly hide. I doubt I would make it more than ten miles from Prague. I have chosen my path and there is no deviating from it now until all this ends. Either Germany falls or I will.'

'So what news do you have for Lieutenant Colonel Moravec?'

'Not much right now; as you can imagine the risk is very high for me at the moment. I have some documents here you can read but you can't leave with them. I won't make that mistake a second time. I hope you have a good memory.'

When their meeting was concluded Bartoš shook Thümmel by the hand. 'I know I probably should not ask you, Thümmel, but I am intrigued. Why is a German risking everything, including his life, to hand Nazi secrets to a Czech government in exile? It isn't just the money we keep for you surely or are you the world's last idealist? Is that it or something more personal? Are you the only man in Germany who despises Hitler?'

Thümmel looked Bartoš in the eye and nodded. 'You are absolutely right, Bartoš.'

'I am?'

'Yes. You really should not ask. Now you'll forgive me but I am late for an appointment.'

He walked Bartoš to the door then and stood on the step watching as the Lieutenant departed, 'Be careful won't you, Bartoš?' Thümmel taunted. 'I've heard Prague can be a very dangerous city.' And then he laughed again.

19

'*The extermination of entire races including women and children is only possible by a subhumanity that no longer deserves the name German. I am ashamed to be German!*'

Wehrmacht Colonel Helmuth Stieff

Heydrich had agreed to address the cream of the SS officer contingent to boost morale. The speech was a distraction he could do without but he told himself to be thankful he was still in a position to give it.

The incident with Bormann had been put into eventual perspective by Hitler's merciful inactivity; evidenced by the very fact Heydrich was still the Reichsprotektor of Bohemia and Moravia; his fall from grace strictly temporary, a mere whim of the Führer's, most probably forgotten within the hour. It had taught him a valuable lesson, though; never to take his position in the Reich for granted again. And he would finish Bormann alright. Just give him time.

The officers waited in the banqueting room where Heydrich had fenced with his subordinate. There was a buzz of anticipation as, for some of the men, this would be their first glimpse of the legendary Heydrich. Of course he kept them all waiting, underlining his seniority, then marched purposefully into the room, followed by a bevy of serious looking aides.

He wore the Iron Cross on the breast of his *feldbluse*, and sported the ever-present fighter pilot badge – for who had not heard of Heydrich's exploits in the air? Envious of Göring's reputation as the First World War fighter ace, holder of the Blue Max and the heir to Von Richthofen's glory, Heydrich had been keen to get into the war himself and win his own medals. In typical style, he had learned to fly and taken to the skies in a ludicrously dangerous diversion. In 1940, he flew combat missions over France to the astonishment of his few superiors. Hitler finally banned him from his fledgling fighter pilot's career when he was shot down over Russia during the early days of Operation Barbarossa. Men from Einsatzkommando 10a were stupefied to see who emerged from the wreckage of the downed Messerschmitt, which crash-landed in the field close to their patrol.

Reaching the middle of the banqueting room Heydrich stopped, turned round and began to address the gathering, commanding attention more on rank and reputation than on the quality of his voice. As a young naval cadet he had been teased for its high, slightly feminine pitch when he spoke. But no one teased Reinhard Heydrich these days.

'Gentlemen, we stand today on the brink of an historic new era. The flag of the SS now flies proudly from the Presidential residency and the protectorate of Bohemia and Moravia is finally a Germanic province, in full step with the Führer's vision in Berlin.'

There was brief, obligatory applause. As he spoke, Heydrich walked amongst the men and they moved silently out of the way to allow his progress, like passive sheep herded by a dog.

'Our previous regime in Prague was a half-hearted, muddled compromise. One cannot truly subjugate a people yet continue to ask its opinion on domestic policy.'

There was a murmur of laughter from the men at this oblique reference to the Czech Provisional Government, which Heydrich's predecessor Von Neurath had indulged. Most felt Germany was a conqueror and should behave as such, not allowing the tail to wag the dog. Heydrich ignored the mirth and continued.

'Let me say this clearly, unequivocally...' he paused for dramatic effect, picking out individuals in his enraptured audience for eye to eye contact, before quietly bringing home the message. 'The Czech people have no right to be here.'

He let the words hang in the air as he paced the room, allowing them to sink in.

'The Czech people have no right to be here!' Heydrich's voice echoed around the palace as he roared the words once more.

Seemingly becalmed, he continued in a normal speaking voice.

'The protectorate is a German land, it has always been a German land. The scandal of the Versailles treaty, at the conclusion of the last war, robbed the German nation of its birthright. We have now reclaimed it. A minority of Czechs, with suitable genetic material, may be allowed to settle here permanently and be integrated into the Greater Reich. The majority, however, will simply be shipped out, either to the General Government in the former Polish territory or further east.'

This last phrase was, as usual, deliberately ambiguous but they all knew it as a euphemism for the enthusiastic work of the death squads.

Heydrich pressed on. 'In the short term the needs of our successful campaign against the Bolshevik threat are paramount. This means enlisting the cooperation of the Czech population. The economy of Bohemia and Moravia must be totally mobilised. For Czechs who are unwilling to adapt there is to be an unstinting policy of suppression. Use every method of state security at your disposal to hunt down agitators, saboteurs, passive resisters and enemies of the Reich.

'The Czech must be made to realise there is only a choice of cooperation and survival or resistance and death. For the most part, the practical Czech is likely to outweigh the misguided patriot. Once again remember, in all of your dealings with him, the Czech has no right to be here. The Czech is subhuman!'

Heydrich dipped his head to indicate he had finished, and was met with rapturous applause from the SS men. The whole address had taken moments but his effect on the morale of the officers was as clear as his expectations of them. Cheering followed as Heydrich and his entourage marched sharply from the banqueting hall.

The Mercedes 540K shot out of the castle with no noticeable concern for pedestrians on the cobbles nearby. They scurried away like chickens evading the farmer's axe. Heydrich, sitting stiff and upright in the passenger seat, afforded Gabčík his first clear look at the man he was going to kill. The Reichsprotektor had a noticeable air of self-importance, as he held his gaze fixedly ahead, refusing to acknowledge there was anything of significance to his left or right.

'Come on, Liběna,' said Gabčík after the car had passed. 'I've seen enough of the castle.'

Liběna had offered to help Josef in his work and he accepted, without explaining his sudden interest in Hradčany. He told her he would look less like a suspicious stranger if he were one half of a couple, enabling him to complete his surveillance unhindered, and she didn't contradict him.

Gabčík had to admit the real reason for Liběna's company – to himself at least. The fact was, after a few days of her tender concern for his damaged ankle, her good-natured teasing and obvious interest in his thoughts and opinions on the world, Gabčík was smitten by her. He wanted to spend time with this girl and learn more about her. His mission still took precedence over everything, of course, but he told himself he was surely capable of pursuing two objectives at once?

As Heydrich's car disappeared from view, Liběna and Gabčík ambled slowly down the steep hill, which took them away from the castle. Josef's ankle was healing quickly but he continued to limp a little. Halfway along the street lay the house of Zelenka's two anonymous girls. They would have the latest of Šafařík's promised surveillance reports, if the man had not entirely let them down, of course.

The *safe to proceed* signal was a vase full of flowers on the windowsill. No vase meant *no message today* or *stay away, it's not safe*. As Josef walked by the window he noticed with relief that a gaudy crystal vase occupied the sill and he quickly looked about him to ensure he was not being watched. As he did so Josef altered his trajectory to bring himself within touching distance of the open window. He spotted the little brown envelope, tucked almost out of sight behind the vase and weighted against the wind with a small stone. Without breaking stride he reached out and scooped the envelope up with his hand, immediately tucking it into the outside pocket of his coat with all the élan of a pickpocket. The pebble dropped at his feet and tumbled off the cobblestones as it bounced away down the hill.

As they reached the end of the steep descent from the castle, Liběna and Gabčík crossed the path of a column of Waffen SS troops marching unstoppably towards Hradčany. Liběna instantly linked her arm into his and drew herself closer to Gabčík, imitating the actions of a woman in love, who instinctively seeks protection from her sweetheart. Gabčík made no attempt to remove her arm.

'Looks more natural this way, don't you think?' she whispered as the troops marched by.

'Yes,' he agreed.

Both pretended the act was intended to allay the suspicion of the passing soldiers. Liběna kept her arm in his as they walked back towards the Manesuv Bridge together as the sky continued to darken around them.

20

*'Heydrich's only weakness was his ungovernable
sexual appetite.
To this he would surrender himself without inhibition'*

Walter Schellenberg, Head of the Reich Foreign
Intelligence Service

Between Panenské Březany and Hradčany Castle lie twelve miles of open road largely surrounded by fields and forest. Later, dwellings that mark the outskirts of suburban Prague appear, flanking the route. The buildings increase in age and grandeur the closer the traveller gets to the old core of the city, where cobbled roads lead right up to the Castle. Jan cycled the entire route on his first clear day, with a cover story if he was stopped by a suspicious German patrol.

'You are visiting a sick relative in the country, a farmer who I have already arranged to support the story should the Gestapo choose to investigate it,' assured Zelenka, 'otherwise you will look too conspicuous cycling up and down the road, whatever your true intentions.'

As he pedalled he glanced from left to right, hoping to spot natural cover behind dense foliage or a rocky outcrop. He could then report back to Gabčík that he had found the ideal place for an assault on Heydrich. It proved a forlorn hope. By the end of the first day Jan realised the task would be far more difficult than he ever could have imagined. Large sections of the road were long and straight with little cover on either side, save for a few thin bushes and an occasional undernourished tree – hardly capable of keeping the men and their equipment hidden from view while they waited for their target to pass by.

'How was it?' asked Gabčík that night.

'Cold as a witch's tit,' was all he received in reply, for the temperature had made the task an even more thankless one.

Kubiš realised a far more detailed analysis of the route was required and he took on the task with a methodical zeal. In the coming days, he spent hours on his belly, ignoring the biting cold, as he lay flat on the frozen hillsides that overlooked Heydrich's route. Kubiš counted the traffic. He monitored and logged the frequency and extent of German patrols and the occasional passing military convoy. He located corners where vehicles would be forced to slow down, leaving them vulnerable to attack, then found no natural cover or suitable firing point nearby.

It took Kubiš two weeks to painstakingly examine every yard of the route and still he found no likely spot. There were well covered areas where it might be possible to leap from the bushes and fire on the state car but it would be moving too fast to ensure any level of accuracy. Changing the plan to catch Heydrich in a sniper's sights was ruled out early on. Kubiš and Gabčík were both more than competent marksmen but even experts with years of experience would find it difficult to hit a moving target at speed from what would be, by necessity, a withdrawn position. Nowhere on the route could they get close enough for a rifle shot, yet be far enough from the road to escape detection and there would be little prospect of getting away afterwards.

Kubiš spent further days walking the surrounding countryside looking for a suitable escape route, before eventually coming to the grim conclusion that any pursuer would have a distinct advantage over them. If the two men tried to flee on bicycles they could only head back down the road towards the city and would be trapped in minutes. A car, even if they could secure one, would be far too conspicuous, as they were seldom seen on country roads these days. If they tried to escape on foot and across country there were vast tracts of open land, making it almost impossible to elude patrols equipped with dog handlers and virtually unlimited manpower.

Each evening Jan would return home to Aunt Marie's house exhausted and downcast. The enormity of their task had begun to hit him. Occasionally he would walk a part of the route with Josef, who was forced to agree with his gloomy forecast, but for the most part he worked alone.

Gabčík was otherwise occupied. He had his own role – the gathering of intelligence and the close surveillance of Heydrich while the general was in the confines of the city. He collected and analysed Šafařík's reports, which now came directly from Zelenka; a less risky proposition than the repeated use of an opened window on a busy side street as a letterbox. Sometimes Zelenka himself related the details during regular meetings with them both at Aunt Marie's house.

'You asked for a more detailed breakdown on the movements of members of the illegal government, starting with Heydrich. Šafařík has done a good job. It's all here. Where he goes and who he sees, with what frequency and for how long.'

'And how does he get this information?' asked Gabčík.

'Straight from the man's diary in most instances. His appointments book is widely seen, as the household must react to his itinerary, but he does have an infuriating habit of changing his appointments at the last moment. Other more informal arrangements Šafařík has worked out from gossip circulating in the castle. He is particularly illuminating when it comes to Heydrich's mistresses.'

'Really? Go on,' urged Kubiš.

Zelenka consulted a page of notes Šafařík had provided, giving the two men a précis of its highlights.

'He is rumoured to spend time with a local girl but we don't know who or where. The only concrete reports we have, concerning Heydrich's current consorts, are the repeat visits to a theatrical actress and the regular appearance of the wife of an SS Colonel who is currently stationed in the east. The former he apparently meets in a hotel, the latter visits him quite blatantly in a room at the castle.'

'The cheek of the man,' said Gabčík.

'Her husband is probably being shelled in some frozen foxhole on the eastern front while she is busy with Heydrich,' agreed Kubiš.

Zelenka continued. 'Apart from his regular appointments with one or other of these mistresses, Heydrich's day seems to consist of a series of meetings with senior Nazis or treacherous Czech statesmen. These are almost always held in fortified buildings. The more mundane administrative tasks are carried out at his desk amid the tight security of Hradčany.'

They all knew any assault on the castle would fail ludicrously before an assassin had gone beyond the first sentry. No one saw the value in a heroic but ultimately suicidal gesture.

'At night, Heydrich either returns to his estate or embarks on an evening's carousing with other German officers. These are usually impromptu affairs, held in a variety of locations, and are impossible to predict. Is any of this helping at all?'

Zelenka looked up from the paper, his face sporting a look of feigned indifference but he was unable to hide his curiosity as to how the surveillance report might fit in with their mission.

'Yes, it is most useful,' Kubiš reassured him without elaborating further. 'Please commend Šafařík on his work; if he can get us more reports on other senior men that would be equally helpful and I do have some questions I would like you to take back to him.'

When Zelenka finally left them alone Kubiš said, 'The only realistic chance we have of killing Heydrich is on the journey between his home and Hradčany. It has to be done on the open road, when he travels in that Mercedes with just one bodyguard. At all other times he is too heavily guarded.'

'I agree and if we wait a while, till the Prague spring weather begins to show, then he might even oblige us by travelling with the top down.'

They were confronted with an unavoidable truth. The mission would require a great deal more planning than either of them had anticipated. Naively they had promised Moravec an attack within ten days of their arrival. Still, it was better to strike late and be prepared than botch the job in haste and see Heydrich survive, thereafter to travel with a truckload of armed escorts. That would serve no purpose at all, except to ruin the chances of a second attempt from any team that followed them.

They agreed henceforth to move slowly, assembling as much information on Heydrich and his routine as possible, amassing clues patiently like a detective tracking a criminal, waiting for the right moment to close in. It was in this manner that days became weeks and winter turned to spring, and still they were no nearer their target.

Heydrich was on his way to meet the double agent he had just unmasked. The man he had long suspected of providing German military secrets to the Czech government in exile was currently under lock and key at the Petschek Palace, being interrogated at length by Schellenberg.

The first breakthrough had come weeks ago, with the arrest of the resistance man carrying information that could only have come from a senior figure. For Heydrich, the sole organisation not entirely above suspicion was the Abwehr, Germany's military intelligence organisation, whose loyalty to Hitler under its leader Admiral Canaris was always open to question. Paul Thümmel, a high ranking Abwehr officer, immediately became his chief suspect.

'How long have I known you, Walter?' Thümmel was pleading as Heydrich made his entrance. 'Come on, this is preposterous.'

The fear of the Abwehr man was visible even in the semi-darkness of the interrogation cell. His eyes were darting and desperate, the sweat clung to his face like raindrops but he was still trying to play the innocent.

'I take it he has not confessed to you, Schellenberg?'

'No, he has not. He denies everything, in fact.'

'Mmm perhaps we should fetch the pliers or possibly a branding iron. What do you think?'

'I think this is an outrage!' interrupted Thümmel, 'and when my friends in Berlin hear of it they will have your rank and your career, Heydrich!' The words were expressed forcefully but they all knew this was the last desperate plea of a doomed man.

'Yes, you do have those influential friends, Thümmel. You're a party member of long standing after all; a gold badge holder, one of the first one hundred thousand to join.'

'That's right, Heydrich, and you'd be wise to remember it.'

'Oh I did remember and it is why you have yet to experience our less subtle methods of interrogation. You are hardly going to confess without them though, which has turned my investigation of your activities into a painstaking affair. It involved the cross-referencing of dozens of pieces of information in a search for some positive proof of your treachery.'

'What treachery?' asked Thümmel, his voice cracking.

'I had your movements analysed. I went back years in fact and it became apparent you were always in the vicinity when a leak was spotted or a breach of security suspected. You did not realise it at the time, Thümmel, but whenever you met your foreign paymasters you left footprints, which, years later, I was able to follow. Of course the evidence is circumstantial….'

Thümmel snorted. 'I'll bet it is.'

'But damning nonetheless. No one wants a fuss, least of all a trial, so there won't be one.'

'The Führer will never stand for this.'

Then came the truly chilling words for Paul Thümmel. 'Actually, the Führer is in complete agreement with me. It's very sad, Thümmel, you were once one of the most important men in military intelligence and now look at you. Tonight you will swap the uniform of a senior German officer for the harsh cotton garb of a prisoner. I will then have you installed as a resident of Theresienstadt. You will be held in solitary confinement under a fictitious name. Have no doubt whatsoever that your stay there will be permanent.'

'Go to hell, Heydrich,' but his voice broke when he said that.

'No, Thümmel, it is you who is going to hell and no one can help you now. Come on, Schellenberg, this is a waste of our time. Let's leave him to contemplate his future, shall we?'

'Better be careful, Walter.' There was no fire left in Thümmel for he knew the game was lost. 'You'll be next, of that I'm certain. I hope you'll remember me when they come to get you.'

'Goodbye, Thümmel,' answered Schellenberg without emotion as the cell door closed on his former comrade.

Heydrich was in buoyant mood for the rest of the day. Thümmel had been one of Admiral Canaris' most senior military intelligence men and a particularly close friend of Bormann, which made this victory all the sweeter.

Now Heydrich could surely convince the Führer the only trustworthy organisation in the Reich was the SS.

Back in London meanwhile, Agent 54 disappeared off the radar forever.

21

*'This man was the hidden pivot around which the
Nazi regime revolved.
The development of a whole nation was guided
indirectly by his forceful character'*

Walter Schellenberg on Heydrich, from his memoirs

Gabčík wanted to be sure Liběna was on her own in the house. Every Saturday morning her parents wandered from stall to stall in the market place fruitlessly searching for produce, so this seemed the ideal time to approach her.

He has rehearsed the words several times in his head but now to his genuine bemusement realises he is still nervous as he approaches Liběna, while she bakes bread in the kitchen. Josef's throat is dry and he has become a coward, afraid of the rejection he is convinced is about to come his way. He curses himself for caring that a girl a good ten years younger than him might not think he is good enough – yet he cannot deny that lately he has begun to yearn for her.

'Liběna, good morning, I was wondering, when you have finished your baking, if you have no other chores to do that is, whether you would like to walk out with me this afternoon.'

Lord, that has to be the longest sentence he has ever uttered. *You idiot, you did not even give her the chance to answer your*

'good morning' before blundering on like a wounded bear
through the forest. What must she think of you now? You've
ruined everything and will have to avoid her out of sheer
shame. She is looking at you like you are a mad man.

Liběna smiled before answering with an enviable calm.
'Yes, Josef, thank you. That would be lovely.'

With that she returned to her baking, leaving Gabčík
standing silently behind her for a moment.

'Good,' was all he could manage, before making a less than
dignified exit, wondering why it is that women were so much
better at this sort of thing than men? It was some minutes
before he had composed himself sufficiently to look back and
enjoy the moment when she said 'Yes'.

That first afternoon together Josef took her for coffee and
sweet pancakes. It had gone well and their conversation was
easy, with a lightness and assurance from Liběna he had not
anticipated. He now had the distinct impression she had been
expecting his invitation – that he might have been a little late
proffering it even, in her mind at any rate.

Luck was still holding out for the newly promoted Captain
Alfréd Bartoš. Agent 54 had been arrested on a day when he
was not scheduled to meet with his new controller and there
was no way of describing Bartoš' relief at avoiding his own
capture. With Paul Thümmel now in permanent retirement,
Bartoš began to devote his energies to the gathering of
intelligence in conjunction with his new contacts in the Jindra
resistance network. He established strong links with the
resistance and used them to travel around Prague amassing
facts that could be sent back to London – information he
strongly believed would hasten the eventual capitulation of
the enemy. He favoured this diligent, methodical approach
over the spectacular gesture, the sabotage of a railway line,
the guided night bombing of a factory, which like as not only

served to enrage the Gestapo into ever more draconian acts against the population.

In this aspect he found an ally in Ladislav Vaněk, the head of the Jindra network. The army officer's military rank and natural authority ensured him a place of equality alongside Vaněk. Subsequently when the Home Army controller received his regular reports from Zelenka, on the movements of Gabčík and Kubiš, Bartoš was invariably at his side. The Captain would then win further acclaim from London with regular reports that the Anthropoid team was alive and well and seemingly proceeding with its operation as planned – a mission about which, to his undisguised exasperation, Bartoš was permitted to know absolutely nothing. His frustration reached a peak during the latest briefing from Zelenka. As usual there was much speculation as to the intentions of the two men sent by London. Vaněk listened to the latest reports of their movements and finally asked.

'This surveillance on Hradčany… you don't think they are planning an assassination?'

Bartoš was disbelieving. 'Do you?'

'Well, I don't think they are planning to break in and steal the crown jewels.'

Bartoš was quiet for a moment then he continued thoughtfully. 'There were rumours back in England, nothing more than that, of plans to assassinate collaborators – high profile people who openly cooperate with the Nazis. Some of the men talked of being linked to such missions.'

Vaněk was interested now. 'Who was discussed?'

'No one specific; as I said, they were only rumours but I would assume government figures; Hácha perhaps or maybe Emanuel Moravec. I don't suppose an Education Minister has too much protection do you? They could get at him, in theory.'

'I hope Beneš has more brains than that! We are barely surviving out here as it is. Can you imagine how the Germans will react if they kill a member of the government? They would hunt us all down like dogs for sure. Now is not the right moment for such gestures.'

He looked to Zelenka for agreement but the former schoolteacher remained silent. Vaněk pressed him.

'What is it, Zelenka? Why are you so quiet all of a sudden?'

'No reason.'

'If you know something then it is your duty to tell us. What is it?'

Reluctantly, Zelenka answered his controller. 'It's not for sure but I may have an idea what Gabčík and Kubiš are doing here in Prague.'

'Really?' asked Bartoš.

'Yes, I can't be certain, but I think they are here to kill Reinhard Heydrich.'

'That would be crazy! I don't believe they could contemplate such a thing!' Vaněk became wild eyed at the prospect. 'Captain Bartoš, you must speak to them. You must promise me you will do everything in your power to prevent this. Assure me of that,' he pleaded.

'Don't worry, Jaroslav, I won't allow what we have here, what you have built here to be destroyed because of the rash acts of two men,' he shook his head for emphasis. 'It would be catastrophic.'

'How will you prevent it?' asked Zelenka.

'I'll order them to stop! Both men are still in the army and I am a captain in that army. They must do as I tell them and stand down. Put simply, if they persist with this ridiculous plan I will simply forbid it!'

22

'I therefore invite you to a meeting'

Memo from SS Obersturmbannführer Adolf Eichmann,
Central Office for Jewish Emigration, on the Wannsee
Conference, 20 January 1942

The white stone building backed onto the shores of a
lake. A more peaceful location it would be hard to find
in all of Germany, thought Heydrich.

The Reichsprotektor sat at a large conference table, waiting
for the other delegates to settle themselves. The fourteen
men fussily removed an array of pens, pencils and official
documents from their monogrammed attaché cases. They
had flown in that morning from all corners of the Reich's
European Empire, before being driven in separate cars to
the grand house in Berlin that was only ever used for the
most important of meetings. Their arrival represented the
culmination of weeks of tireless effort on Heydrich's part. If
the day proved a success he would be able to look back on the
travails of early winter with the satisfaction of one who has
placed his troubles entirely behind him.

Since that fearful day at the Wolf's Lair, Heydrich had
set himself a new task. He now realised the need for some
powerful allies and had begun to win over as many senior
figures in the Reich as possible. First, Albert Speer was invited

to tour Prague. Hitler's architect was seduced by the irresistible lure of unfettered access to its pretty little streets. The man became positively euphoric at the thought of levelling half the city to create enormous museums, grandiose state palaces, and concert halls of an elaborate vulgarity. Between them, promised Heydrich, they would create a new imperial city worthy of its place as a second capital of the Thousand-Year Reich.

Next, Joseph Goebbels was lured back to the city to view the type of propaganda display for which he himself was rightly feted. Witnessing the carefully ordered spectacle of Czech labourers working diligently to produce German armaments convinced Goebbels the regime was a model one, whose practices should be swiftly adopted throughout the occupied territories. Both men would report their positive findings directly back to the Führer and there would be nothing Bormann could do about it.

The German war effort, by contrast, had not gone as smoothly. The campaign in the east became hopelessly bogged down in the winter snow and the Japanese attack on Pearl Harbor meant Germany was now at war with the United States. The latter incident had annoyed Heydrich immensely. As a result, he had been forced to postpone this most vital of meetings.

Fortunately, Heydrich could rely on the loyalty and tenacity of the man charged with coordinating his Wannsee Conference. Lieutenant Colonel Adolf Eichmann was an implacable type who first came to attention with his diligent work in the general's Central Office for Jewish Emigration. Heydrich liked Eichmann's solid approach to the task and was amused by his physical appearance – without his uniform he would look more like a Jew than most Jews thought Heydrich, with his large ears and nose and thin bloodless lips. His studies of Hebrew and Yiddish were detailed enough to attract some suspicions but Eichmann's Nazi credentials were impeccable. Heydrich understood. He merely liked to know his enemy. Eichmann was the genius who devised a plan to tax rich Jews to pay for the deportation of the poor ones. He had even attended the same school as Adolf Hitler. What a pity he chose to marry a Czech girl – a move that would surely limit him from going to the very top, even with the Reichsprotektor as a patron.

Today's gathering was arguably the most important of Heydrich's career. The general had summoned the heads of a diverse group of governmental agencies, together with the controllers of the major European territories. Now he had to convince them all to work in unison for him. There was less than a handful of men in the Reich ambitious enough to even attempt such an undertaking and fewer still who possessed the talent required to turn it into a success.

Heydrich began by calling the meeting to order. He then instructed his subordinate to read out a memo from Hitler's deputy.

'The order is from Reichsmarschall Göring and addressed to the Chief of the Security Police and the Security Service, SS OberGruppenführer Heydrich,' Eichmann told the gathering of self-important souls assembled around the heavily waxed wooden conference table. He bowed his head almost imperceptibly in his superior's direction, cleared his throat and continued in his customary flat and emotionless tone.

'Complementing the task that was assigned to you on 24 January 1939, which dealt with the carrying out of a solution to the Jewish problem, I hereby charge you with making all necessary preparations in regard to the final solution of the Jewish question in the German sphere of influence in Europe.' Eichmann could have been a civil servant reading out the latest munitions targets.

He paused again and was greeted by a tangible silence from

the assembled dignitaries – men who had just had their power and influence on this most contentious of issues removed at a stroke thanks to the formal intervention of Göring.

'Wherever other governmental agencies are involved, these are to cooperate with you. I charge you furthermore to send me, before long, an overall plan concerning the organisational, factual and material measures necessary for the accomplishment of the desired solution of the Jewish question.'

This missive had the required effect. There were many in the room who feared Heydrich personally; and those cavalier enough not to had just been presented with undeniable evidence of the general's authority on the issue. They would be working for him.

'Well, I think the implications of the Reichsmarschall's words are clear enough, gentlemen. The purpose of this meeting is to once and for all end the Jewish problem in Europe,' said Heydrich.

Stuckart was the first to speak – his phrases those of the world-weary lawyer. 'We have never even arrived at a true and universal classification of the Jew or the half Jew, let alone been in a position to...'

Heydrich stopped the Secretary of State for the Interior with a raised hand. 'I too have been present during interminable debate about the qualifications of Jewry – what to do with half Jews, quarter Jews, those married to Jews, Jews with decorations from the First World War and so forth. I do not intend to waste the majority of this meeting in further debate. There will be time for the study of fine detail later.

'The key point is there are eleven million Jews in Europe. Eleven million and they multiply like bacteria. The question remains of what to do with them all. You will no doubt be pleased to learn I have given this matter a great deal of thought of late and much work has already been undertaken on our behalf. If I can draw your attention to the papers in front of you.'

Heydrich paused for a moment while a dozen pairs of hands unfolded an equal number of draughtsman's plans.

'Let me understand this correctly,' said Friedrich Kritzinger, from the Reich Chancellery. 'You have brought us here to assist with a solution to the Jewish Question, yet you appear to have already devised this solution.'

'That is precisely what I am saying. There can be only one final solution. That much must be clear to all of you by now – what remains is the method required to implement it. You will be familiar with the basic layout of this camp. It is loosely modelled on Dachau but there are some important differences. Dachau was devised as a correctional facility, within Germany, for enemies of the state and party. It was largely a work camp. Auschwitz, however, contains special facilities. The huts you see marked in bold on the plans before you are gas chambers. We have recently perfected the use of the nerve agent Zyklon B, a form of cyanide, to the extent that we can now safely use the gas in enclosed chambers like these to efficiently resolve our problem with the Jews once and for all. This new special treatment is far more effective than any method previously attempted.'

'To give you a sense of the scale involved, two months ago, twelve hundred antisocials and political prisoners were taken from Buchenwald to Bernberg Euthanasia institute and subjected to the first large scale testing of the gas. They were dealt with in little over an hour, a quite considerable leap forward in technology. There are other camps under construction across middle and Eastern Europe; in Treblinka, Sobibór, Bełżec and Chełmno. All will be equipped with the new gas chambers.

'Many of you are fully aware of the extraordinary executive measures in place to combat the clear danger of world

Jewry. You have all accepted, by your presence in the highest reaches of this administration, the need to rid the Reich of their insidious influence. The progress made thus far is commendable. We have taken on the most arduous of tasks in a spirit of selflessness and with a laudable energy considering the restrictions of war.

'When this work is complete we will receive the gratitude of the entire civilised world. Germany will be proud to say it led the way where other nations stood idly by. Be assured there are thousands who will applaud our endeavour in this matter even within nations which are currently our enemies at war. But we must do more, much more. The Americans have joined the conflict and the Russian war has proved to be a far harder campaign than expected. Let there be no doubt that both nations will eventually fall before us but their unavoidable defeat will take time and enormous resources of men and equipment.'

'What has this to do with the Jews?' asked Dr Martin Luther, the Foreign Office Under Secretary of State, displaying a singular failure to grasp the key principles of the argument before him.

'Everything. We must speed up our special treatment of the Jews before the work becomes an unwelcome distraction.'

Eichmann leaned forward to interject, in what he probably considered to be his calm and helpful tone. It merely left him sounding like an adult trying to explain something to a particularly dim-witted child. 'Everyone knows they caused our defeat in the last war by stabbing us in the back. Let us not lose this one because too many of our men are diverted from the frontline to deal with them.'

Heydrich nodded his agreement.

'What will we do, Eichmann?' chided Stuckart. 'Ship them all off to Madagascar?'

Heydrich suspected the good doctor was annoyed at the

curtailment of his specialist lecture on the various categories of Jewishness, as he was unable to keep the inherent insult from his voice. Eichmann had indeed constructed just such a scheme before war had intervened, preventing the deportation of millions of Jews to this enormous island off the south east coast of Africa. Eichmann ignored Stuckart and Heydrich treated the question as if it were entirely rhetorical.

'May I ask what exactly is meant by the term Final Solution?' asked Kritzinger, in a tone that indicated he saw himself as the only one willing to cut to the very core of the argument.

'Extermination,' answered Heydrich without hesitation. 'Don't minute that word, Eichmann. For the purposes of record use "transported to the east".'

'You will note from the plans in front of you that gas chambers are not only possible to construct but their wide-scale use is imminent. We estimate they could mean the annihilation of every Jew in Europe in less than one calendar year.'

He certainly had them now; they were hanging on every word of his briefing. The men in uniform, and they were the majority, nodded their enthusiastic approval. Those who oversaw territories in the east competed with one another to begin the use of this exciting new technology.

'Take my Jews first,' pleaded SturmbannFührer Lange, the senior SS man in Latvia. 'Do you know how many firing squads my officers have had to organise in the past month alone?'

'No, no, you must take mine,' argued Dr Bühler, the Secretary of State responsible for the former Polish territory, now known as the General Government. 'These Polish Jews are the worst and I have 350,000 clogging up Warsaw alone.'

It was the central ministries, those trumped up politicians in suits, who were the problem, with their law degrees and stately moderation. Some appeared sceptical but one or two were noticeably shuffling in their seats and looking uncomfortable. It was only then Heydrich realised Kritzinger was staring at him as if he had gone quite mad.

'You are talking of herding people like cattle... into execution cells and... putting them down,' he said indignantly.

'I assure you it is quite humane, certainly more so than the bullet or the bayonet. In addition, it is a thousand times more efficient.'

'It is an outrage!'

'What alternative would you suggest? After all, one does not kill rats with a revolver.'

It was the sheer size of the undertaking that daunted Kritzinger. Heydrich could see that now. He had such a civil servant mentality – incapable of visualising an entire continent cleansed of Jewry.

Freisler, the Ministry of Justice man, was scrutinising the layout of a proposed camp. 'And will these thousands of Jews march calmly to their deaths without offering any resistance?'

'Yes, when the odds are overwhelming. Besides, the buildings resemble showers and there is no need to inform them of their impending demise. Herding them in with a bar of soap each should have the desired effect.'

'And, of course, the soap could be reused,' smirked Lange, to amusement from all corners of the table.

Heydrich did not join in the laughter. Instead he continued to address the group, though his eyes never left Kritzinger's for a moment.

'Do not delude yourselves. You are already part of the process, contributing towards the solution to the Jewish problem. You are aware of the work of the *Einsatzgruppen* and have said nothing. You have never once queried the wisdom of the high policy against the Jews.'

'Perhaps we should have,' replied Kritzinger but his voice was beginning to crack, under the calm, stolid menace of Heydrich's gaze.

'It is too late for that. The work is already far advanced. You fail to comprehend this discussion is not about the annihilation of the Jews. That is already decided upon and occurring as we speak. I am merely seeking to make the process more efficient. You turn pale at the productivity levels of the gas chambers. Do you desire to kill more slowly? Is your objection then merely a question of mathematics?'

When Krizinger spoke again his voice was weak and he was unable to match Heydrich's stare for shame. 'I am still not sure what you want from us all.'

'It is very simple. I want your approval, your compliance, and your full and unreserved support. What I need is trains, camps, gas chambers and cooperation, nothing less than that. Before you leave here today, I wish you all to give assurance of your personal assistance in the operation. This I have promised to deliver to Reichsmarschall Göring directly. I am obviously keen to ensure my report contains no noteworthy omissions. He is not known for his patience in this matter. Is that understood?'

'Yes, clearly,' answered Kritzinger on behalf of everyone. The Ministerial Director sounded entirely defeated.

'Good. Lieutenant Colonel Eichmann will write up the minutes, I will personally check and edit them and you will each receive a copy. Once everyone here is clear of his role and responsibilities in this affair all of the copies will be destroyed. No minutes are to remain. It will be as if this gathering never took place.

'Gentlemen, thank you for playing your part in the creation of history. With your cooperation the future of Europe is assured. The continent will be combed of Jews from east to west.'

23

*'We have become immune to any increase
in the great screaming of world Jewry'*

SS journal *Das Schwarze Korps*

Gabčík took Liběna for an evening at the *Lucerna*, an imposing art deco picture house whose ambition represented the city's optimism for the future before the Germans marched in. The film was a harmless, pre-war melodrama starring Hana Vítová, bland enough to have escaped the ravages of censorship. Afterwards he had taken her dancing at the Palace Ballroom, holding her close, enjoying the smell of her skin and the softness of her hair.

Before he knew it they had been stepping out, as she called it, for weeks; with trips to cinemas and dance halls. In between there were long walks across the city together. He would have to admit it felt like the most natural thing in the world. He finally confessed to Kubiš that he was seeing the girl and, to his great relief, Gabčík's friend seemed to sense his discomfort at this admission and merely wished him the very best of luck with her.

They were a couple, Liběna and Josef, who would have thought it? They discussed things he would have once seen as inconsequential and Gabčík found he wanted to provide them for her nonetheless. The house in a certain street, the plain wooden table where the friends and family could dine in the evenings, the brass bed with the down pillows. And Gabčík, who had owned little and cared less till now, began to realise the importance of these things. More, he dared to think of a future. If only he could complete his mission and somehow survive it.

Zelenka had promised Kubiš a pleasant surprise and, sure enough, when he returned to Aunt Marie's house that evening he found Jo Valčík, his old comrade from SOE training, sitting at her table.

Valčík grinned at him. 'There's nothing left, Jan. I've eaten it all.'

'It's not the food I'm worried about,' beamed Kubiš. 'It's my girl I'll be keeping from you, though she would find that little boy's moustache as hilarious as I do.'

Valčík pretended to be hurt. 'Please, I've not been growing it long. A necessity following our hasty departure from Pardubice.'

The three men dined together from Aunt Marie's table. They watched as the matriarch of the Jindra network defied the shortages by serving up a generous helping of smoked pork. Kubiš realised that, as in all things, this remarkable woman had her ways of defeating the German system and that night they dined as well as any Czech in the capital. Aunt Marie carried enormous clay bowls in from the kitchen full almost to the brim with black barley and horseradish, which she held easily in her fleshy arms as if they were no heavier than newspapers. Then she immediately sat down with the men as an equal, switching from the mother of the group to her less obvious role as the eyes and ears of Jindra.

'Now we have found a haven for Valčík we should discuss other matters. Your mission for instance, Jan,' and something in Zelenka's voice gave Kubiš a premonition of trouble.

'So,' he asked quietly, 'when were you thinking of telling me the target is Heydrich?'

Kubiš' heart sank. Though he had suspected it would be impossible to cloak their true intentions for long, he had hoped to avoid a confrontation with the resistance man who had been such a help since their arrival in Prague. Jan decided to make light of things.

'I thought you would work it out for yourself soon enough.'

'It was obvious in the end,' conceded Zelenka. 'Of all the comings and goings at Hradčany your follow up questions invariably came back to Heydrich.'

'You are going to kill a Nazi general?' asked the clearly astonished Valčík.

'No,' deadpanned Kubiš, 'we're going to buy him a beer and reason with him, ask him politely if he will leave our country.'

'Oh my God.'

Kubiš found he could at least derive some amusement from Valčík's obvious state of shock. Zelenka, though, he could not read. The Jindra man was calmly polishing his glasses with a handkerchief, his gentle monk-like face as inscrutable and expressionless as ever.

'What is it, Zelenka? Think it can't be done?'

'Oh, I think it can be done,' he replied before putting his newly polished glasses back on and carefully pushing them to the back of his nose with his middle finger. 'There are some, however, who would question whether it should be done.'

'Some?' asked Kubiš, alarmed now. 'How many know of this?'

'Not so many, Jan; Bartoš, Vaněk, one or two others in Jindra. I have to report back to them on the assistance I give you. It's my duty. They worked some of it out for themselves.'

'It's your duty to resist the Germans, not tell the whole world of our mission.'

Zelenka did not rise to this. Instead he gave Jan a frown, which indicated his argument was both flawed and beneath a response. Kubiš sighed then continued more reasonably. 'What are the objections of the others?'

'They think killing Heydrich will bring down a huge amount of trouble on them, which it will, of course. We barely survived the last Nazi reprisals, lost a lot of good people. They feel it is better to lay low and wait for a better opportunity.'

'And you? What do you think, Zelenka?'

'Me?' He answered as if it were of no consequence what he thought, then he paused for a moment to take out a battered old brass cigarette case, offer all of them a smoke and light all four. Kubiš accepted his even though he wanted to knock the tin out of Zelenka's hands, grab the man and shake him till he offered an opinion.

'I think there may never be a better opportunity. I think if London wants Heydrich dead then they have their reasons and we should do all we can to grant the request. Personally I have never heard of anyone, bar Hitler, more deserving of an early grave than Heydrich.'

'Good, then you will help us?'

'Yes, Jan, I will help you but it is not that simple. Bartoš and Vaněk want a meeting. They will try and persuade you to stop this.'

'In that case I'll let Josef do the talking.' And he grinned at Zelenka. 'Have you ever tried to argue with the man?'

Zelenka nodded. 'I'll get a message to them. Think of a time and place. They would greatly prefer to meet outside Prague, for security.'

'That's acceptable to me. What about you, Valčík? Will you help us kill Heydrich or does the very thought bring out the pacifist in you?'

'What?' replied the indignant Valčík. 'You mean miss this and let you two get all the glory? Besides you would only make a complete cow's arse of it without me. So tell me, what is your plan?'

'Besides killing Heydrich you mean?'

'I mean how do you intend to get close enough to kill him?'

Kubiš appeared uncomfortable. 'I'll be honest with you, we don't know yet. We have been watching him for weeks. There's not an inch of any route the man has taken that I don't know, but we are still no nearer getting to him now than we've ever been.'

Valčík couldn't hide his disappointment.

Zelenka spoke. 'Once we knew your target for sure I began making enquiries among our most trusted comrades; don't worry, Jan, I have been discreet. I asked for news of any sign of weakness in Heydrich's daily routine. There must be something there we can exploit.'

Kubiš remained resolute. 'I never said it was going to be easy, Valčík, now did I, but we'll get him.'

24

'We know that some Germans get sick at the very sight of the
SS black uniforms – we don't expect to be loved'

SS Reichsführer Heinrich Himmler

Kubiš walked out of the tiny railway station, alone
except for a couple of traders and a forlorn looking old
lady, who trudged along with the wearisome gait of
one who might actually welcome death.

Where the hell am I? he wondered bemusedly. He knew
Prague right enough but, in all his years, had never seen
the need to venture more than forty miles outside it to visit
the tiny town of Kutná Hora. What attraction could this
settlement to the east of the capital contain for Josef, the man
from Slovakia?

'You'll see,' Gabčík had told him infuriatingly, unable to
hide his glee. 'I have the ideal place for this meeting with
Bartoš and Vaněk. I am taking you all to church.'

Unlikely, thought Kubiš. Gabčík never disrespected religion
– it did not pay to when you were a soldier, requiring all the
help you could get, divine or otherwise – but he was hardly a
three times a day worshipper.

'Just get there,' insisted Gabčík unyieldingly. So Kubiš
trudged off into the town for his rendezvous with the
resistance.

Gabčík had travelled on a separate train for security and he was waiting for Kubiš, who was wholly unprepared for the sight that greeted him. 'What in God's name is it?' asked Kubiš, genuinely alarmed.

'The Church of the All Saints,' replied Gabčík.

'I know that, you said. I mean what is *that?*' and he pointed ahead of them.

'Oh,' replied Gabčík as if he had only just noticed, 'that, Jan, is the remains of thirty thousand people; their bones at any rate.'

Kubiš blinked into the dark and empty church and, sure enough, as he had suspected and Gabčík has just confirmed, the whole building is full to bursting with bones; human bones, many thousands of them.

'But how...?' Bartoš cannot complete his sentence. He is simply unable to comprehend the sheer scale of human life. Vaněk and Zelenka meanwhile are looking about them in confusion.

Gabčík told the story with blackly comic detachment. He could be discussing a sporting event over a beer.

'The cemetery has soil in it that is said to have come all the way from Golgotha – brought back from a crusade. When people heard about it, and this is eight hundred years or so ago, they all wanted to be buried there because it would bring them closer to God, so the old and the sick started making pilgrimages there when they thought their time was almost up.'

'A few years later, there was a great plague and the place became very popular. As soon as you spotted the symptoms you started the journey to Kutná Hora and if you didn't make it there was probably someone left in your family who'd put your body on a cart and drag it here, in line with your last, dying wish. Throw in a couple of wars as well and pretty soon you have a cemetery, made for a few hundred townsfolk, that is full to bursting with thousands of bodies from all over Europe.'

'Fine, all well and good, lots of bodies,' Kubiš tries to sound calm, 'but why *this*?' and he waves an arm expansively at his surroundings.

'About eighty years ago the place was being looked after by Cistercian monks. Realising they had a bit of a problem with all these bones, they went to an artist – Rint he was called, I'll never forget his name – and they gave him a most unusual commission. "Do something with our bones, Rint," they said, "anything you like really, but keep it tasteful." Well, I suppose old Rint must have *thought* it was tasteful.'

Bartoš ventured further into the Church of the All Saints and his mouth gaped in horror. Above his head was a huge chandelier entirely fashioned from human bones. This enormous construction had candles protruding from bleached human skulls, the skulls sat on little ledges, conveniently fashioned from what Kubiš assumed were pelvic bones, but unlike Bartoš he was none too keen to get close enough to check. The skulls stared sightlessly ahead but all of the mouths were full. Each contained a solitary limb, wedged horizontally between the jawbones. Zelenka stared at the nearest skull and it looked like a dog that's successfully scavenged outside a butcher's shop. Beneath the skulls, literally dozens of leg and arm bones were vertically suspended, hanging down like stalactites to enhance the elaborate trimmings of the chandelier.

Kubiš tried to tear his eyes away but there was nowhere to look. Every available surface in the church contained a similar abomination.

'What were they thinking, to make art from the remains of men?' asked Bartoš.

'Christ, even the Nazis would not create such a thing.'

Kubiš is about to turn on his heel when his eye caught a final blasphemy. On closer inspection a truly enormous mound of bones was revealed, piled high on top of one another, and imprisoned behind an arched window set back into the wall of the church. The window contained the remains of hundreds, their skulls looking out at passers-by, as if to say, *we were living once too – now look at us*. It was an open, mass grave, for all to see and marvel at the fragility of man. And Jan wondered – what thoughts, what good hearts and deeds were lost forever at the deaths of all these people? Is this how they could end up, he and Josef and Anna, their bones scattered among anonymous thousands?

'It's horrific.'

Bartoš shook his head in disgust and wonder.

'How did you know about this place?' Kubiš asked the man from far off Žilina.

'I was visiting family in Prague and my cousin brought me here, when I was maybe seventeen. It scared the hell out of me even then I can tell you.'

'Why,' Vaněk asked, 'did you bring us here, Josef?'

'I thought it was a suitable location to discuss the killing of a Nazi. Can you think of anywhere more appropriate?'

He was challenging the resistance man and they all knew it. Gabčík sat down in one of the aisles in the empty church and Kubiš joined him. Bartoš and Vaněk sat in the one in front and Zelenka, significantly perhaps, chose the seats occupied by Jan and Josef. The discussion had a surreal quality as all five men faced ahead, looking towards the altar.

Bartoš, unsettled by the array of bleached bones, began. 'I will come straight to the matter we wish to discuss. This attack on Heydrich must be called off.'

'On whose authority?' Gabčík spoke swiftly, his adrenalin up and arguments prepared thanks to the warning Kubiš had given him.

'I am a ranking officer here, Gabčík, a captain in the army and you are still expected to obey my orders.'

'Not when mine come from a higher authority. Do you feel you somehow outrank the President now, because if you do I have not heard of it?'

Captain Bartoš rounded on him then. 'Don't be insolent. The chain of command must supersede any orders you had back in London. I am here in Prague and aware of the true situation the network finds itself in. I am better equipped than a politician to determine the right course of action on the ground. If you try to assassinate Heydrich you will fail and die in the attempt. Even if you do succeed you will unleash a terrible retribution on the population and that includes all of us.'

Gabčík was immediately dismissive. 'You may well know the situation on the ground, but so do we. We can see how the people are living, like slaves, and you want us to do nothing. You might as well turn up at Gestapo HQ with a white flag or shoot yourself in the head right now for all the use you are doing.'

'Josef…,' cautioned Kubiš but Gabčík would allow no interruption.

'Men are being sent to Germany as slave labour, Jews are being shipped out never to return, innocent people are arrested, tortured and executed every hour of every day. Right now someone is being lined up against a wall and shot or guillotined in the Petschek Palace. Our country is being destroyed and you ask me to do nothing? What right have you to ask that? We should be doing more, not less.'

'But the Germans will…'

'Let the Germans do what they want but when we hit Heydrich it will hurt them all. This act will be like a knife through Hitler's heart. Then he will know there is still resistance in Prague. They have not entirely crushed us yet and they never will.'

'Josef, I am begging you,' pleaded Bartoš, choosing reason above threat, 'the Germans will kill everybody.'

'They can't kill everybody, there would be nobody to make their weapons, change their bed linen, polish their shoes, serve their drinks. The more they kill, the more hatred and resistance they bring down upon themselves.'

'I am ordering you not to go ahead with this mission.'

Gabčík stood up and gave the captain a look of such anger Kubiš feared he might even strike the man.

'And I am telling you no. I have never disobeyed an order in my life but I will not obey yours now. Unless you provide me with complete proof that President Beneš or Lieutenant Colonel Moravec wish this action to be called off it will go ahead. Do you understand me? Because I will not discuss it with you any further. You are just a captain.'

There was anger in Bartoš' eyes but Gabčík was not finished yet.

'And one who seems to have forgotten his duty.'

Bartoš, flushed and humiliated, at first had no reply to this and Gabčík strode from the building.

'Gabčík! Come back here.' Bartoš belatedly found his voice but Gabčík was gone.

Without a word Kubiš rose to his feet and followed him.

Now it was Vaněk's turn to attempt reason. 'This is madness. Zelenka, you must do something. You must go after them and stop this hothead from carrying out his crazy mission.'

Zelenka sighed, for he knew that he too was about to defy his superior and the clash of loyalties caused him pain.

'Gabčík may be a hothead. He may be indelicate in the way he puts forward his arguments but I am afraid, I have to say, I think this time he is right. We cannot just do nothing while our nation continues to descend into darkness. I'm sorry.'

Zelenka walked from the church then too. He left Bartoš and Vaněk alone in the church surrounded by the bones of thousands of men.

Outside the argument had already begun. Gabčík marched off at a brisk pace fuelled by the adrenalin of his defiance. Kubiš called after him to wait but his friend continued to pound away down the street. They had gone some distance when an exasperated Kubiš halted Gabčík with a shout.

'What the hell is the matter?'

Gabčík spun round. 'I'd like to hear it.'

'Hear what, Josef?'

'Why you said so little in there.'

'I let you speak for both of us, and I think you did a pretty good job.'

'Really, are you sure?' asked Gabčík, clearly rattled by his confrontation with the captain.

Kubiš bridled also. 'What do you mean? I am on your side.'

'Are you certain about that, Jan, or perhaps you'd rather we abandoned the attack like Bartoš wants. Then you can spend every day from now on with Anna if you please.'

'Hey, fuck you, Josef. I have never given up on this mission.'

'It looked like we did not speak with one voice in there. What I want to know is why?'

'Because you did not stop talking for one second, you great idiot, then you stormed out of there. How the hell was I supposed to get a chance to speak while you were telling everyone what they should say and do? Answer me that!'

'I just need to know if you want to go ahead and do this, or would you rather run off and marry your girl instead? I'll do it alone if I have to.'

That was it for Kubiš and he snapped, advancing on Gabčík and shoving him violently in the chest.

'Fuck you, Gabčík, you know nothing!'

Gabčík was stunned at this show of Jan's temper, which was all the more disturbing because it was seen so infrequently. He reacted in typical fashion.

'I know your mind is not on this and if you shove me again there'll be trouble!'

'My mind isn't on this! Do I take my woman on surveillance operations? At least I don't use Anna as my bag man. What will you do, Josef? Replace me with a nineteen-year-old girl?'

'Why not, when you act like one?'

Gabčík's heated final words acted as a signal and the two men immediately advanced on each other, both set to land punches; another moment and they would have been brawling in the gutter. They were no more than a yard apart when two middle-aged women rounded the corner and stopped sharply in their tracks at the unexpected sight of grown men about to come to blows. The spell was immediately broken and the understandable fear of arousing suspicion or prompting arrest instantly calmed Gabčík.

'Sorry, ladies,' he spluttered in embarrassment as he stepped back to let them pass. 'It's just a game…'

By the time they had crossed his path Kubiš was already marching furiously down the street. Gabčík called his name in irritation and Kubiš rounded on him.

'Take the next train, Josef. I don't want you on mine! It was your idea to come out here!' Then he rounded the corner and disappeared from view.

25

*'All means, even if they are not in conformity
with existing laws and precedents, are legal
if they serve the will of the Führer'*

Diktat from Adolf Hitler

When Gabčík returned on the afternoon train, he discovered he had another problem, for Liběna had disappeared. She was not waiting for him at her house as agreed and he received a particularly frosty reception from her father, who merely grunted in recognition as he entered the parlour. Realising something was amiss, Gabčík did not even bother to remove his raincoat. Instead he turned and walked out of the door.

She was still weeping when he found her. Liběna was sitting on their bench in the Municipal Park, as he had instinctively known she would be. Oh Lord, would he ever become immune to her tears? He thought it unlikely. And now he would have to make light of her fear again; Liběna's constant and understandable trauma that she was on the verge of losing him.

Even the weather conspired against Josef. Instead of a bright and all-forgiving sun, bursting through the leaves on the surrounding birch trees, he was forced to make his assurances under a dark and maudlin sky. The scene was of a grey drabness suited to her mood.

Taking no encouragement from his surroundings Josef walked up to the bench, sat down next to her without a word, and put his arm around her shoulders. Liběna did not look up. Instead she dabbed at her tears with a handkerchief.

'What's all this?' he asked. 'I thought we talked about everything. I thought you understood the situation.'

'I understand that you will leave me soon.'

Gabčík sighed his disagreement.

'My father tells me not to become too attached to you.' She let out a bitter little laugh at Fafek's belated powers of deduction. 'He says you will not stay here long, that you will try to assassinate Reinhard Heydrich and will very likely be killed in the attempt.'

Jesus, who in the resistance had told Fafek, or had he somehow worked it out for himself? Either way he must be desperate for his daughter to stay away from him now.

'If you survive you will leave Prague when your mission is over and I will never see you again,' Liběna concluded.

'Your father has a lot of ideas,' he began, buying some time, 'most of them completely foolish.'

He was momentarily lost for what to say next then decided on, 'I would have thought you were old enough by now to realise fathers do not always know everything.'

This was a wise choice of tactic and it temporarily calmed Liběna. She was the last person to assume her father was perfect and he knew it.

In truth, up to that point, Gabčík had never really contemplated a time beyond their mission. It was true that, once Heydrich was dead, he would have to go into hiding, either in Prague or the surrounding countryside, but he anticipated the hunt for the killers would eventually die down and he would then be free to continue his life; his life being Liběna.

'I have no plans to run off and leave you when my mission, whatever it may be, is over.'

'But you could be killed.'

'And so could anyone. All over the world there are people dying every day in this war.'

She fell silent then, her head drooping forward and he took it she was unconvinced.

'What have I said about all of this?'

'No, Josef, not now.'

'Yes, Liběna, now. I mean it, it's important. I need you to say it back to me, now more than ever. I have to be convinced you will be alright.'

'I don't like to think of it. I don't want to consider going on without you.'

'But you must promise me you will. You must promise me, for my sake. I need to know I can concentrate on my mission. I can't have my mind distracted from it by worrying about you. I need to hear you say that you will do everything necessary.'

'I will,' she answered reluctantly, and fresh tears fell.

'Then say it.' He was gentle but insistent.

'I will do everything necessary to survive.'

'And what will you do first?'

'I will take the package you gave me,' she answered him by rote.

'And who will you go and see?'

'Hlinka, the forger.'

'Then who?'

'Your Uncle Jaroslav in Žilina.'

'Good, very good, Liběna. And what then? How will you go about your life?'

And she looked up at him half pleadingly, as if to say don't make me go on with this cruel game, but he met her eyes with his and frowned a response until she relented.

'I will take each day in turn.' Liběna said it defiantly. 'Each day in turn,' she repeated firmly, looking directly into his eyes as she spoke, and he let the matter end there.

Now all Gabčík sought was the opportunity to bring Libĕna back from her melancholy, so they could enjoy the precious, irregular moments they had together.

'You know my view, it's all in the fates. Maybe we will live to be a hundred and maybe we will not.' He had tried to sound jovial but she answered him with a silence, so Josef continued by teasing her. 'And maybe you will love me forever or maybe you will run off with the baker's son.'

'Would he bully me the way you do?'

'Probably not.'

'Then he is in with a chance.'

He pulled Libĕna closer to him, so the back of her head rested against Josef's chest and his arms enveloped her entirely.

'Of course maybe, just maybe, we will grow very old together and have children, and so many grandchildren that I forget all of their names and you will have to constantly correct me.'

He kissed her hair.

'Then I would have grown fat and be the size of a house and you would not want to look at me anymore.'

She said it sullenly but he knew she was starting to relent, playing along with the game now. Her pretended sulking showed him the little crisis had passed and he leaned over her, kissing Libĕna full on the lips.

'I will never tire of looking at you.'

By the time Sergeant Karel Čurda reached Prague, via the safe houses of the Jindra network, his nerves were in shreds. Zelenka christened him the worrier, for he had noted Čurda's doleful eyes and permanently furrowed brow and the way he held his hands clamped nervously together when he sat, as if praying, and perhaps he was.

Any sudden noise, a bang on the door perhaps, would

make Čurda flinch visibly and he was clearly ill at ease in the company of more than one or two resistance men at a time. Zelenka could understand it, of course. Čurda had endured a torrid time since his return. The mission that brought him here had ended almost before it began and he had barely escaped with his life. Čurda had seen the man who sheltered him betrayed by an anonymous hand then shot dead in the street. If that were not enough ill fortune, he had then learned the fate of his good friend Ivan Kolařík. The man had killed himself with cyanide rather than be tortured to death by the Gestapo.

If Čurda had really lost his nerve, Zelenka would not push him back into danger. Still the man should surely try to be a little more active than he was currently. If Čurda had his way he would sit in the safe house all day and simply stare out through the window, watching the street outside, monitoring its comings and goings. Surely he would go mad with frustration if he stayed there any longer?

As soon as Zelenka returned from Kutná Hora he delivered a bag of provisions as an excuse to check on him. He was about to leave Čurda once more in his solitary state when, on an impulse, he stopped.

'Čurda, I am off to talk to someone who may have some interesting intelligence for us. I thought you might like to come with me. It will get you out of this house for a while and I could use another set of ears on this one. It may help your friends Gabčík and Kubiš with their mission. It's not far, we could walk it together.'

'Well, I would like to help you Zelenka, of course. You have all been so kind to me since I arrived in Prague, sheltering and feeding me like this...'

'That is our duty, Čurda. You do not have to thank us for this.'

'It's just we were expressly forbidden to know anything

about each other's mission; ordered in fact. Back in England they would make us swear not to talk about what we were going to do over here. In case we were ever captured. I would hate that anybody could later say I disobeyed a direct order by getting involved in Gabčík and Kubiš' mission. You do understand that, don't you?'

Zelenka reached for his coat and slipped it on.

'Don't worry, Čurda, yes, I think I understand,' and he left without another word.

Čurda watched Zelenka through the window as he walked away. It had been an uncomfortable moment but he would gladly endure many more of them if he could stay away from this resistance work. Once in Prague, Čurda had given up all thoughts of armed struggle against the Nazis. The Germans were organised, well equipped and patrolling the streets in numbers. It was clear they could never be driven out, only a fool would try. Instead he would settle for the quiet life. He had false papers and a safe room with a good Czech family. There was enough food and the house was warm. Hell, with his subsistence money there was not even a pressing need to get a job. It was almost the good life.

Each time Čurda thought of the last moments of Ivan Kolařík it made him sick to his stomach. He promised himself whatever happened he would never endure the same fate as his friend.

Kubiš looked petulant, hurt, like a woman, thought Gabčík, as he watched his friend walk into the bar at U Fleků, the four-hundred-year-old beer hall they had chosen for a meeting place, but he was not going to point that out for fear of another almighty row.

Jan reluctantly sat down and his friend challenged him immediately. 'So, have you decided? Are you going to kill Heydrich or me?'

'Both I think,' answered Kubiš. 'Then I will shoot Anna's father as well, so all my troubles will vanish in a day.'

Gabčík nodded sagely. 'Sounds like a good plan.' And he slid a freshly poured glass of beer over the table to Kubiš.

They were treading warily, each trying not to inflame the other but both too proud for conventional apologies. Their nervous verbal sparring was as close as either would come to it.

'I am glad I didn't hit you, though. I mean, I would hate to have ruined your good looks,' added Gabčík.

'That was very thoughtful and bruises are so conspicuous in Prague.'

'They are becoming less so. You could always say you had an afternoon at the Petscheck Palace.'

'Not many get to say that. Can you honestly say you have met anyone who actually came out of there again?'

'No,' and Gabčík exhaled deeply. 'Look Jan, what do you say we kill Heydrich together first, and leave killing each other till after the war, eh?'

'On balance that sounds like a sensible idea. Hell, the Germans will probably save us both the trouble.'

'I realise you are as committed to this operation as I am. I just wish you had said something to Bartoš so he got the message from us both.'

'And I told you it was impossible to interrupt you, as it always is when you lose your temper, and besides that I did not feel comfortable.'

'What do you mean, because he is a captain?'

'No, fuck Bartoš, not that no, it was the location.' Kubiš seemed embarrassed to continue. 'Frankly, I felt uncomfortable speaking in that church, with all of those bones around me.'

Gabčík laughed but this time it was the amusement of a friend.

'If you chose the sight to confound Bartoš and Vaněk,' Kubiš continued, 'then I think you did a good job. You certainly unsettled me.'

Gabčík was serious for a moment. 'No, that was not the reason I chose Kutná Hora.'

'Why then?'

'I chose it to remind everybody that all men are mortal. You are mortal, I am mortal, but so is the bastard Heydrich.' Gabčík said it with conviction and instantly Kubiš began to comprehend. 'We have started to treat him as if he is impossible to kill but he is not a devil, though he acts like one. He is only a man. He is flesh, he is bone and he is blood, and we have forgotten that. And I tell you this, Jan, he is a lot closer to God today than he thinks.'

26

'Untermensch'

German word meaning less than human, used by Hitler to
describe Jews, Poles and all Slavs, including Czechs

'The trouble with you, Walter, is you never want to get
your hands dirty.'

Heydrich spat the words at Schellenberg, with a
spite slowly nurtured by alcohol. The Reichsprotektor swirled
his brandy in its glass in snatched rhythmic movements,
as if keeping time with the argument as he reproached his
subordinate.

'It's all very well just so long as you don't have to do the dirty
work yourself, isn't it? So long as someone else is prepared to
climb down into the gutter and do it for you.'

Schellenberg's usual sense of dread was becoming similarly
inured by the brandy, which Karl Frank, Heydrich's deputy in
Prague, continued to pour repeatedly, following his insistence
the bottle remain at the table. Schellenberg's fear of Heydrich
was ever present but he could not allow such charges to go
unanswered.

'That is hardly fair, Reichsprotektor. You yourself
congratulated me on the successful completion of numerous
hazardous missions on behalf of the Fatherland. Why,
following Venlo, the Führer himself…'

'Shut up about Venlo... I'm not talking about Venlo, Walter.'

Heydrich slurred his subordinate's name so badly Schellenberg belatedly realised it would be useless to debate the point. The Reichsprotektor was drunk.

'I'm talking about high policy, the actions that matter, the grand vision. Doing what is necessary to secure a Thousand-Year Reich. Not just a few missions.' He spat the last word as if it were an illness.

'No, it takes more than that. More!' Heydrich's head lolled giddily and he set his glass back down on the table with a loud bang, caused by drunken misjudgement of distance. The noise reverberated in the restaurant that was, by now, noticeably absent of other diners. A waiter misconstrued and came scurrying over to serve them, only for Frank to wave him away violently.

Heydrich almost seemed to have forgotten his point. Then he caught Schellenberg eyeing him nervously and the thread of his argument began to return.

'Take Salon Kitty. A perfect illustration.'

Schellenberg let out a sigh. 'Reichsprotektor, we have discussed this matter repeatedly and I simply could not get involved in such a scheme. It had nothing to do with the intelligence service.'

Heydrich leaned forward in wild-eyed contradiction.

'It had everything to do with intelligence!' and he fixed Schellenberg with a look of unfettered fury.

'I agree, Walter,' chuckled Frank, who seemed oblivious to the dangerous current passing between the two men. 'Salon Kitty was definitely an intelligent move.' And he laughed uproariously at his own weak joke, impervious to the fact that he was chortling alone.

Schellenberg began to feel trapped once more. Would Heydrich always hold such events against him, bringing them out with impunity whenever his mood turned sour?

But of course he would.

Heydrich had launched Salon Kitty back in the thirties. It was the most extravagantly debauched scheme the SS ever cooked up. Here was a real, fully operational brothel, operating in a semi-legal capacity, with genuine whores who knew more than a trick or two, and all reserved for the finer people in society: ambassadors, politicians, senior army officers and the numerous visiting foreign dignitaries Berlin played host to in any given peacetime year.

Every room a hedonist's haven and all of them bugged, with microphones lodged in double walls. Each and every sexual practice noted and filed away for the day it would come in handy against the enemies of the state, domestic and foreign. Any piece of small talk, sex talk, and pillow talk recorded by an army of listeners who manned the place twenty four hours a day – with pictures through spy holes of every act man could imagine and some he probably could not; masochists and sadists, troilists and onanists, voyeurists and fetishists, all captured lovingly on film for the greater good of the Reich. Not a single whore who was not a volunteer, and how shocked was the disapproving Schellenberg, dispatched to find these amoral courtesans, at the ease with which they filled Salon Kitty with good German girls, each one of the finest stock? He had simply refused to get directly involved and Heydrich had been forced to delegate the task to Arthur Nebe, chief of the criminal police, and a far more natural choice to sniff out potential whores. Everyone a patriot, willing to lie for her country then lie down for it; trained to ask the right question at just the right time.

'Tell Frank why you would not get involved in Salon Kitty. Go on tell him. He wants to know, don't you, Frank?'

Heydrich took yet another swig of brandy. Frank had stopped laughing now.

'Yeah, sure, why not, Walter?'

'Reichsprotektor, I really don't see…'

'Tell him!!!'

Heydrich slammed his hand down onto the table with a crash. The glass he still held in his hand shattered on impact, pitching the last of the brandy onto the white linen tablecloth, staining it the colour of long dried blood. Heydrich appeared shocked for an instant and Schellenberg realised his superior was so drunk he had forgotten he was holding a glass at all. The Reichsprotektor surveyed his hand but miraculously there was no cut. Seemingly satisfied, he turned his attention back to Schellenberg.

'Just tell him,' he commanded, quietly.

Though Walter dreaded these outbursts and always felt sick at the wild uncertainty of the outcome, he had little choice but to play his superior's game and hope he would somehow survive the examination.

He swallowed slowly, turned to face Frank, who now looked almost as nervous as Schellenberg, and said. 'It was a matter of honour.'

Heydrich began to laugh. It was a low, nasty, snickering laugh, rich in contempt.

'Did you hear that, Karl?' he slurred. 'A matter of honour.'

Frank, not knowing how to react, simply grinned and mumbled something inaudibly noncommittal. It did not matter, for Heydrich was challenging Schellenberg to his face again.

'So, you will not choose whores for a brothel dedicated to obtaining secrets for the Reich, yet you will happily take those secrets and make use of them in your role as an intelligence officer?' He did not permit Schellenberg the luxury of an answer. 'That is what I am talking about, Walter. You don't mind that these places exist, you prosper from their presence, and do nothing in practice to prevent a brothel filled with nice German girls sucking and fucking their way through half the foreign diplomatic corps, just so long as you don't have to choose these women yourself. Heaven forfend that you might actually have to meet one of them, touch her hand in greeting, issue her with orders, because that would be beyond the conduct of a gentleman. Am I right? So, I have to find someone who is less of a gentleman than you to handle things. Then everything is acceptable and there is nothing to offend your delicate sensibilities.'

He let out a humourless chuckle. Frank, desperate to back the right horse, began to laugh weakly along with his superior. Heydrich continued to stare at Schellenberg, who could find no fault in the brutish words of his drunken boss, because they were entirely true. Heydrich was far from finished.

'But if we all held your views there would be no Salon Kitty and none of your precious, invaluable secrets would ever come to light. What would you do now, Walter? If we went back in time and the decision to start the brothel was solely yours, knowing what you know now, aware of the secrets we have gained from the place, would you open her up or not? Answer me – no, don't answer me, I know the answer already – you would wash your hands of it, like you always do – because you're weak, Walter, weak.'

Schellenberg no longer fears for his life. His leader's voice has calmed and somehow Heydrich is managing to speak clearly for the moment, despite the truly gargantuan amounts of brandy he has consumed. Something tells Schellenberg it is not his life or liberty that are under threat this night, but the carefully ordered and mannered justification of his position within the Reich that is being slowly eroded in front of him. It greatly troubles Schellenberg that there is some truth in Heydrich's assertion – that he may actually be the watered down, half Nazi hypocrite the general describes.

Then, the inevitable conclusion of his leader's argument.

'Take the Jews, for example. Now that is just what I am talking about, Walter. You do not share the responsibility we all shoulder for the destruction of this plague, this bacillus. You refuse to become directly involved. Or rather it is not that you refuse, it is more that you do not put yourself forward to play a part in this most vital work.'

'My duties with AMT VI are most time-consuming.'

'An excuse, a ridiculous excuse. Senior men are supposed to delegate their work. Are you saying that I have time to spare that you do not?'

'No, I merely...'

'I am trying to run this ludicrous country as well as commanding the entire fucking secret service. I am in charge of that, am I not? You do concede that at least, Walter, that I am still in charge?' and Heydrich's eyes widened with paranoid delusion at the perceived ambition of Schellenberg.

'Of course I do.' Walter spoke quietly, his voice free from challenge, desperate to avoid further debate on just who holds the true power.

'So, if you accept that it is not time that is your enemy, you must concede it is your appetite for the task. And that is where you are hopelessly misguided. We are engaged in a battle, and it is a fight to the death. It will end either with the complete destruction of Jewry or the eventual annihilation of the Fatherland. There is no middle ground and only one choice. We do not want careerists who join the SS and the party just because everybody else does. We need committed men, warriors who are prepared to wipe the enemy from the face of the earth. It is time you made up your mind and chose your camp, Walter. Whose side are you on?'

Schellenberg began to resent this probing, for Heydrich had opened up a bitter wound and was attacking him where he was at his weakest. He had managed to avoid the worst excesses of Nazism and his role never brought him into direct contact with the *Einsatzgruppen*. Certainly, he had heard about the firing squads, the lynch parties and the orchestrated pogroms but they were nothing to do with him. He was a member of both the SS and the party but one had to be to progress. He could never have gone so far in his career if he had refused to join either group – the very idea had not even entered his head. So, he could accept the actions of other, less balanced individuals as part of the overall system in which he prospered and that was Heydrich's point.

Schellenberg's reply was careful, considered and expressed in a deliberately firm manner. 'My loyalty has never been in doubt. I have been faithful to my country, obedient to my superiors and steadfastly loyal to the Führer. I have never flinched to carry out all that is necessary to sustain the Reich. There is really no reason to question me further.'

'Are you an enemy of the Jews or not?'

But Schellenberg is developing a stubborn streak and now seems intent on silence.

'Answer me, Walter.' Heydrich locks his eyes on Schellenberg, who is attempting to deport himself with an officer's solemnity in the face of this drunken verbal assault. When no reply is forthcoming, Heydrich makes up his mind. He leans forward until he is disconcertingly close to his subordinate's face and hisses the words, 'Jew lover,' at the outraged Schellenberg.

'General, you go too far!' Schellenberg looks for a moment as if he wishes to strike his leader. Almost immediately he regains control of himself, rises unbidden by his superior, scraping his chair a little unsteadily along the ground as he steps away from the table, then says simply. 'I really must excuse myself, gentlemen. It has been a long day and I have an early flight to Berlin in the morning. Good evening to you both,' and Schellenberg walks from the table.

'Walter! Walter, come back here. I haven't finished. Walter!'

Schellenberg does not pause. Instead he walks through the front door of the restaurant leaving Heydrich to realise that, in some strange way, he has lost the argument but is too drunk to understand why.

Heydrich insisted they drink on. The evening continued through a slurred and rambling conversation covering their mutual hatred of the Jews and Frank's deep loathing of all things Czech.

Drunkenness led to a complete suspension of discretion, so nervous waiters easily overheard Frank's heartfelt opinion that the entire population of Prague should be exterminated to make way for more healthy Germanic folk. Moments later he leaned forward to summon a shocked maître d' and ordered him to fetch more brandy.

Finally, neither man could take any more and they stumbled out into the street, the cold breeze fanning the flames of their drunkenness. The driver was not Heydrich's usual man and he was glad of it. He did not want Klein, who had a day's leave, to see him like this. Instead he was driven from the restaurant by a nervously formal young *Rottenführer* he had never seen before, probably seconded for the evening from a less senior man.

As Heydrich took his seat in the car, he could see Frank climbing unsteadily and with an exaggerated caution into the back of his own vehicle. The State Secretary had a newly delivered, armour plated Mercedes Benz 540K; a wholly unnecessary precaution in Heydrich's view. He had been urged to follow suit but never quite found the time to allow his vehicle to be withdrawn for the necessary alterations. He supposed he would get around to it eventually.

Lina was visiting family back in Germany, so a quiet and solitary night could be taken. He spent the journey home in a sullen silence, brooding aggressively on the events of the evening, which compounded his belief that he was losing the faultless judgement for which he was rightly noted. His two closest subordinates had witnessed the debacle from near at hand and they would lose respect for him, if they had any to begin with. It seemed they no longer even feared him now. Schellenberg had simply walked away from the table without permission when it suited him. And Heydrich had let it happen; partly because he knew he had over-stepped the mark with his accusation of Jewish sympathies, but mainly because he was too drunk to stop him.

As the car made its slow, twisting way down the side streets of Resslova, Heydrich began to nurture a new and terrible thought. Perhaps Hitler had found out his most shameful secret, despite all his tireless efforts to wipe out the past. Yes, that was it. That had to be why the Führer had given him a look of such loathing in the Wolf's Lair. Bormann had somehow found out then made Hitler aware of the one thing that could destroy Heydrich. The secret he had done everything within his immense power to suppress.

As he brooded on this new and awful possibility his overwrought mind recalled a different age. He was a child then, and the world was not the ordered place he had made it in later years. Oh, how they had taunted him in the playground at Halle, with the particularly malevolent relish only a child can summon; the memory of it so fresh, now that his self-pity has been coaxed unresistingly to the surface by brandy. Years would pass before he could leave the accusations and the terrible omissions from their clubs, their groups and their games, behind him.

Even at the naval academy the whispers had followed him, leading to fresh torments from his fellow cadets. By then it had reached the point where he was no longer sure if their allegations were true or not. His mother assured him he had no cause for concern, that his father's name had occasionally been misrepresented, due to the inadvertent addition of Bruno's own stepfather's surname – Suss – in official correspondence, yet the nagging doubts remained.

As the years went by Heydrich tried everything to expunge the shame of his past. He had even had his mother's middle name omitted from her gravestone, in case anyone made the connection, and the subsequent devastating conclusion. Elizabeth Sara Heydrich. Not a German name. Oh no.

'Stop the car. Pull over,' Heydrich commanded.

The corporal did as he was ordered and the general barely had time to open the car door before the streams of vomit spattered onto the pavement. Heydrich retched for what seemed like minutes. Finally, it was over and Heydrich pulled the door closed and slumped back in his seat, his eyes streaming from the effort.

The lateness of the hour ensured there were no onlookers at the Panenské Břežany. Corporal Frick walked around the car to open the door for Heydrich. He watched in horror as the general tripped and pitched forward, landing heavily on his face, bouncing on the gravel with the pliant indestructibility exhibited by only the truly drunk. Heydrich let out a gurgle of protest as he sprawled helplessly on his hands and knees.

'Let me help you, Herr Reichsprotektor.'

The panicked driver, unused to the ways of this most powerful man, trotted forward, desperate to assist him. He took hold of Heydrich's left arm, placing his other hand on the right side of the general's torso, and began to haul him aloft.

'Get your filthy hands off me!'

The driver let go of Heydrich with such haste the general was unceremoniously dropped back onto the ground. With supreme effort, Heydrich slowly hauled himself to his feet, swaying wildly in front of the terrified man.

'Breathe a word of this to anyone and you will find yourself in the east, at the head of a punishment battalion,' he hissed.

Frick's eyes filled with fear and, in his panic, all he could think to do was come to attention and salute, with a parade-ground stiffness.

'Get out of here.'

Heydrich turned his back on the man. He did not hear the car depart, drowned out as it was by a persistent ringing in his ears.

Heydrich dropped the key more than once before he was able to successfully open the door. He nudged it closed behind him with his shoulder, crossed the hall then clambered up the stairs, at times on all fours, gasping for air as he went. When he reached the final stair, he pulled himself upright then stopped suddenly at the sight that greeted him. What was this, some sort of taunting, spiteful joke at his expense? Who could have done it? Placed such a thing in his way when he was at his most wretched.

On the landing in front of him was a large mirror. Any visitor would be greeted by his own reflection as soon as he ascended the staircase. Heydrich had never even noticed it before. It was an irrelevance. Now, standing on his own at the top of the stairs, with illuminating moonlight shining brightly through a nearby window, he was confronted with a hideous apparition, a vile distortion of himself. Through a veil of drunkenness, there stood a man in the uniform of an SS General but, instead of a strong Nordic nose, he possessed the elongated beak of the Jew; where once a wholly noble Germanic face looked out at the world, now Heydrich was convinced he saw the inferior features of Judaism forcing their way to the surface. In his paranoia, he felt he was changing, right there in front of his own eyes, metamorphosing into the creature he despised most. Hitler was right, the Jews were a disease and they were taking control – not just of Europe but now of his own body, robbing him of his strength, clouding his judgement, slowly killing him.

Heydrich scrambled at the holster on his belt, taking two attempts before he was able to pull the Luger from its grasp. He raised the weapon and pointed it unsteadily out in front of him, where it veered violently between waist and shoulder height as he tried desperately to level it at the looking glass. With a supreme effort, he managed to hold it steady for an instant.

'Filthy Jew!' he screamed as two bullets astonishingly found their mark.

The glass shattered in its frame and the shards tumbled to the ground, turning end over end like a crystal waterfall.

Heydrich's world rotated on its axis. What was happening? The solid frame of the wrecked mirror seemed somehow to be magically detaching itself from the wall, and it began to roll onto its side in front of him.

The Reichsprotektor was so drunk he did not feel the impact as his body crashed limply to the floor. He was completely unconscious even before his face found the soft welcoming fibres of the landing carpet, and he slept as he lay, splayed unnaturally on his side, his legs a comical scissor shape. Heydrich's right arm was pinioned beneath his body, and the Luger lay on the ground behind him, pointing back the way he had come. As alarmed servants began to emerge, the general let out a solitary adenoidal snore before lapsing into a deep, impenetrable haze of brandy and self-loathing.

27

'We Germans, who are the only people in the world who have a decent attitude to animals, will also assume a decent attitude to these human animals'

SS Reichsführer Heinrich Himmler,
on the population of Eastern Europe

A crowd had gathered to witness the President address his subjects. Old man Hácha stood in front of the Jan Hus monument, now covered up with Nazi banners, while he spoke to his people. As he stood on the podium it was clear he was reading from a crib sheet, as he reinforced the need for Czechs to back their German allies in the fight against Stalin. Hácha's rambling monologue was delivered to a hard faced audience which merely stared back at him. Words are cheap, thought Gabčík, who stood to the rear of the crowd.

It was another half hour before Gabčík spotted Heydrich. Finally, the Reichsprotektor made his discreet entrance at the back of the monument, as Gabčík knew he would. With Kubiš he had already contemplated then dismissed a plan to attack the general here, while he delivered his scheduled *Winterhilfe* speech in front of today's press-ganged crowd. In the end they had both concluded it was too risky. Now, the plan seemed worthy of a second look.

Gabčík tucked his hand into his coat pocket and wrapped it round the cold metal stock of the pistol. All he needed was a split second; a chance to fire a clean shot at the man while he stood on the podium addressing the crowd, and all this would be over. Then he could make a break for it in the confusion, losing himself amongst the panicked people. But he would need to be closer.

Heydrich's high voice began to fill the square, distorted by the microphone. 'I urge the good people of Prague to support their German brothers fighting the evil of communism,' he droned in the unenthusiastic monologue of one exhibiting the symptoms of extreme tiredness.

Gabčík began to edge his way slowly forward, sliding carefully between the people in front of him, until he was halfway across the square. Never for a moment did he let his eyes divert from the pasty figure of Heydrich as he droned interminably on about German soldiers sacrificing themselves on behalf of the Czech people.

Finally, when Gabčík made it to within a dozen yards of the podium, he at last stopped moving, to take in the scene around him. Only then did he belatedly realise the magnitude of the act he was contemplating. From Gabčík's new vantage point he could make out men from a detachment of the SS who had ringed the podium. More soldiers watched proceedings from opened windows in high buildings, overseeing the square. Closer to hand, plain-clothes members of the Gestapo made their presence all too obvious amongst the crowd.

Gabčík realised he would never make it to within pistol range before he was arrested or simply shot down. He was so near now, agonisingly close, almost enough to kill this man but certainly at the expense of his own life. And what if he missed?

Before long Gabčík became nervous he might be stopped randomly and the weapon found on his person. Sick with frustration, he slunk away from the gathering, returning sullenly home, without ever mentioning a word of the episode to Kubiš.

Novotný the watchmaker slowly eased the glass face free from the rest of the pocket watch. He was a skilled and experienced craftsmen but, as he carefully wrapped the fragile little circle in a soft piece of cloth, he could feel the moisture on his fingertips – his nervousness caused not by the routine nature of the repair but the proximity of the Reichsprotektor, who had already warned him to be particularly careful with his father's timepiece.

'You have twenty four hours to repair and return it in full working order,' instructed the general. 'It must be ready by tomorrow night.'

Neither felt the need to discuss further the disastrous consequences for the watchmaker if it were not. Novotný kept his ear close to the ground and he knew the reason for Heydrich's deadline. The general wished to have this significant item with him as he attended a special concert at the Wallenstein Palace. Heydrich himself seemed to be taking an immense interest in final preparations for the event. Surely this could be the only reason for the imposing presence at Hradčany, that very afternoon, of the heavily pregnant Lina Heydrich.

Novotný had been installed at a desk outside Heydrich's office; the better to focus his mind on the job in hand. He was perfectly positioned to witness the fearsome whirlwind of the woman's breathless demands while he gently coaxed the pieces of the ancient pocket watch apart. Servants and middle ranking German officers alike were dispatched on imperative errands with a similar degree of brusqueness and lack of social grace. From time to time Heydrich would appear for further earnest discussions with his wife on seating plans and floral arrangements, reminding Novotný of the level of preparation usually reserved for important state occasions.

There eventually came a point when there could surely be no matter left unaddressed by Frau Heydrich and she finally pronounced herself at least partially satisfied with proceedings. The whole castle seemed to sigh in relief.

Heydrich chose this moment to emerge from his office again and congratulate Lina on both her impeccable taste and the immense hard work required to organise so many servants. In response Lina pronounced herself quite overwhelmingly exhausted. Heydrich, by contrast, seemed in good cheer and playful mood.

'I have just received word from the Führer, my dear. He wants to see me in Berlin the day after the concert.'

'Really?' asked his preoccupied spouse.

'Yes, and the thing is…' deadpanned Heydrich, pretending indifference, '…it is possible I may not return to Prague.'

'What do you mean?' She was listening to him now.

'Yes, it seems, from what I have heard, that I am about to be reposted.'

'Oh, Reinhard no, surely not.' Her agitation was palpable.

'I fear so, my darling.'

'No, it would be a tragedy, after all of the work I have done on the estate.'

'Oh, I'm sure we will be able to keep the house. You could stay here and fly out to see me whenever you like. Or, if you prefer, you could come and live with me at my new posting.'

'And where might that be? Even further east?' she exclaimed sourly.

'Well, of course one can never be entirely sure with the Führer, but I think there is a good chance that it will be… Paris.'

'Paris!' And her face showed joy for the first time that day. 'Oh, Reinhard, is it true?'

'Let's just say I have it on very good authority.' And he beamed back at Lina, enjoying her happiness.

'You were teasing me!' she squealed in chastisement but there was no anger left in her now.

28

'Have patience, the day of revenge is approaching'

The signal for action from the Czech service of the BBC

When the Heydrichs departed, Novotný diligently carried on with his repairs. As soon as the watchmaker was finished, however, he packed up his tools, ensured the safe delivery of the pocket watch and immediately went to look for a friend on the Hradčany staff.

Novotný found the joiner working on an ancient dilapidated cabinet.

'Šafařík,' he whispered, 'I have important news. The day after tomorrow, Heydrich is to leave Prague forever,' and Novotný explained everything.

Šafařík wasted no time. As soon as he had received a verbatim report on the Heydrichs' conversation from Novotný, he went round the castle making further discreet enquiries among his fellow servants, disguising them as the natural curiosity of a paid underling. He soon discovered the Reichsprotektor's immediate staff were preparing for one of his regular trips to Berlin and was satisfied the watchmaker had not misunderstood. Although nobody could confirm Heydrich's next destination was Paris, there was a good deal of speculation he would soon be moved away from Prague.

'A new posting,' explained the maid who tidied his office. 'A promotion by all accounts,' she added, sounding almost proud of the fact, stupid girl.

Further investigations revealed Heydrich's driver Klein had been granted a few days' leave, starting the day after Heydrich said he would be in Berlin, and the Mercedes was due to have a complete and thorough mechanical check at the same time, keeping it off the road for several days. Šafařík concluded Novotný was entirely accurate in his summation. Heydrich was leaving.

It was all Šafařík could do to stop himself from running across the road with his news. Instead he waited until his normal hours of work were over then he took this priceless information to the girls in the apartment by the castle.

One of them, Helena, set out immediately, trawling the safe houses in an effort to locate Zelenka. She eventually found him at the fourth time of asking, sitting in the back room of a shabby coffee house with Hlinka, the forger, at his side. Whatever business they were discussing, Zelenka quickly brought it to a conclusion when he saw Helena, for she had never come looking for him before. On receiving her message, he kissed the diligent girl on both cheeks, thanked her for her persistence in locating him, and dashed off to find Kubiš.

At Aunt Marie's house the resistance leader passed an increasingly anxious two hours, waiting for Jan to return from his latest surveillance trip. As soon as he crossed the threshold Zelenka sat him down at the table then set out everything he had heard.

Kubiš did not bother to disguise his alarm. 'Christ, that ruins everything. When is this concert?'

'Tomorrow night, at the Wallenstein Palace, but the whole place will be crawling with security. He has invited a large number of SS, Gestapo and *Wehrmacht* officers. I have a contact working in the headquarters of the Abwehr. Their senior men are all expected to attend apparently, much to their irritation.'

'And he will leave the very next day?'

'Yes, but not till the afternoon. Šafařík says he is expected to attend a meeting with Hácha in the morning, before he flies out.'

'This meeting, it will still go ahead even though he is to be posted away from Prague?'

Zelenka nodded. 'It has not been removed from his diary, which is the usual practice. We can normally rely on the fastidiousness of the German military.'

Kubiš fell silent for a moment while he racked his brain for a solution.

Zelenka asked him gently. 'What do you want to do, Jan? Call it off? You don't even have a suitable location. Rushing into this greatly increases your risk.'

'Would you call it off?' challenged Kubiš.

'I don't know, but it's not my neck on the line, is it?'

'If we let him fly out of here like nothing ever happened then he has won. Heydrich would go unpunished for countless murders.'

'He could be brought to justice eventually.'

'There is no guarantee of that and you know it. Who can tell how this war will go? If Heydrich ends up in Berlin or Paris, he may be untouchable. Certainly, a Czech would never get near him. Do you want to leave our vengeance up to someone else?'

'Of course not. I want you to hit him and make him pay for his crimes. I just don't know how you are going to do that now.'

'Neither do I, but we promised the President we would fulfil this mission and I have no intention of giving up on it yet. Can I trouble you for one of those awful cigarettes you smoke?'

Zelenka reached for the tin and selected a hand rolled cigarette, with loose strands of tobacco hanging from its sides, for each of them. They both lit up and puffed silently away for a moment.

'Can you get a message to Gabčík tonight?' asked Kubiš finally.

'Of course.'

'Tell him I need to have an emergency meeting with him tomorrow. I'll think of a time and venue before you leave.'

'I'll ensure it.'

'In the morning I will walk the route again. There is no ideal place for an operation like this, so the best I can hope is to find a location that makes a shot at the man possible and does not bring a battalion of soldiers down on top of us two minutes later. Who knows, maybe I'll discover the ideal place now that I simply have to.'

'You never know, Jan, you just never know,' agreed Zelenka. 'It certainly helps to concentrate the mind, I'll say that much' and he took a long reflective drag on his cigarette.

They met the following evening in one of those quiet little restaurants so beloved of agents across the globe. The family-run *vinárna* was never too busy to talk, nor was it entirely empty. A couple of apathetic waiters plodded from table to table, with no interest in anything except what was ordered, middle aged men who could be relied upon to drop the plate sullenly on the table then leave you to it. The presence of two strangers discussing business would be overlooked.

Gabčík was already there, facing the door, as all spies in foreign countries are wont to do, a glass of local beer poured in front of him, half of it gone already in the few moments he had been seated. Perhaps he was as nervous as Kubiš. There was an empty glass there for him too and another bottle with its top removed. Kubiš undid his raincoat, letting drops of water spill onto the dark, warped wooden floor. He hung it on a hook on the wall near to Gabčík's table then sat down in front of his friend. Jan's hair was sopping wet from the rain and water slid down his back when he sat, but it was a small price to ensure his counter-surveillance ritual was followed in advance of this most vital of meetings. To get there Kubiš had taken three buses and walked down a maze of side streets only lengthy veterans of Prague could know as well as he.

'I ordered *Vepřový Řízek* for two, didn't think you'd care,' pronounced Gabčík by way of greeting.

Kubiš nodded. The traditional fried pork dish would do as well as any other. He had no appetite and, if it were not for the sake of appearances, would have avoided food altogether. He was happy to be spared the distractions of a menu.

Kubiš poured his beer and both men watched as the bubbles rose up the glass to form a foaming head. He took a rejuvenating gulp before setting it down and confirming the news Gabčík had received from Zelenka the night before. Heydrich would be leaving the next afternoon but not until he had visited Hradčany in the morning at his normal hour and in the usual vehicle.

'What time does Heydrich's car leave Panenské Břežany?' asked Gabčík.

'Nine o'clock.'

'Every morning?'

'Without variation. Always nine, give or take a moment or two. The man is like clockwork.'

'Has he ever had an escort?'

'Apart from his driver, no.'

'Motorcycle outriders even? A couple of men to go ahead and clear the way?'

'No need, there is barely any traffic. No one can get petrol.

Almost every vehicle he sees will be German military.'

'And you are sure it would be impossible to take him at the gates of the mansion?'

'It can be done, Josef – when his driver slows to take the bend out of the gateway – but I think we would never get away afterwards. There is the SS barracks down the road for one thing and no way out except the road into Prague. They would have us in minutes.'

'I think you are right,' conceded Gabčík reluctantly.

'Also, there is not enough cover by the entrance. We could easily be spotted by a routine patrol and jeopardise the whole attack before it began.'

Gabčík raised a hand in supplication. 'I'm convinced. Where then?'

'It's the same problem we have always had. Where can we wait for him without attracting attention? It must be somewhere we can attack without too many civilians in the way. One, we don't want to kill any bystanders if it can be avoided. Two, we cannot be in too large a crowd. It will hinder the escape and we have to remember there are some in Prague who do not want Heydrich dead. They might try to play the hero if they think it will profit them. You need a clear shot and you won't get it if some collaborator hurls himself at you during the crucial moments.'

'So it cannot be in the heart of the city and it cannot be in the countryside because there would be no place for us to run. We need to be close to the safe houses.'

'Which leaves the suburbs,' confirmed Kubiš.

'You have a place in mind?'

Kubiš nodded. 'Holešovice.'

Gabčík thought for a moment. 'Where exactly?'

'You remember, weeks ago it was, when we were scouring the whole area for a likely spot? I thought it showed promise then. The tram stop.'

Gabčík's eyes narrowed. 'Remind me. Describe it to me exactly as you remember it.'

'I went there again this morning. It's by a tight corner. We could join the rush hour crowd there. It is busy enough but not so bad that we can't break out afterwards. Trams are coming and going all the time. From early in the morning they are full of office workers. Then later it stays busy with the wives heading into town for groceries. Enough people I'm telling you. We can blend in. Valčík has agreed to help and he can give the signal once he sees the car coming towards us.'

'So we join the crowds and we wait. And when Heydrich comes round the bend…'

'His car will slow down…'

'And bang, we hit him.' Gabčík illustrated his point by quietly bringing his right fist into the palm of his left hand.

'That's the way I see it. I think we could do it and maybe stand half a chance of getting away afterwards. On bikes, back into the city, amid all the confusion. I would say it could be done. We have both committed to die if we have to but who says we have to?'

'I agree. They all think it is suicide but I have every intention of killing the bastard Nazi and staying alive.'

'So, we are agreed?' asked Kubiš. 'It's Holešovice.'

'Agreed.'

There was a solemnity in the moment and the two men shook hands as if they had just taken an oath together.

'Now let's go through every detail,' said Gabčík, 'moment by moment, so there can be no mistakes.'

29

'Blond Moses'

Derogatory nickname given to the young
Reinhard Heydrich by his fellow naval cadets

The Wallenstein Palace was a picture of opulence, its
entranceways flanked by towering arrangements of
flowers and guarded by soldiers, whose dress swords
and silver buttons gleamed. To witness waiters pouring
French champagne or handing out canapés, symbolically
assembled using delicacies imported from all corners of the
Reich's European empire, was to forget there was a war on at
all, thought Schellenberg.

As was his custom, the head of Foreign Intelligence declined
the rich food and held onto a single glass of champagne until
it had long since lost its fizz. He did endeavour to mingle
with his fellow officers and the gilded ladies of Prague who
accompanied them, for he did not want to be accused of
delivering any form of snub during this most auspicious of
occasions. Then, just as he was about to creep away to a quiet
corner of the gardens for a moment's respite, Heydrich hailed
him.

The party was about to go in it seemed and the
Reichsprotektor had decided to bestow a quite singular
honour on Schellenberg – the privilege of sitting next to his

master while the orchestra struck up the opening chords of a most eagerly awaited concert. For the first time in years, and to a much larger audience than ever before, the collected and interminably dull works of Heydrich's late father Bruno would be publicly performed.

Was there no one else of sufficient importance for Heydrich to choose as his companion during hours of this awful faux Wagnerian rubbish? It seemed not. Every officer in Prague, from the Gestapo, SS and Abwehr, was at the concert, itself a ridiculous security risk in Schellenberg's view, but, when one considered it, there was nobody here whom Heydrich would regard as a part of the true elite. For the past week a stream of regretfully declined invitations had been steadily arriving from the likes of Goebbels, Speer and Göring. Himmler too was indisposed it appeared and the Führer had also regretfully declined, though not in his own hand, for the card quite clearly contained the childlike signature of Martin Bormann.

Surprisingly, Heydrich was still in good form, laughing and joking with his surrounding acolytes, for the evening, even with the most senior men absent, appeared to be going well. Eventually the whole group, led by Heydrich and Lina, traipsed along the scarlet carpet that ushered them towards the Palace's golden staircase. Here they paused while animated photographers competed to capture the finest images of the Reichsprotektor and friends, as if he was royalty or a film star.

It was then Heydrich paid the bemused Schellenberg something akin to a compliment. 'Good idea about the Mozart, Walter. I think it will work.'

Oh God, and it had been said in a form of mischievous half jest as well. A week ago, when Heydrich had been looking for suitable music to begin the concert and pad out his father's insubstantial repertoire, he had asked Walter for an opinion on an opening act. Schellenberg had offered Mozart, on the spurious grounds that Prague was his second home, but surely even the general would see the folly of putting a genius further down the bill than a largely ignored nonentity. Not so. Heydrich thought it an excellent and fitting idea.

'But which piece?' he had pondered.

'Requiem,' answered Schellenberg, immediately cursing himself inwardly for his out of character mischief making. Offering the funereal piece as an opening to the programme might easily offend his volatile superior so he quickly added, 'For its power. If you think it is appropriate.'

'Entirely!' and Schellenberg had been startled by Heydrich's enthusiastic endorsement.

And so the two men took their place in the balcony, alongside Lina's spreading bulk, with the orchestra and choir deliberately poised, ready to strike up the first bars of Mozart's Requiem as they took their seats. Heydrich had delayed their arrival, insisting they wait outside in the corridor while everyone else sat down. Only when he received the signal from a harassed looking junior officer did they make their final entrance, to accompaniment from the opening triumphant strains of *Rex Tremendae*.

Thankfully nobody was foolish enough to ruin the music by applauding, but all eyes turned on Heydrich and he took his time. He even gave the conductor a slow regal bow, acknowledging the man's obsequious sense of timing. This was the crowning moment of Heydrich's tenure in Prague. Here was a chance to redeem a father's neglected memory, underlining his superiority, watched over by the last remnants of the Prussian military class, all forced to turn out and pay homage to him. The general had come a long way since they had thrown him out of the Navy for conduct unbecoming of a gentleman when he broke off an engagement to another girl to marry Lina.

As the music rose to fill the room, Schellenberg was struck

by the look of vainglory etched on Heydrich's face, as clear and distinct as the buttons on his best dress tunic. He thinks he is the Sun King, a modern God, thought Schellenberg as the sound of the choir rose and swelled in homage to the all-powerful Reichsprotektor.

30

*'Of all the Slavs, the Czech is the most
dangerous because he's a worker.
He has a sense of discipline, he's orderly...
he knows how to hide his plans'*

Adolf Hitler, January 1942

27 May 1942

The sky was white from a sun shrouded by early morning clouds that refused to disperse as Gabčík pedalled his way up the hill towards Holešovice. He arrived at the tram stop and untied his briefcase from the handlebars, leaving his bicycle, a ladies' model borrowed from Aunt Marie, leaning against a wall. The spot was carefully chosen so he could easily run back for it.

Gabčík draped an oversized raincoat over an arm and in his other hand he carried the briefcase, which contained the disassembled Sten. He wore a cap to disguise the colour of his hair and the humble suit of an office worker. As he crossed the road towards the tram stop he spotted Kubiš, similarly dressed, standing among the commuters. His friend immediately produced a cigarette and lit it; the signal that all was as expected and the attack should go ahead as planned. Kubiš had been at the scene for half an hour already and his blessing meant the last obstacle to the mission had been removed.

As he reached the tram stop, Valčík left the huddle of workers and started slowly up the hill without acknowledging his co-conspirators. He would take up a spot along Heydrich's route that the general's car could not avoid.

Gabčík chose a position to one side of the tram stop, standing apart from the rest of the crowd. The coat draped over his arm provided cover as he set the briefcase down on the pavement then went onto one knee over it. To an onlooker, he could have been checking if his wife had remembered to pack the day's lunch. Gabčík used the raincoat to shield the Sten and, without looking into the case, began to assemble it – a simple task as he had done it so many times in training. With the gun complete he was able to slide the strap onto his shoulder, which he concealed by hanging the raincoat over it. When he got to his feet he found he could hold the machine gun pointing barrel downwards and it was entirely obscured. It looked as if he had draped the raincoat over himself purely to save the bother of carrying it. When he was certain the weapon was hidden, he picked up the briefcase in his free hand and stepped back against the wall. With preparations complete he could begin his wait for Heydrich. Everything was now in place – except the target.

Klein stood smartly by the passenger door of the Mercedes wondering what could be keeping the general – a man noted for his regimented punctuality in the mornings, even after the heaviest of drinking sessions. Usually the car swept up the gravel driveway at Panenské Březany just before the stroke of nine, and Klein would clamber out in time to witness Heydrich emerge through the mansion's main door. They would then be off again within seconds.

But not this morning. Klein had been waiting for more

than half an hour and he cut an irritable figure, craving a cigarette but not daring to light one for fear Heydrich might make an immediate entrance and take him to task for his ill-discipline.

Was this some form of end-of-posting lethargy on the general's part? Like everyone in the bars and barracks, Klein had heard the stories. Heydrich would leave him as soon as his trip to Berlin was over. The rumours were many and varied; he was taking over in France, he was going to work at Hitler's side where they would jointly mastermind the winning of the war, he was replacing Himmler, whom the Führer had grown tired of. Who knew which story was true but the speculation kept the NCOs of the Waffen SS entertained over their beer. Klein liked to pretend he knew what was going to happen but could not possibly say, for reasons of national security.

'Wait and see,' he would tell them all with a knowing smile and they would curse his sense of loyalty. Of course, he had no more idea where Heydrich would end up than they did. The mighty general was hardly likely to confide in his loyal driver and bodyguard. That was never his style.

Damn the man, thought Klein, what the hell is going to happen to me when he goes? It was the end of a cushy little number, that was for sure. And Heydrich, never one for sentiment, was not the sort to take a faithful bodyguard with him to Paris or Berlin. Klein was a realist. He knew by this time next week there'd be a number of middle ranking officers who would delight in bringing Heydrich's man down a few pegs just for the mischief of it, and there would be no more cups of coffee in fine town houses while the Reichsprotektor was rolling around upstairs with a mistress. It was too bad really.

Klein glanced at the closed main door of the mansion – still no sign of the general. He kicked the car's front tyre bitterly.

The rush hour crowds had long since dispersed, leaving Gabčík exposed, standing in an open spot. A casual observer would obviously assume he was waiting for a tram but might easily wonder why he never seemed to board one. Initially he had been able to move forward slightly with the crowds to avoid attention as each tram arrived. Then he would edge slowly and unobtrusively back again as if he had just noticed that it was not his tram after all and he would actually have to catch the next one.

By now he had abandoned such follies, for he was a solitary figure. Gabčík imagined he could barely have looked more suspicious and was surely inviting the enquiries of any soldier or police officer passing. Of course he was armed and could easily gun down anyone who proved too inquisitive but the attack would have to be abandoned, Heydrich would escape his just fate and there would be no second chance.

Where was the Nazi? What the hell was keeping this normally fastidious German officer? Had his plans been altered? Was he no longer heading for Hradčany? Perhaps he had left Prague a day earlier than Šafařík had thought. What if the nervous little joiner had tricked them? After all, he had no desire to be mixed up in an assassination. All of these thoughts and more raced through Gabčík's over-heated mind. Opposite him, he could clearly make out Kubiš, who had positioned himself in the shadows at the other side of the road. Presumably his friend was also wondering whether all of their preparations were to be in vain.

Heydrich led the pony along by its reins, glancing back over his shoulder to check that all was well with little Silke. Her mother held the child tightly in place while the little girl's tiny hands loosely gripped the front edge of the fine leather saddle. She swayed contentedly back and forth, in time with the movement of the docile creature's footsteps. Silke's head was down and she seemed intrigued by the pony's thick grey mane. Heydrich was delighted she showed no outward signs of distress.

'I think we have a little champion on our hands here, you know. She has taken to it as if it were the most natural thing in the world.' He could not help his pride.

'Yes,' agreed Lina breathlessly, 'always a good idea to start them young. Don't you think?'

Heydrich could hardly have been in a better mood. Last night's concert had been an enormous success and everything was as it should be in the Protectorate. Soon he would be at the Führer's side once more where, if he were not completely mistaken, the governorship of France would be the latest prize to be offered to the golden boy of the Fatherland. He noted with satisfaction that he would have to find even more of his legendary energy if he was to turn round the sluggish performance of the occupying forces in Paris.

With this in mind he resolved to spend a little extra time with his children that morning. After all, who was senior enough to complain if he was late into the office? And if his job in Prague was almost done it mattered little if he arrived an hour or so after his normal time.

Heydrich turned back to Silke. 'We'll have one more ride around the house then, shall we, Silke? Just one more then daddy really will have to get off to work.'

Kubiš was communicating with his eyes. From across the narrow street he gave a questioning look, which revealed he was as baffled by the absence of their target as his friend was. He made a move as if about to cross the street for a consultation and Gabčík hurriedly raised his free palm to stop him. Kubiš returned to his vantage point with a bewildered look.

Gabčík did not know what to do. It was nearly 10 am and still there was no sign of Heydrich. How long could they leave it until somebody inevitably became suspicious of the two men standing on opposite sides of the road all morning without any evident purpose?

Had they been betrayed? Set up by Šafařík or one of the girls in the flat perhaps or maybe Bartoš had tipped off the Gestapo because of his fear of reprisals. Even now a lorryload of German soldiers could be about to round the bend and capture them. Outnumbered in that manner they wouldn't stand a chance and would be gunned down. Then both their deaths would have been pointless.

Gabčík cursed under his breath and told himself not to be so stupid. Bartoš may have strongly disagreed with the operation but he was no traitor and besides nobody but Valčík, Kubiš and himself knew the exact time and location of the attack. They would be safe as long as they remained calm and stuck to the task in hand. The delay was beginning to rattle him though. Where was this infernal Nazi?

Heydrich sat tall in the passenger seat next to Klein as the driver took the road to Prague at speed. He held a document case tightly on his lap and enjoyed the feel of a light May breeze in his face as the open topped car sped swiftly along.

Sunshine brightened the countryside around them and in his good humour Heydrich took the trouble to enjoy the scenery. This wasn't such a bad country after all. When it kept off from raining and the eastern chill did not cut through you like a knife, the place became really quite presentable. He'd had some fine times in Prague when he thought about it and would look back on the city with affection as his career progressed to the very heights.

'The road is dry and clear, Reichsprotektor. I think we will make good time this morning,' offered Klein.

'There is no hurry today,' Heydrich answered dismissively but his driver did not slow down.

At a little after half past ten, with Gabčík wondering for the hundredth time if they should call off the attack and return home, the signal finally came. At first Gabčík convinced himself it was merely sunshine reflecting back off the mirror of a car but no, there it was again; a flash repeated at regular intervals that could only have come from Valčík's position. Heydrich's car was on its way.

Gabčík shot a glance over at Kubiš but he had already seen the signal and confirmed as much with a single tense nod. His hand reached into a coat pocket for one of the adapted grenades.

Gabčík ran across the road until he was positioned at the sharpest corner of the bend. He gripped the Sten gun tightly under the raincoat and glanced in the direction of Valčík's signal. Sure enough, an indistinct dark shape was moving towards them along the road. Gabčík wiped each palm in turn against the sides of his trousers but found they were moist with sweat again within a moment. He could make out the state car more clearly now and, as it travelled steadily towards him, it became distinguishable as Heydrich's Mercedes, a vehicle they had watched for five months on countless surveillance operations. Now it would pass him for the last time whether the attack was a success or not. Gabčík knew he would have one chance and only one chance to kill Heydrich. He had visualised this moment endlessly since the beginning of the operation and the realisation that Heydrich's arrival was imminent shortened his breathing.

The car would have to slow down to take the bend in the road. When it did, Gabčík would step forward and cut the Nazi general in half with a well-aimed burst of gunfire. Only when he was certain he had inflicted mortal wounds on the man would he turn his attention to the bodyguard, despatching him with a second burst. Then he would run to the bike and pedal away to a safe house, leaving Jan to decide whether the detonation of a bomb was still needed to cause a distraction.

At that moment the tram appeared. It was packed with people and edging its way towards them from the foot of the hill. All of the passengers would be imperilled by an assault in its proximity but the two men had already agreed the risk of injuring, even killing, bystanders was acceptable as long as their mission was a success. The tram took an age to pass Gabčík and the moment that it blocked his view of the target seemed to stretch. Finally it crawled its way beyond him.

The car was almost upon him now and reducing speed just as Gabčík had relied on; or was it that everything seemed to slow, as Gabčík's senses went into a false state of adrenalin and deep concentration? He emptied his mind of all thoughts except the instinctive action required to raise the gun and fire. Now he could make out the gleaming silver star of the Mercedes mascot. It glistened against the sunlight and, as the car came nearer, he could see his target clearly behind the windshield. Heydrich seemed oblivious to Gabčík's presence, shielded from it as he was by the bend of the road and the fortuitous angle of overhanging tree branches. Gabčík had a moment to steel himself, to take a breath and hold it, before stepping out to the edge of the pavement. He waited until the car's momentum would have to take it beyond him, even if the driver applied the brakes suddenly, then he let the raincoat drop to the ground.

Perhaps it was the sudden movement of the light material that caught his eye but Heydrich spotted Gabčík then, turning his head to stare straight at him. When their eyes locked, the German showed no emotion at all, as if this Czech was of no significance whatsoever. As the car drew level with Josef it was moving at little short of a walking pace. Gabčík raised the Sten gun, put his left foot forward for balance and pointed the machine gun straight into Heydrich's chest. The range was point blank and the target unmissable. There was a fleeting fraction of a moment when he could take in the shocked and fearful look on the SS man's face then he pulled the trigger.

But nothing happened.

Instead of a rattling wall of fire, which would shatter Heydrich's rib cage and destroy his vital organs, there was a dull snick. The Sten was jammed.

'No!' Gabčík howled in frustration and immediately started to wrestle with the gun. He couldn't let Heydrich get away but if his bodyguard did the sensible thing he would speed past Gabčík in a moment.

There was a hastily barked command from Heydrich and the car came to an abrupt halt. That was fine by Gabčík. There would be a second chance to kill the bastard if he could just clear the stoppage in the gun. He tugged at it frantically, holding the Sten high so he could check if the mechanism was jammed or if he had somehow inexplicably failed to assemble it correctly even though he had done it so many times before.

As Gabčík tugged at the gun, his peripheral vision picked up Heydrich's figure rising from the car. He realised the SS man had turned to face him and was now standing tall in the passenger seat. Heydrich raised his Luger and pointed it calmly into Gabčík's face. *Jesus no, he has beaten me to it.*

Before Heydrich could fire there was a deafening bang and the whole car shook with the force of an explosion that could only have come from Kubiš' grenade. Heydrich let out a sharp cry, a mixture of pain and distress, and fell against the back of his seat. As he lolled forward again it was clear he was still in one piece and Gabčík realised the bomb had missed its target. Jan must have been as astonished by the failure of the Sten gun as he was and had thrown the grenade early to try and save his friend. In his haste it had not landed inside the car, as they had practised so many times, but instead exploded near the rear wheel of the vehicle, sending lumps of shrapnel flying up at all angles.

It was then Gabčík noticed Jan. He was running blindly towards his bicycle but was holding his face in his hands, letting out an alarming cry of pain as he went. Even from a distance Gabčík could make out the blood that poured through his fingers. Too close to the impact of his own bomb, Kubiš had taken some of the blast himself and now he ran frantically for his bike but Klein was after him. Kubiš pulled the bicycle away from the wall and swung his leg over it in virtually one movement. He then pedalled madly away in the opposite direction, heading straight for a crowd of stunned onlookers, made up of passers-by and those who had hurriedly disembarked from the tram at the sound of the explosion. At this rate, thought Gabčík, they would surely block his path.

With no way to help his friend, Gabčík dropped the useless Sten gun and attempted to make his own escape. He could not reach his bike as the damaged car was between it and him and he was cut off. Already Heydrich was hauling himself from the wreckage of the vehicle. The Reichsprotektor was on his feet hollering and gesticulating after the fleeing Kubiš.

'Get after that bastard!' he grimaced and Klein pulled a Luger from his holster then broke into a full sprint, which threatened to bring him quickly within range of Gabčík's injured friend.

Gabčík ran in the opposite direction. Looking back, the last thing he saw of Kubiš was the bike going full pelt towards the crowd of onlookers. Just as it seemed Kubiš could make no further progress, he drew a pistol from his coat and, with one hand holding the handlebars of the speeding bicycle, he fired two shots into the air. There were screams as the crowd scattered, parting like the Red Sea and onlookers were knocked over to left and right in their haste to get out of his way. As the bicycle reached the edge of the crowd a large gap had opened up. Jan shot through it to safety and disappeared.

Gabčík, now running at full pelt, was about to round the corner when a bullet from Heydrich's Luger whistled past his ear. Another hit the ground between his feet and he was forced to fling himself behind a telegraph pole as the German sent a third after him. Gabčík drew his Colt and instinctively returned fire but he could not get a clear sighting of Heydrich who was slumped on one knee, attempting to clamber unsteadily to his feet and give chase.

A bullet slammed into the far side of the telegraph pole and Gabčík realised he was cornered. If he tried to move, Heydrich would easily gun him down in the street. From this range he could barely chance exposing his position to return fire but he knew he must move soon or be completely trapped when reinforcements arrived.

Gabčík bent his wrist round the pole and let loose a blind round in Heydrich's direction. He then risked a glance at the advancing German. At first he thought Heydrich was hit, for the Nazi toppled forward, collapsing like a drunk. As Heydrich sprawled onto the pavement clutching his ribs, he shouted at the returning Klein to once more give chase.

Gabčík needed no further prompting and he ran flat out from the scene. Klein pursued him and the two men hared at full speed down the hill towards the city. Gabčík pumped his arms like a sprinter, trying to power his way free from the athletic German following him. The pavement passed beneath his feet like a blur and he had to flail his arms wildly more than once as his momentum threatened to send him crashing to the ground.

As he went round the corner at the foot of the hill, Gabčík realised he had a head start on his pursuer but he was too exposed out here and who knew what he might bump into around the next bend? Surely by now there would be German soldiers heading towards the sound of the blast. Gabčík had to get off the main road and hide himself in the alleyways, until he could plot a route back to one of the safe houses, but he couldn't do that with Heydrich's bodyguard in full pursuit.

Then he spied a solution; a small butcher's shop, which would certainly have a rear entrance for deliveries. If Gabčík could reach the front door before Heydrich's driver came round the corner he could disappear from view and confuse his pursuer for a moment. That was all he would need to get through the shop and out the back way, where he could lose himself in a maze of side streets.

Gabčík thundered through the shop door a second before Klein raced round the corner. The German stopped in his tracks, momentarily unsure of his next move, just as Gabčík found himself face to face with the owner of the shop. The butcher's name was emblazoned on a canopy above the door outside and Gabčík took a chance, breathlessly addressing the startled man.

'Brauer, I am a patriot. Show me your back door. Quickly, the Germans are after me.'

To his astonishment Brauer, a fat man with a red face and balding crown topped with a thin ginger wisp of combed over hair, appeared shocked at the very notion.

'No, never, get out of my shop! Get out!!'

Rage welled up in Gabčík. Who was this coward, this traitor to his country who would not help him in his distress? Had he a moment longer and the means to do it quietly he would have happily killed the collaborator.

'Bastard,' he hissed and ran through the shop looking for the back door.

Brauer dashed outside into the street and began to shout for help and the forces of law in that order. Klein spotted the distressed butcher immediately, realised his quarry must be in the shop and ran towards it.

Gabčík could not believe his ill luck. First he finds a traitor and now a dead end. The anticipated rear exit was completely blocked with trays of butchered produce, carcasses suspended on hooks and wooden slabs for working these raw materials into useable cuts of meat. There were no shortages for this collaborator, who must surely have connections with the state police to enjoy such privileges. The entire detritus of the butchery trade blocked Gabčík's progress and he had no time to fling it all to one side. In a frenzy of anger and fear for his life he turned and ran back through the shop.

Klein entered the building just as Gabčík was leaving it. Both men reached the doorway from opposite sides, at speed and exactly the same time. Gabčík tensed his body and charged the startled Nazi with his shoulder. There was a bone shuddering collision, which threatened to knock Gabčík completely off his feet but, luckily for him, it was Klein's stockier frame that ended off balance and he crashed to the floor. Gabčík, with his lower centre of gravity, landed in a tripping, hurdling motion, just outside the front door. He instinctively reached for his gun. Before Klein could retrieve his discarded Luger, Gabčík turned and fired twice, in the double-tap manner he had been taught by the SOE. He shot by reflex and with no time to aim. Though he was off balance the bullets found their mark, striking Klein in both legs and the SS man screamed in pain.

Gabčík did not wait to finish Klein off. Instead he ran out into the road and waved his gun at Brauer to get him out of the way. He had the satisfaction of seeing a steady stream of urine pour from the collaborator's trouser legs as he sprinted past him and away. A moment later Gabčík spotted a tiny alleyway and flung himself down it, not pausing for a second until he had put several blocks between himself and the butcher's shop. By the time help arrived to attend to the wounded Klein, Gabčík had a head start and his would-be captors were left with no clue as to his whereabouts.

Heydrich tried to haul himself onto an elbow but a sharp jolt of pain passed through his torso and he slumped onto his face. Sprawling helplessly on the pavement in agony he became vaguely aware of movement all around him but it was not the presence of the returning Klein he could sense. The Reichsprotektor rolled over onto his back, causing another surge of pain beneath his ribs, and he realised a small crowd of Czechs was beginning to mass around him. They walked slowly and unsurely towards Heydrich, a man none of them had seen before at close quarters. He could pick out their alien Slavic faces clearly. They were *untermensch* but he had been hurt and his first impression of his injuries was that they were serious. He needed help and quickly; and with no sign of Klein or any other German presence he had to appeal to them. When he spoke it was a supreme effort.

'Help me,' he pleaded.

No one moved to his aid. They merely stood and gawped at him, their looks somewhere between confusion and curiosity.

'Help me,' he said again, this time turning it into an order, 'get me to a hospital.'

But still they did not move, merely continuing to stare down at his incapacitated figure. Why would they not come to his assistance? What were they doing just standing there? Were they just going to let him die here? Oh God, were they going to kill him? Was that it, now that he was helpless and unguarded? Heydrich had to accept they could tear him apart with their bare hands if they chose, then simply melt back into the anonymous sprawl of the city. Surely it could not end like this.

'Help me.' Heydrich weakly slurred the words once more but, as a menacing dark red stain began to spread visibly across his tunic, he received no reply.

31

*'After life nothing will remain but death
and the glory of deeds'*

Adolf Hitler's philosophy
– quoted by Walter Schellenberg

The Bulkova hospital had never seen the like before. SS General Reinhard Heydrich, Reichsprotektor of Bohemia and Moravia, the most senior figure in the occupying forces, transported there in agony in the back of a filthy truck, draped face down across some tins of floor polish like a piece of tarpaulin.

If that were not enough for the little provincial hospital, half an hour later another Nazi luminary arrived, this one in an animated state. It had taken that long for word to reach him on Heydrich's whereabouts, such was the confusion surrounding the assassination attempt. An obviously shocked Heinz Pannwitz, head of the anti-sabotage section of the Prague Gestapo, angrily ordered the detachment of SS men he'd brought with him to clear all other patients away from the unguarded general, as he lay unconscious in an emergency ward.

'I want a sentry at every doorway and teams of men up on the rooftops with machine guns,' he barked. 'Jump to it!'

When he reached the bedside of the shirtless figure of the

Reichsprotektor, he became puce with rage.

'Cover all of the windows with whitewash. A sniper could finish him here while he sleeps!'

Heydrich was under a general anaesthetic, in preparation for emergency surgery to remove shrapnel from his battered body. After a few moments supervising the placement of sentries, followed by several minutes standing around not knowing what to do next, Pannwitz decided he could be of more use elsewhere. Leaving a sufficient number of soldiers behind to secure the area, he set off for the scene of the attack to scrutinise it personally.

There was still confusion in the German ranks but by now he was at least in possession of some facts. From the crippled driver of the Mercedes they had been able to piece together a reliable account of events. Two men had attacked Heydrich's car with a machine gun and a grenade before fleeing the scene and losing themselves in the city.

The whole street was cordoned off by now and guarded by grim faced SS men. At the centre of the scene was the Mercedes, which had borne the full brunt of the explosion. The collapsed car was on its axles, listed to one side like a ship that had run aground, its highly polished metalwork now sporting gashes from the shrapnel. Pannwitz surveyed the scene. What little evidence of the crime there was had been left where it lay and he was thankful for that small mercy. The Gestapo man had taken one look at Gabčík's abandoned Sten gun and the briefcase, which still contained an undetonated Mills grenade, and instantly deduced the origins of this plot lay in London. He turned to the nearest uniformed member of the Czech Police.

'Tell all of your people we will catch the men who perpetrated this outrage and, before they die, a full confession of their links to the British will be extracted. This was no spontaneous revolt!' He said that last bit with some satisfaction.

Then he walked briskly from the scene, looking forward to the moment when he could unleash the maximum enthusiasm and expertise of the *Geheime Staatspolizie* on the two anonymous fugitives.

For now, though, it was the condition of the Reichsprotektor that was of most concern to Pannwitz and everyone else, so he returned to the hospital to receive an early and encouraging report from the general's doctors. Heydrich had arrived in great pain and some distress, as much for the fact that his wounds had to be cleaned by an *untermensch*, a junior Czech doctor, as there was the possibility that he faced emergency surgery, but it seemed at least that he was likely to live. Crucially the shrapnel had missed his vital organs and he had reached the hospital in time for surgery to be carried out to save his life. Professor Hollbaum, the top German surgeon in Prague, was brought to his side and he felt reassured to at last be in safe hands. The fragments of shrapnel were carefully removed from Heydrich's body and a full exploration of the damage carried out. It was confidently felt that, with the administration of the right drugs and a blood transfusion, there would be no need for further surgery. On completion, Professor Hollbaum pronounced the procedure a complete success.

Heydrich's expected deliverance was no thanks to the bungling of German forces in the city. They had dismissed the initial report of an attack as a false alarm and the Reichsprotektor owed his safe deliverance entirely to the actions of a passer-by, a young Czech girl who flagged down a truck. She then persuaded the reluctant driver to lift the general into the back of his vehicle and transport him to the hospital.

'Saved by a Czech,' mused Pannwitz, 'inexplicable.' And he shook his head in wonder at the world.

Later the Gestapo man paced the corridors, waiting for the Reichsprotektor to wake from the anaesthetic; his relief at the doctor's optimism short-lived. Pannwitz was in a state of some agitation by now, for he'd heard Karl Frank had finally been alerted and would be arriving at the hospital to take belated control of operations. Worse than that, an apoplectic Heinrich Himmler was already on his way from Berlin.

After the attack Heydrich crossed over. When he awoke from the operation he was in a new world. One almost entirely made up of pain and encompassed by the three bare white walls he could see from his hospital bed.

In this world, nothing from his previous existence mattered; not rank or privileges, women or wealth. They were a distant irrelevance. He would gladly trade them all now to anyone who could stop the unendurable agony of his wounds. The pain centred on his abdomen but spread in waves over his whole body, rising in intensity until he prayed for unconsciousness again, so he could be spared the anguish for a few precious moments. And he swore, when they captured the men who had put him here, he would take a highly personal interest in the remaining days of their short wretched lives.

When Frank finally arrived, his sense of shock was almost as profound as his keen awareness of the opportunity before him. He would have a chance to impress the Führer himself if he could quickly bring these assassins to justice and, if Heydrich failed to fully recover, who would be a more natural heir to the position of Reichsprotektor?

Hitler had been raging round the Wolf's Lair demanding justice and revenge. Much of this was entrusted to Frank and Pannwitz, in a blistering phone call, which left the former in no doubt as to the ferocity of action expected. Frank was to oversee proceedings and he started that afternoon at the hospital with an emergency meeting involving his most senior men.

'Martial law is to commence immediately,' he told the officers who had hastily assembled before him.

'A 9.00 pm curfew is proclaimed throughout the Protectorate. Anyone caught breaking the curfew is to be shot. Ten thousand Czechs will be rounded up for arrest, including all those deemed to be part of the nation's *intelligentsia*.' He spat the last word. 'We have lists, use them. On Himmler's personal orders one hundred of these are to be shot immediately. And no, it doesn't matter which ones.' He said it impatiently so he might be spared any foolish questions.

Then he added, seemingly as an afterthought, 'All political prisoners held in the capital are to be summarily executed. I want the word to be sent out that these acts are taken in direct reprisal for the cowardly attack on General Heydrich, protector of the Czech people. Begin immediately.'

Within minutes the house-to-house searches began, closely followed by the first arrests. That night the city's streets reeled from the ferocity of the German reprisals and the air was filled with the screams of women and the desperate pleading of their men as thousands of homes were systematically cleared by hundreds of troops in full battle dress. At the same time, what remained of Prague's educated classes was marched off to the ghetto at Theresienstadt. The firing squads killed one hundred and fifty that night. From this point panic slowly began to grip the population of Prague.

A day later Himmler and his personal surgeon flew into the Czech capital. The effect on the atmosphere in the hospital was tangible for Himmler always brought with him an air of barely suppressed threat. It ensured each sentry snapped-to with precision as he passed them, and every officer walked alongside him with the high alert of a soldier leading a patrol through the streets of a bombed out Russian city, never knowing what peril awaited him at the next turn.

An almost whispered 'Doctor,' was all he bothered to enunciate in greeting to a clearly panicked Hollbaum, who had lined up outside Heydrich's room with a posse of white-coated subordinates alongside him.

'Herr Reichsführer,' the good doctor stammered, 'may I be permitted to say what an honour it is...'

Himmler raised a hand to prevent further flattery. 'I merely wish to be informed of General Heydrich's condition.'

'Good, I think,' he answered and immediately appeared alarmed. Was this the wrong word to describe one who has fallen victim to an assassination attempt? 'I mean under the circumstances.'

Himmler frowned at the doctor's statement of the obvious and he attempted to redeem himself with a hastily delivered monologue on the surgery carried out and the drugs administered to aid recovery. All the while Himmler scrutinised the man with an unblinking stare, causing the doctor to be so disconcerted he began sentences without ever knowing where they would end. When he had delivered his appraisal under Himmler's famously passionless gaze, Hollbaum fell silent and braced himself for some form of chastisement. The surgeon was used to dealing with pressure but never had anyone made him feel more wretched than the Reichsführer, whose priestlike features and diminutive frame somehow made him more alarming than if he was a man twice his size. The fear of Himmler was all about his power and knowing that in the Third Reich it was second only to Hitler's.

'Gebhart,' said Himmler quietly to the man who had accompanied him. The illustrious professor, Surgeon General of the SS, shuffled forward to scrutinise the effects of Hollbaum's work on the general. Eventually he emerged to declare the surgery a good job well done, to the intense relief of all assembled.

A pacified Himmler preferred to survey the stricken figure of Heydrich through the window, because, ironically, the sight of wounds close up made him squeamish. His protégé was asleep but appeared half dead to the Reichsführer's untrained eye. It was only the sweat, which matted the hair to his forehead, that convinced Himmler the general was still in the land of the living at all.

'We shall stay by his side until he awakes,' he announced grandly, but when Heydrich spent the next three hours drifting in and out of consciousness he instead decamped to a city centre hotel, accompanied by enough soldiers to capture a small town.

32

'Truth and goodness had no intrinsic meaning for him'

Wilhelm Höttl, Nazi Security Service,
on Reinhard Heydrich

The next morning Himmler rose early, breakfasted lightly then spent an hour dealing with his correspondence. The Reichsführer was in buoyant mood. He had arrived in Prague fearing the worst but his right-hand man had survived an assassination attempt and would soon be on the road to recovery. He wondered how many weeks it would be before he would reach full operational effectiveness again. Weeks? Knowing Heydrich it could be days.

As Himmler travelled back to the Bulkova hospital that afternoon, he fully expected his protégé to be sitting up in bed demanding to know when he could leave the place. What he saw instead shocked him palpably. Heydrich was unconscious, his skin white and lifeless, his pallor that of the cadaver.

'I thought you said he was recovering.' He spoke to Professor Gebhart, in a quiet voice that was infinitely more sinister for its lack of emotion.

'That was my initial prognosis, Herr Reichsführer, but I am afraid that overnight there have been complications.'

'How so?'

'We think, I mean it appears, that fragments of horsehair

from the car seats passed into the general's body with the force of the explosion. These strands are infected. They have been driven deep and are slowly poisoning the Reichsprotektor.'

'Poisoning him?'

'He has developed septicaemia. It's very serious I am afraid. We have tried to treat him with transfusions and sulphonamide to control the infection but I fear it is too advanced.'

'What about this operation to remove the spleen? The one you decided against.'

'That was Professor Hollbaum's decision and, I concede, it appeared a sensible course of action at the time.'

'And now?'

There was a pause while Gebhart found the inner resolve to answer.

'Now I am afraid it is too late.'

Himmler was amazed. 'Are you sure? Can nothing be done for him? Another operation?'

'I am afraid his condition has deteriorated so rapidly in the past twenty four hours that it is now inoperable. He is completely beyond our help. I really am so sorry.'

The Surgeon General of the SS steeled himself for the tirade that would surely follow this admission of failure. Instead Himmler remained completely silent for a moment then he simply nodded and walked through the door to Heydrich's bedside.

Heydrich woke to find the Reichsführer SS sitting calmly by his bed.

'Have you been here long?' Himmler shook his head but did not elaborate further.

Heydrich's mouth was dry and he swallowed hard, attempting to clear his airway. The head of the Schutzstaffeln rose to his feet, poured a glass of water from a jug on the bedside cabinet and gently held it to Heydrich's lips, while his subordinate, propped up against pillows, strained forwards to sip at the liquid.

This seemed to have the desired effect and Heydrich lay back again, noting with satisfaction that the pain, though very much still with him, had diminished slightly. Thank providence; he must finally be getting better. Heydrich lacked the energy for more small talk and instead sought some honesty from his superior. When he spoke it was in slow, wheezing rasps.

'I can't seem to get anyone to give me an answer. Will I be alright? I don't remember everything that happened to me.'

'You have distinguished yourself, Reinhard. The partisans could not defeat you. They came after you with bombs, like cowards, but you sent them fleeing away, ducking from the bullets in your gun. Soldiers all along the eastern front will take heart from your example.'

Heydrich turned his head on the pillow so he could watch Himmler. The Reichsführer SS held his head slightly to one side so the light caught his pince-nez glasses, turning them into mirrors, which obscured his eyes and made his expression an emotionless mask.

'Yes, but what is going to happen to me?' he pleaded.

Himmler cleared his throat before replying in a voice other men might use to comment on the changeability of the weather.

'You are dying, Reinhard.'

Heydrich took a long time to respond and when the words came they broke along with his voice.

'Are they certain?'

'There is nothing more that can be done. Fragments from the bomb have poisoned your blood.'

Once again Heydrich took moments to digest the news

Himmler relayed. At one point he appeared to be stifling tears. Then he said simply and with wonderment in his voice. 'But it cannot be. There is still so much left to do.'

'All great men think like this, Reinhard, but there is no way to cheat providence. For some it is their destiny to leave the stage early but to what applause! You are our brightest light, Reinhard. An example to every SS man there has ever been or will ever be. We will ensure your memory lives on forever. We will name SS detachments after you, Hitler Youth camps, Concentration Camps, city streets even. There will be a *Reinhard Heydrich Strasse* in every capital in Europe. Twenty, thirty years from now there won't be a single schoolchild who does not know your name or the great work you are associated with. There will be a statue of you in every public park. You will be known forever as the example for all to aspire to.'

'But my wife, my children...'

'Will be taken care of in a manner befitting the family of a German hero. Your wife will want for nothing and your children could not be better attended if they were the Führer's own. Imagine the respect and love they will be held in years from now when they are pointed out as the son or daughter of the great Reinhard Heydrich. They have nothing to fear and nor should you.'

The words continued to pour enthusiastically from the Reichsführer's mouth as if he were describing a glorious future for Heydrich and not his imminent death. The wounded man could not take it all in. There had to be some mistake. The doctors were wrong. He was not going to die. It was an impossible notion. He would recover and one day lead his country, he was sure of it. It was not his destiny to pass away inconsequentially in an obscure Czech hospital from a few poisoned flesh wounds. It couldn't happen. He would show them. He would show them all.

33

'The best political weapon is the weapon of terror.
Cruelty commands respect. Men may hate us.
But, we don't ask for their love; only for their fear'

Reichsführer Heinrich Himmler

At that moment in Hradčany, Pannwitz was enthusiastically briefing Karl Frank on the steps taken to capture Heydrich's attackers.

'A reward of ten million Czech Crowns has been offered. That's almost a million Reichsmarks. The equivalent of ten years' pay for most of these *untermensch*.'

'All of the evidence left at the scene of the attack is on display in the largest window of the Bat'a department store. Passers-by are encouraged to stop and look at the bike, the Sten gun, and the briefcase. There is also a mackintosh dropped by one of the assassins which has been placed prominently on a mannequin.

'We have officers from the Czech and German Police working in tandem, backed up by men from regular army units, who are scouring the streets and houses of Prague one by one. This substantial force does not include the usual resources at the disposal of the Gestapo and the SS. More than twenty thousand men mobilised to look for just two. It is the biggest manhunt ever staged in the history of the

Reich!' he concluded with some satisfaction.

'Yes, Heinz, I have heard of the results,' answered Frank without enthusiasm. 'They are dragging people from their homes, destroying a great deal of property in an entirely random fashion, running up and down the streets in full battle order and shooting out old ladies' windows. Oh, don't get me wrong, I have nothing against keeping the population on its toes and if that involves the crushing of a few innocents then so be it, but this activity is bustle for the sake of it, a decidedly fruitless exercise. In the absence of a legitimate target for vengeance our men are lashing out in all directions. Where are my suspects? We don't even have any proper witnesses; it's embarrassing to you and me. Imagine what they are saying about us in Berlin.'

Pannwitz bristled. 'Sometimes police work takes time but I am confident that eventually, with the reward…'

'Eventually is not near soon enough. All I have so far with which to placate the Führer are the acts of vengeance taken in Heydrich's name. Three thousand Jews have been transported from Theresienstadt in the past two days, on a special train. They will be immediately exterminated in the new concentration camps; an appropriate gesture since they were largely erected due to the vision of the general. In Sachsenhausen Concentration Camp they executed hundreds the instant they learned of the attack and in the eastern territories all of the special SS work against the Jews has been named Operation Reinhard in his honour. All of this brings the Führer some solace but, if you know the man at all, this can only be temporary. Until we deliver the assassins there will be no rest for either of us.'

'I understand, State Secretary.'

'I hope you do, Heinz,' Frank concluded. 'I sincerely hope you do.'

'I will redouble my efforts, of course,' Pannwitz promised.

And he made as if to rise but, unable to hide his curiosity, he asked, 'I understand the Führer has asked for a big show,' and he shifted uncomfortably in his seat, 'some reprisal that will send a clear message to the population?'

'I'll leave the detective work to you, Pannwitz,' answered Frank, 'that's what you are good at after all,' and he smiled mirthlessly. 'You leave the sending of messages to me.'

It took another day for Heydrich to realise he was not immortal. The spasms of excruciating pain that racked his body, as the poison coursed through his veins, slowly but surely eroded his belief in the divine providence of his destiny.

There eventually came a point when the pain was so unbearable that even death was preferable to further suffering. By now Heydrich could not move his head from the pillow and he craved a sleep that would not come thanks to the nagging persistence of his wounds. Finally he realised the doctors were right. There was no hope left.

Reinhard Heydrich would not live through this war to witness the preordained victory of Germany's armies. He would not enjoy the exalted status afforded to one of the foremost architects of a postwar Reich and he was to be cheated of the position he coveted beyond all others; leader of the German race. His tears were caused as much by an understanding of the bitterness of his fate than the overwhelming pain of his wounds.

Earlier he had given Himmler a message for his dear Lina – instructing her to wait until the time was right before remarrying with a clear conscience and ensuring his boys had the appropriate masculine influence of a stepfather. The fellow would have to be of the finest type and the truest Aryan blood. Himmler had promised to prevent any match that did not live up to their highest ideals of German manhood. Heydrich's thoughts then turned to his little Silke and the grim realisation that he would never again hold the baby girl in his arms. The fact that many hundreds of thousands of German families across the Reich would experience similar grief before this titanic struggle was over never crossed his mind.

One of his last clear thoughts, before he slid into unconsciousness a few moments after midnight on the fourth of June, was to curse his assassins, those unknown men who had put him here and robbed him of everything he had and all that he desired.

'Damn them,' he whispered so softly that Himmler could not make out the words, 'damn them all the way down to hell.'

There was no anguished death rattle as the Reichsprotektor slipped out of his coma a little more than four hours later. A soft, choked gasp was the only sound as Reinhard Heydrich finally crossed from this life into the next one.

Himmler had remained by his side until the very end, had been quite insistent on the point in fact, leaving all of the medical staff hugely impressed.

'See how he cares for his men,' exclaimed one of the German doctors.

The Reichsführer waited until he was sure Heydrich's body was completely lifeless then rose from his chair and walked over to the cabinet next to the deceased man's bed. Pulling open the drawer he brushed aside a number of personal effects that had been placed there for safekeeping; Heydrich's leather wallet, containing money he could no longer hope to spend, along with the photograph of a family he would never see again, a rather cheap and battered looking old pocket watch and finally the item Himmler was looking for. From the bottom of the drawer the Reichsführer SS removed the key that had never left Heydrich's possession since he had become the head of the *Sicherheitsdienst* eleven years before.

Himmler held it up for closer scrutiny. He needed to be sure it was the right key. When he was satisfied, he put it in his pocket, took a last look at the lifeless figure of his subordinate, with its grey skin, lolling mouth and sightless eyes then left the hospital.

The next morning Schellenberg was surprised to personally witness Himmler's early arrival at Hradčany. The head of AMT VI saw it as his duty to be at Heydrich's office before anyone else in an effort to show some leadership following the traumatic death of their superior.

He was sensitive enough not to occupy Heydrich's seat, however, and instead positioned himself opposite the empty chair, as he had done so many times before when the man was very much alive. Heydrich had ordered, cajoled and berated Schellenberg on a variety of matters from this desk. That will never happen again, he thought to himself ruefully. He was just going through the morning despatches when the Reichsführer SS walked in accompanied by a half dozen soldiers in black uniforms.

'Sorry to disturb you, Schellenberg, but I really think we need to have these files removed as swiftly as possible.'

Himmler indicated the huge wooden cabinets at the back of the room.

'I would hate to see them fall into the wrong hands after all of the diligent work General Heydrich has done. I'll have them taken to Berlin this morning for safekeeping.'

He ordered the men to begin the process of transporting the heavily laden filing cabinets from the room. Schellenberg felt Himmler observed this process with more than a little satisfaction.

'They should make interesting reading, Walter, don't you think?'

'Herr Reichsführer?' Schellenberg tried to feign innocence,

desiring no association with Heydrich's private archive.

'Yes,' confirmed Himmler, adding almost to himself, 'I wonder what he has written about me.'

Taborsky was concerned for Beneš. Ever since first word of the attack on Heydrich had reached them his President had been entirely preoccupied with its outcome, at the expense of sleep and the ruination of his meals. It was the inconclusive nature of those early reports that bedevilled him. Was Heydrich dead or alive and, if the latter, what was the state of his injuries? Would he be bed-bound for the duration of the war or was he already marching the corridors of Hradčany angrily plotting revenge on his assailants, hindered only by flesh wounds, a broken arm perhaps. And what of the brave attackers? No news had been forthcoming on the condition of Kubiš and Gabčík. They had simply disappeared. It seemed they escaped the scene of the attack but where were they now? Miles from the capital, holed up on some isolated farm perhaps, or had they been belatedly captured by the Gestapo and were even now undergoing unimaginable tortures?

Only that morning Taborsky had checked on Beneš to find him staring silently down at his desk. He watched as the President lifted an ancient, leaky fountain pen, made a characteristically indecipherable note then crossed it out again a moment later, before screwing the paper into a ball and consigning it to the wastebasket. No calls were allowed to disturb him and all appointments rescheduled.

Every few hours his secretary would knock quietly at the door, enter when he heard no response, and witness the head of the nation sitting in his hard leather chair, elbows on the desk, head down, fingers sometimes pressed against his temples, lost in private contemplation. A tray would be set gently on the desk, with coffee, or a pastry destined to remain uneaten. Its virtually untouched predecessor would be removed and Beneš left alone once more, to continue his passable imitation of a man in a trance.

Taborsky was in the office later that same day when a call was finally allowed through because its origin was Porchester Gate. Beneš answered it on the first ring.

'František,' he said urgently, 'go ahead.'

Beneš picked up his pen and spent a few moments scribbling on a virgin sheet of unlined, white notepaper. The President was careful to allow no emotion to distract him from the imperative task of accurately recording all of the details. He would use the same notes to draft a memo to Churchill and Eden afterwards and wanted to ensure he would not be embarrassed by inaccuracy or omission.

The call lasted perhaps two minutes, no more, and was almost entirely one sided. Beneš listened intently and finally ended the dialogue with, 'Thank you, František. Thank you so very much,' and replaced the receiver.

Taborsky's spirits lifted for a moment. The President's secretary was no fool and he had been able to link the departure of Beneš' agents months ago, to the news that had so animated everybody in their little embassy in Aston Abbotts. The attack on Reinhard Heydrich was all anyone was talking about. What remained was the need for an accurate report on the Nazi's condition. Taborsky waited almost a minute for Beneš to lift his head and deliver the presidential pronouncement.

Finally Beneš looked over at his secretary and his face broke into a smile.

'Got him.'

34

Heydrich's funeral was a macabre spectacle, most notable to Schellenberg for the two hours he was forced to stand as part of the honour guard in full dress uniform, at the height of an unusually warm day. Schellenberg delved deep within himself, trying hard to find a smattering of genuine grief but he could feel nothing, other than the trepidation caused by an uncertain future. Heydrich may have been a ruthless, impossibly demanding superior with a penchant for random acts that could inflict terror on his subordinates but he was the devil they knew. Lord knows what fate had in store for them now. It was a thought that preoccupied Schellenberg during two long days of ritualised mourning in Prague and Berlin.

The first night SS men lined the streets of the Czech capital holding flaming torches, while the general's coffin was transported to Hradčany at snail's pace on a gun carriage. The next morning, as the coffin lay in state, thousands of fearful Czechs walked by it to pay their respects in a fruitless bid to avoid further reprisals. Eventually Heydrich's body made its final journey by train to Berlin for a full state funeral. Schellenberg travelled with it.

The ceremony was notable for an abundance of adornments to both the coffin and the Mosaic Hall of the Reich Chancellery where the funeral was conducted. Elaborate SS runes, gargantuan Nazi emblems and hundreds of white lilies competed for the eye's attention in the most vulgar and ostentatious funeral ever to be held in the Third Reich.

Hitler was typically verbose in his oration. He proclaimed Heydrich a martyred hero of the Fatherland and vowed vengeance on all who had a hand in his death.

'He was the great wolf leader of the Wolf Pack!' apparently and how Heydrich would have loathed that ridiculous description, thought Schellenberg.

'The man with the iron heart!' concluded Hitler while in private he expressed supreme irritation at his Reichsprotektor's idiotic scorn for security.

The Führer's last act was to publicly embrace Klaus and Heider. Heydrich's two small boys were the sole representatives of his family, due to the infancy of baby Silke and the absence of the traumatised and heavily pregnant Lina.

Genuine expressions of grief or regret were noticeable by their absence. When mourners gathered after the ceremony, and felt obliged to comment on the passing of the blond beast, many of the party's upper echelon had to rein in their sense of relief. Even Himmler, mentor of Heydrich for close to two decades, could breathe a little easier now his pathologically ambitious deputy was no longer in a position to covet his job.

Only Canaris chose to publicly express his sadness. Schellenberg was astonished at one point to witness the Admiral weeping. 'I have lost a good friend,' the head of the Abwehr told everyone with conviction. It was a staggering claim from the rival most vulnerable to Heydrich's endless plotting.

When the funeral was over, the mourners, representing the

very highest officers and officials of the Fatherland, wasted no time in leaving the building. The absence of a widow and the youth of Heydrich's uncomprehending brood made their undignified exits far simpler.

It's time for me to leave too, thought Schellenberg. Karl Frank had offered the chance of revenge but he had declined. 'Come back to Prague, use your experience and all of your skills to help me track down his killers. Nobody was closer to General Heydrich than you, Schellenberg.'

If that were true, the statement spoke more about Heydrich than it ever would of Walter Schellenberg. He told Frank it was precisely his closeness to the general that disqualified him from tracking down his killers. 'I would not be objective enough in this matter. You need a cooler head. I'll leave it to you, Karl,' he said. 'I know you will succeed.'

For some intangible reason Schellenberg had a bad feeling about the whole affair, instinctively wanting to remove himself from the hunt. It's time to bow out. It ends here for me, he had decided. Schellenberg did not know exactly why but he was sure no good could come out of any of this.

Within minutes of the climax of Hitler's oration the Mosaic Hall was empty, save for a single sentry assigned to stand over the body, and Schellenberg who, out of duty, stayed till the last before saluting the coffin of his friendless leader. *It's as if he never existed* thought the head of Foreign Intelligence as he turned on his heel and walked from the room.

SS Hauptsturmführer Max Rostock knocked on the door of Karl Frank's office, entering only when he heard a muffled permission from within.

He found Frank sitting behind the desk formerly occupied by the Reichsprotektor. The Brigadeführer had explained, rather too publicly for some, that this was for operational reasons – to enable him to coordinate the twin effort of catching the assassins and ensuring good order in the Protectorate from a recognised central point. Most saw it as the latest step in Frank's patently obvious attempt to secure the position of Reichsprotektor for himself. In taking the desk he was seizing the command, a psychological move designed to make it harder to deny him the position later.

To witness Frank occupying a desk with a picture of Frau Heydrich and her offspring still resting on it was a distasteful sight. Few who met the general mourned him but that did not mean they would appreciate such an obvious dance upon his grave. Frank wasted no time at all in ensuring Heydrich's trappings came to him. It was a shame he was already married thought Rostock for, had he been a single man, he would surely be round at Panenské Břežany now, comforting Lina Heydrich and ruffling the children's hair. He would have taken Heydrich's driver onto his staff too no doubt, if the poor man was not now incapable of walking.

The two men exchanged formal greetings and Rostock was allowed to sit down, while Frank explained the purpose of his summons.

'I have been in close and daily contact with the Führer since the despicable attack on Reichsprotektor Heydrich,' the State Secretary explained with just the right level of frowning self-importance. 'He feels, as I do, that a grand gesture is required to show the Czechs the futility of such acts. The careful, managed handling of that gesture will fall to you, Max.'

Rostock realised he ought to acknowledge the appointment. 'Thank you. I will not let the Brigadeführer down, whatever the assignment.'

Frank continued as if he had not spoken. 'The target has been chosen by my deputy, Horst Böhme, after lengthy investigations. It is a village in Bohemia near Kladno called...' Frank seemed to have forgotten the name of the unfortunate place and he had to drag a map over from the corner of his desk then let his long fingers crawl to an area that had been circled. 'Lidice,' he proclaimed at last.

Rostock decided he should demonstrate he was paying attention by asking an incisive question or two. 'This village is linked with the attack?'

'Not exactly. It is not as simple as that.'

Frank paused and he looked directly at the young captain opposite him. The thirty-year-old was an ambitious man with a hard, serious face and his eyes were as unflinching as his resolve. Frank stared into them for a moment, as if he were examining the man for the possession of certain qualities, then finally he smiled.

'I don't think I need to be coy with you, Max. No one doubts your commitment. We have yet to fully establish a direct link between the village of Lidice and the men responsible for Heydrich's death. However, we feel it is only a matter of time, and time is a luxury we cannot afford.'

'The Führer is concerned if the Reichsprotektor's death goes unpunished it could lead to a spate of similar attacks on senior officers across Europe. This village has had links with the resistance in the past. Only last year we caught a parachutist who carried contact addresses from Lidice on his person. The villagers are undoubtedly guilty of something. There is no smoke without fire after all. What we must ensure, what is most important to the Führer, is that Lidice acts as a suitable deterrent to anyone planning a similar assault. The villagers would doubtless applaud the attack on General Heydrich and that in itself is sufficient reason to act.'

'Very well, I understand.' And Rostock did, only too well. 'What exactly would you like me to do? Are we describing a similar operation to the work of the *Einsatzgruppen*?'

'No, we should go much further than that. Lidice must be a name that sticks in the minds of the Europeans under our dominion, thirty, fifty, perhaps one hundred years from now.' Rostock was intrigued but he let Frank continue uninterrupted. 'Are you familiar with Carthage?'

'Carthage?' The name rang the most distant of bells for the Hauptsturmführer but he could not place its significance. 'I'm afraid I am not.'

'Then allow me to give you a brief lesson in history. The Carthaginians had an empire once, centuries before the birth of Christ, which stretched the width of the Mediterranean. For seven hundred years it prospered, until they encountered a more advanced and superior culture in the Romans. The two empires initially struggled for dominance and Carthage even boasted some early victories; you must have heard of Hannibal and his elephants?'

'Yes, of course. At school I...' But Frank brooked no interruption.

'These were mere delays before the inevitable collapse of the city to the Romans, which came at the end of a siege lasting more than three years. Imagine that, Max; such patience, these Romans, so implacable.' Frank's admiration was expressed with a furrowed brow and tightened fist. 'Anyway, that is not the point of the story. The fact is Carthage was a visible symbol of defiance for years and the Romans were eager to ensure it never rose again, nor serve as an inspiration to other rebels. The world would have to see that resistance to the empire was futile. So, do you know what they did, Max?'

Rostock gained the impression Frank was enjoying the telling of his story so, even had he known the outcome, he would have lied. 'No, I am afraid not Herr Brigadeführer.'

'They killed everybody. Every man, woman and child in the city was put to the sword, except a few who were marched in triumph through Rome. They burned all of the buildings to the ground and destroyed the city entirely. Then they went further.' And he stabbed his finger onto the surface of the desk to show he was finally reaching his point. 'The foundations were dug up and scattered, the soil was ploughed through and every last trace of Carthage systematically removed over a period of months. By the time the Romans were done it was possible to deny the city ever existed. It could have been a mere legend. No more Carthage, no more defiance.'

Frank seemed to be reflecting on the words he had just uttered and Rostock deemed it unwise to interrupt his thoughts. Finally the Brigadeführer continued.

'That was a city, Max; a city like Prague perhaps. I am entrusting you with the destruction of a mere village. Do not let me down. I want to send out a signal to these subhuman people every bit as powerful as the Roman message to their subjects. Months from now I want to walk across fields and find no evidence that Lidice once stood there – not one single brick. Is that understood?'

'Completely, Herr Brigadeführer.'

'Good, see to it and soon.'

Ever eager to please a man of rank, Rostock was keen to show his enthusiasm for the task he had been allotted, for he knew it was the path to advancement.

'I will be ready to begin tonight, with your permission.'

'You have it Hauptsturmführer, now go about your mission.'

Rostock took this as a dismissal and he rose from the chair, saluted his superior with a raised arm and an exchange of *Heil Hitlers* and made for the door. As he reached and opened it he heard Frank's voice behind him.

'Max?' and Rostock turned to see a look of pure vindictive hatred on the State Secretary's face. 'Remember, not one brick.'

35

'Corn will grow where Lidice once stood'

SS Brigadeführer Karl Frank,
State Secretary of Bohemia and Moravia

10 June 1942

Rostock wore the frown of a man whose prospects are wholly dependent on the efficiency of others. The men of his unit were assembled, briefed and ready to go. He would even take the trouble to address them personally in advance of this most important of tasks.

Initially he had fretted. Not a natural speaker, he worried he would be unable to find the words necessary to inspire them. Frank's colourful comparisons with Carthage were beyond him. Instead he would have to find a way to appeal to their sense of vengeance while deflecting them from any thoughts of mercy towards the civilians they were about to destroy.

Rostock stood before the men under his command at dusk that evening. His voice was strong and it carried clearly across the parade ground.

'You are all decent men, good soldiers,' he began. 'Perhaps some of you may have…' he searched for the appropriate word, 'misgivings… following the orders from your sergeants. I tell you now… put them from your mind.'

'The people of Lidice are agitators bent on the ultimate destruction of the Third Reich. They played a major part in the death of General Heydrich and he will be avenged.'

Rostock saw no need to trouble his men with the moral vagaries of Lidice's tenuous link to the resistance. It was better they went into the operation seeing their enemy clearly in the faces of the villagers.

'Remember, you are *Schutzstaffeln* – the finest soldiers ever assembled in the history of the Fatherland. Act accordingly. I know you will not let your sergeants, myself or your Führer down.'

The village of Lidice – population just 489 – had received visits from the Gestapo before and those who bothered to peel the curtains back an inch to investigate proceedings were not unduly alarmed by the sight of soldiers disembarking in front of their homes. They were obviously looking for someone or something. Fine, let them look, it was hardly the business of anyone except those brave enough or foolish enough to assist the resistance in their schemes. Most simply went back to bed, unaware of the impenetrable cordon of men and vehicles slowly encircling the village.

'Nothing gets through, not even a rabbit,' Rostock warned his men.

As dawn broke, loudspeakers called the people from their homes. The more reticent were coaxed into the streets at rifle point during the house-to-house searches that followed; four soldiers per house, moving quickly. While one group separated the men over fifteen years of age from the women and children, another smaller band of soldiers took mattresses from the bedrooms and delivered them to the back of a large barn.

The women were herded towards the trucks with their children, the men into the school hall. A collective wail of despair emanated from the women as they were forcibly parted from their menfolk. Some of the wives bent almost double, holding their hands outstretched as if they could actually reach the men and touch them, though they were yards away by now and separated by armed soldiers. Many of them called their husband's name, others invoked the help of God. The cries of the women and children could be heard above the noise of the vehicles until they were driven away.

When all was ready the first ten men were marched from the school building in an orderly line and made to stand before the wall of the barn. Now they would discover the purpose of the mattresses. These were placed on their ends and leant against the brickwork behind them to prevent ricochets. Rostock ensured his NCOs moved their men quickly. The first victims of Lidice barely had time to register their surroundings before a line of rifle-bearing Germans faced them. The few remaining seconds of their lives were, for the most part, passed in dumb disbelief. The order to aim then fire caused a decimating burst, which cut the men down.

No sooner had they fallen to the ground than a young lieutenant moved in, using his Luger to finish off anyone continuing to show signs of life. By the time he had completed his duty the second group of incredulous villagers was marched into place. Rostock witnessed this line and twenty more like it as they were herded from the building and finished off by the firing squads. It was a textbook exercise in SS efficiency and he congratulated himself on his planning.

The men faced their executioners in different ways, as one would expect. Some walked with a silent solemnity, accepting their deaths, facing the firing squad with dignity and, presumably, religious beliefs still intact. Some men wept and others prayed. A number passed into the next world more vocally but it mattered little to Rostock if they cursed his men or pleaded with them for mercy. They would all share the same fate.

'Why do they do nothing, sir? Why not try and run, or rush us and fight with their bare hands?' one of Rostock's senior NCOs had asked when the executions were almost over. 'If they all attacked at once it would be difficult to control and maybe one or two would make it.'

'The hopelessness of their situation prevents it,' Rostock explained.

He glanced at one of the next victims, a man in his early twenties who was staring at the heap of bodies behind him as if they were all children playing a game and would surely rise to their feet again in a moment. Then he too joined them.

The executions were carried out at an incredible rate. By 9.00 am there was not a man left alive in Lidice, and the Jewish work detail, brought in from Theresienstadt, began to move the first of the one hundred and ninety nine bodies to the freshly dug earth of a mass grave nearby.

Rostock supervised the second phase of the operation in Kladno. The wailing of the children when they were taken from their mothers was the hardest part to endure. A handful, the eight most promising specimens, were sent to German families for Aryanisation, the remainder despatched to the new concentration camps. As they were prised from their mother's grips, red eyed and weeping desolately, Rostock could not help thinking they almost resembled German children. He had to harden his heart temporarily until the *untermensch* were loaded onto separate trucks and driven from his sight.

By evening the job was done and the sky above Lidice illuminated by the flickering lights from scores of houses set ablaze. Tomorrow the blasting teams would destroy what was left, the rubble would be cleared and the land ploughed under. Rostock, witnessed the spectacle from an armoured car parked on a ridge and told himself it was a fine sight. His men had made him proud. They were good soldiers; organised, professional and disciplined men. The Romans could not have handled the exercise more efficiently.

Čurda had almost known contentment. For a few uncomplicated weeks he treasured the sanctity of a family home, benefited from soft, clean linen on his bed and enjoyed the luxury of a full belly.

All that changed following the reckless and ill-judged assassination of General Heydrich. Prague was in uproar and now, like every other parachutist in the area, he was a hunted fugitive. Zelenka had tried to persuade him to go into hiding with the others. The resistance man had a new safe house somewhere and had sent Aunt Marie to collect him personally.

'Lieutenant Opálka is already there,' she explained.

'Already where?'

'It's a safe place in a church; you do not need to know which one. Come with me and I will take you there. It's the only way, Karel. It is too dangerous for you in the open, you know that.'

'Yes, alright, I agree but you must give me another day to get matters in order.'

'What matters?'

'There are some things even you are not permitted to know, Aunt Marie. You have your secrets and I have mine. This is to do with my mission.'

As soon as Aunt Marie had gone, Čurda immediately left the family he was staying with and went on the run.

Why could they not just leave him alone? He had nothing to do with the attack on Heydrich and was damned if he was going to be found guilty by association with the man's killers by hiding out in the same location. It was Gabčík and Kubiš apparently – trust those fools to play the hero. What had they done? He would be better off alone, thank you very much. The whole world was looking for the two assassins now and one could only imagine what the Nazis would do to them both when they were caught.

No, he would be just fine on his own. He would keep his head down, stay apart from the meddling fools in the resistance and remain firmly out of harm's way.

36

'Prague is paralysed. Silent with awe'

Propaganda Minister, Joseph Goebbels

After two weeks of house-to-house searches, mass arrests, wide scale use of torture and hundreds of executions it was a simple task to catalogue the number of significant leads. There were none.

The pressure on Karl Frank and Pannwitz to deliver something, anything, was growing by the hour. Both knew they had nothing positive to report back to Berlin.

'How can two assassins disappear in the middle of a city when they are being hunted by twenty thousand men?' asked an increasingly exasperated Frank.

'There is one tactic we have yet to attempt,' offered Pannwitz.

'And what's that?'

'An amnesty.'

'An amnesty?' Frank was clearly unimpressed.

'I think it could be worth a try. I'm not suggesting we go soft on the *untermensch*. Far from it, let's continue the terror tactics, highlight the folly of resistance by all means but show them there is an alternative. Increase the reward and offer this amnesty; a few days to encourage people to come forward.'

'We are already encouraging people to come forward.'

'There may be those who know something but are scared to come to us because they are too close to the assassins or the resistance. We must get those people to trust us. Let the word go out into the city that we understand and can possibly overlook a spirit of resistance but assassination goes too far. Tell the population anyone who comes forward with information leading to the arrests of Heydrich's killers will be granted an amnesty for himself and his entire family, no matter what acts he may have been associated with before. Promise them protection along with the cushion of a substantial reward.'

Frank appeared perplexed at the very notion. 'Well, I tell you honestly, I don't think it will work, but in the absence of any other masterful plan, I will permit you to try.'

'Thank you, Brigadeführer.'

'But only for five days. If no one comes forward by then, we return to more traditional methods.'

'Agreed.'

'I think you are wasting your time, though.'

'I am not so sure. The people of Prague are terrified. Give them a choice of fear and hope, and let them decide.'

'I hope you're right, Pannwitz. Whatever you do, you have to find them and quickly.' And he showed his exasperation by exhaling audibly. 'Damn it, they can't just simply vanish. Where in God's name are they hiding?'

The Czech Orthodox Church of St Cyril and St Methodius occupies the corner of Na Zderaze Street. The large white stone building, with its distinctive external courtyard, strong metal gates and carved stone icons lies just yards from the banks of the River Vltava in the very heart of Prague. Here, Father Vladimír Petřek once again received the faithful, reflecting ruefully that there had been a marked increase in the number of worshippers of late. Petřek could take no credit for the inflated size of the congregation, for this was not about his powers of oratory and had everything to do with the terror inflicted by the Nazis. It was rumoured the Germans would use their firing squads to literally decimate the city, executing one in every ten citizens of the capital; a punitive act not used since the days of Ancient Rome. Like all rumours no one could accurately trace its origins but it passed among the population with an alarming rapidity, spreading quicker than any virus.

Some came to the church to pray for the souls of loved ones who had been put to death, others to plead with their God that they and their families might be spared the next round of arrests.

'What must I do, Father, to keep my family from harm? Tell me how to protect them, please.'

Many clutched copies of newspapers containing a reference to a family member, friend or lover amid the endless lists of the newly executed, printed daily and with a seeming relish by the Nazi controlled publications.

Petřek could offer little to the recently bereaved beyond the inadequate comfort of his presence and the Lord's good word. A handsome man with a full head of dark hair, a moustache and beard, he would meet the mourners at the door of his church, for Petřek had learned they would often break down as they entered its sacred confines and he would have to support them to a pew. As these unfortunates knelt in prayer on the cold stone flagstones, they could hardly have imagined Heydrich's assassins were hiding beneath them.

Underneath the public section of the church lay a disused crypt that was once a final resting place for its priests. The bodies had long since been removed and the crypt now provided shelter for a small group of fugitive parachutists, including the two most wanted men in the Third Reich; Jan Kubiš and Josef Gabčík.

The seven men currently occupying the crypt were still very

much alive and determined to remain so. Gabčík, Valčík and Kubiš had been joined in the catacombs first by Lieutenant Opálka, then Jaroslav Švarc from the mission codenamed TIN. Their assassination team was forced to abandon its attempt on a Czech collaborator because of the heightened security of the Nazi terror.

'You made it too hot for me out there, that's for sure,' Opálka told Gabčík and Kubiš.

The little band of fugitives was completed when Sergeants Bublík and Hrubý, from a sabotage squad codenamed Bioscope, also sought the sanctuary of the church.

It was Zelenka who had approached Father Petřek, through an intermediary, requesting a temporary safe haven for the men. Petřek was eager to assist the struggle against the Nazis, a force he considered to be as near to pure evil as any he had ever encountered.

'Heydrich is engaged in the Devil's work. The men who attacked him are the new crusaders. However, I am bound by duty to seek permission from Bishop Gorazd.'

If Petřek was worried about his Bishop's view on the moral complexities of sheltering unashamed assassins, he need not have been. Gorazd proved resolute.

'The greater sin is on the head of the Nazis. Any act designed to combat their evil tyranny is therefore a justified one.'

That same night, one by one, the parachutists were transported into the delivering hand of the church.

Since that day it had fallen on Petřek to feed the men and be their sole contact with the outside world. At first the two assassins had been desolate. Their mission was believed a failure with Heydrich seemingly on the way to recovery. Gabčík, in particular, repeatedly blamed himself for the jamming of the Sten.

'Of course it is my fault. It was my weapon, I should have checked it.'

'Josef, you checked it a thousand times. What was it the British called the Sten, after those shops?' he asked before finally remembering. 'The "Woolworth's Special" because it is so cheap!' but Gabčík was inconsolable.

Kubiš had arrived at the church with face wounds that were thankfully far from serious. Zelenka arranged for a doctor to dress them before he entered the crypt. Now he merely sported light scarring on his cheek and forehead, caused by tiny fragments of shrapnel and his skin carried the discolouring associated with blast burns.

'I look like I fell asleep too close to the fire,' he conceded.

Even in this relatively uninjured condition, however, he could not hope to last on the streets of Prague for more than minutes with the Nazis on such a heightened state of alert. The temporary role envisaged for their haven was already beginning to seem woefully optimistic.

The crypt was a dark L shape, no bigger than twenty yards in length, with a honeycomb of niches on both sides where the ancient corpses had once been stored. The men slept in these niches trying to forget that the bodies of Father Petřek's forerunners had formerly occupied them.

During the day they sat on the red brick floor, which was always partly covered with their equipment that had been steadily smuggled in by the resistance. Among the weapons and bedrolls were items of outdoor clothing that doubled as blankets during the night. Some of the men had taken pictures of loved ones from their wallets and placed them in positions of relative prominence, close to candles or in little nooks in the brickwork, where they could be seen and provide some small comfort through the long hours of isolation.

The air was musty through lack of oxygen – the only breeze coming from a small grille above the men's heads that faced out into the street. It was positioned in the smallest section of the L shape, which they avoided to prevent even the slightest possibility of detection.

If the prospect of weeks or even months underground initially depressed the men, all of their spirits were immeasurably lifted when Petřek brought them the news of Heydrich's death.

'We did it, Josef. We did it.' Kubiš was elated, bunching his fists and waving them in front of his face, while the other men came forward exuberantly to pat them on the back or embrace them, offering heartfelt congratulations amid cries of *well done* and *good job*.

'No, you did it, Jan, with your bomb,' said Gabčík.

'We are a team,' replied Kubiš sharply as Hrubý enthusiastically pumped his hand in congratulation. 'We have always been a team and it was the team that finished Heydrich. Would you have claimed all of the credit for yourself if the Sten had not misfired and none of the grenades was needed? Of course not. We planned this mission together, we carried it out together and it was a success. Now shut up and take some of the credit.'

Gabčík smiled for the first time since the attack.

Valčík beamed at them both. 'Enjoy the moment. Not many believed two soldiers could take down an SS General. I bet Hitler shat himself when he heard the news.' And he laughed, 'You did it, boys.'

'And you played your part,' nodded a joyful Kubiš, determined to share the credit. 'This is a great moment for our nation.'

Even Gabčík had to concede it now. 'We struck back, Jan, and we hurt them, hurt them hard.'

Opálka came towards Josef then and, for the first time in the crypt, reestablished the previously irrelevant protocol of rank. The lieutenant came to attention and saluted the NCO crisply.

'Well done, Sergeant Gabčík, well done,' he said proudly.

Gabčík returned the salute, 'Thank you, sir.'

Opálka repeated the act for Kubiš while Gabčík enjoyed the moment. He could now look his President in the eye. His mission was accomplished.

37

'Unfortunately this earth is not a fairy-land, but a struggle for life, perfectly natural and therefore extremely harsh'

Martin Bormann

Petřek waited for his congregation to disperse before locking the church doors from within and descending into the crypt to visit his charges. For the parachutists inside, his delivery of food and news was the highlight of their long and restless day.

To gain access to the crypt Petřek used a trapdoor by the altar before carefully descending a dozen stone steps to the catacombs. That afternoon, as always, he called out to the men below to reassure them he was not the Gestapo. He was careful not to make too much noise in case his voice carried to the streets outside. An arthritic knee and the weight of the provisions he had brought to sustain the men through another day of seclusion restricted his movement and he puffed a little as he took the steps one at a time. Valčík met him at the bottom to assist with the burden of the bags, taking them from him while the priest's eyes adjusted to the minimal light provided by a few carefully positioned candles.

Petřek sat down among the men and they leaned forward expectantly to hear the latest news of the Nazi terror. Petřek had bright intense eyes that a parishioner had once memorably described as dangerous looking and the fugitives had come to regard him as a man lacking neither courage nor strength. Today, though, he was reluctant to meet their gazes for he had, that very morning, received word on Lidice. How could he begin to explain what had happened there?

Petřek had given the men his word that he would pass on all news from the outside world, no matter how terrible, and so he regretfully commenced his story, sparing them no detail. When he had finished the grim tale, Lieutenant Opálka looked at him disbelievingly.

'A whole village? You are sure?' he asked as if the priest must surely have been mistaken.

'It seems so,' confirmed Petřek and he instinctively muttered a short prayer for the lost souls of Lidice.

'Because of us?' asked a desolate Kubiš.

'No, not because of you,' Petřek assured him, 'do not blame yourselves for Lidice when that unspeakable crime sits on the shoulders of others. The Nazis kill men and women in our country every day. They were doing this before you arrived and they will continue to do it whether you fight them or not. What is important is that you struck back. The Nazis may carry out these atrocities in the name of their dead general but they do such things for only one reason. They believe that might is right and all that matters is strength and power but this cannot be a sustainable philosophy. Not when good men like you refuse to accept your fate and continue to stand against them.'

'I hope you are right, Father Petřek, I do,' said Kubiš, 'but right now I cannot think of anything worth the lives of so many people,' and he picked up his bedroll and walked away from their little huddle, unable to disguise his grief.

Despite the risk, Petřek spent another hour in the crypt reasoning with the men for, if he could help them in no other way, he was determined to at least absolve them from the guilt of Lidice.

Čurda took to drink the way a baby takes to its mother's milk; naturally, unquestioningly and without conscious thought. The shots of Slivovitz, taken with the regularity of a doctor's prescription, were now a necessary requirement to get him from one end of the day to the next. Without them the fear became unbearable, for Čurda was quickly approaching his breaking point, as he moved around the city, lodging with relatives, who were the only people left he could trust. Every day there were more arrests, a new wave of executions and the endless repetitious threats; anyone involved in the plot to kill Heydrich would die, but not before he had seen his entire family killed in front of his eyes.

This was not a war in the way Čurda, as a soldier, understood one. There were no rules of engagement and your mother was just as likely to take a bullet as you were. It was the end of the world and all reason, goodness, decency and mercy had been driven out forever. He was living in the dark ages where the only important thing left was survival, the sole worthwhile notion to prevail, to rise each morning and continue to breathe until nightfall when there would be a few short hours of disturbed and fitful rest before the process began all over again the next morning.

He preferred to drink standing up, tucked into a corner of a bar or leaning low against the wooden counter top, exempting himself from the well-meaning interference of strangers, as he repeatedly raised his glass. Čurda would spend hours in this manner, contemplating the bitterness of his fate, steadily beginning to hate the men who had sent him back here with useless forged papers and foolish notions of resistance, while resentfully spending their subsistence money on shot after shot of spirits.

Usually his drinking was quiet and contemplative as he tried to work out a solution to his problems. Čurda just wanted to get away from here but how and, even if he could break free from the resistance and leave Prague, where would he go and what would he live off? The search for solutions to these practical problems was postponed that night by the shocking news that reached him shortly before he sought refuge in the bar. One of Čurda's relatives told him about Lidice and he knew then that all possibility of salvation was lost.

News of Lidice's fate soon filtered through to the capital. The Nazis wanted to ensure the population learned what would happen to anyone who helped the resistance. It seemed to Čurda that there was simply no way to defeat a terror such as this one. The regime held no respect for anyone and was as content to murder women and children as men to achieve its ends. Rumours were sweeping Prague. It was said the Germans would murder everyone in the capital if that was what it took to get someone to hand over Heydrich's killers. How could Čurda continue to hide in the city if they were going to slaughter everybody?

Čurda slumped against the bar, his whole body shaking in terror. He looked like an exhausted prizefighter who has been expertly punched in the stomach. He seized a near full glass tightly in his hand and wolfed down the entire contents in a single burning swallow.

How could anyone survive in the face of such absolutism, such awesome, cruel and unforgiving power? It took Čurda's breath from him and what remained of his resistance.

The very next morning he stood before the huge black banners with their white SS flashes that flanked the entrance to Gestapo Headquarters at the Petscheck Palace. Like everyone in Prague he knew of the five day amnesty. Despite the terror in his heart, Čurda walked unsteadily up the marble steps, reported to the first Nazi he saw and told the man he had important information relating to the killing of General Heydrich.

38

'The trumpet blows its shrill and final blast!
Prepared for war and battle here we stand.
Soon Hitler's banners will wave unchecked at last,
The end of German slavery in our land!'

The Horst Wessel Song –
official marching song of the Nazi party

'Just remember this will all eventually end. The Nazis won't keep looking for us forever. They will have to stop eventually,' said Hrubý.

'Yes, sure, perhaps by next Christmas,' replied Valčík grimly. 'Then maybe we can leave here.'

'So, only six months to go then you can have the best Christmas you ever had,' reasoned Hrubý, determined to play the optimist. 'Is that so unbearable when you have a whole long life ahead of you?'

'Christmas could not be worse than last year.' Kubiš was joining in the small talk now. 'For my dinner I got a tin of pressed meat and a precious can of condensed milk poured over an apple. And I had to spend the day in the pub with that bad tempered bastard over there.' He pointed at Gabčík who snorted a laugh in response. 'It took more than a few pints of beer to restore my natural good humour.'

'That's all you need for a perfect Christmas, a good drink,' reasoned Valčík. 'Well, perhaps not all. A nice warm fire, a bottle or two of beer, some shots of Slivovitz and someone prettier than you lot to sleep next to, that's all I need,' and he smiled at the prospect.

'What about the food?' said Opálka. There were murmurs of agreement from men who had received little more than bread and cold meat or cheese to sustain them for days now.

'What I would give for some fried carp and potato salad,' the young lieutenant continued. 'In my town there are men who go door to door selling the carp at Christmas time.'

Bublík spoke from a prone position, head propped up against his bag, 'Steaming hot bowls of *Oukrop*, made with goose fat and garlic, served with slices of black bread.'

'Don't let's think about it,' groaned Gabčík but his eyes grew distant at the mention of the traditional garlic soup.

'Or how about a roast goose with white cabbage and dumplings?' offered Kubiš.

'Stop, you're making me homesick,' Gabčík tried to look pained but then he smiled. 'What sweet things will there be?'

'Moravian tarts with cinnamon and poppy seeds,' announced Kubiš triumphantly. 'Or strudels; enormous ones, stuffed with apples and sugar.'

'No more please. I can't take it,' protested Gabčík. His stomach actually growled audibly, to the amusement of all.

Possibly it was the reminiscence from a better world that pushed Kubiš into it or perhaps the biting drop in temperature, which the men had complained about all afternoon, but he suddenly announced. 'I have had enough of living down here like a rat. I am going to sleep upstairs.'

'You can't do that, Jan. What if someone checks up there in the night?' Valčík countered.

'I'm taking my bedroll up to the choir loft. I'll lock myself in. An entire congregation could enter the church and still not know I was there. At least it will be dry and warmer as well.'

Opálka was already getting to his feet. 'Sounds like a good idea. I am sick of lying here in the gloom.' And he picked up his bedroll, weapons and ammunition. Bublík followed suit.

'Well, I suppose it can do no harm. If you keep your heads down,' cautioned Gabčík.

'We will. Care to join us?' asked his friend.

'I don't think so, Jan. I feel safer down here. At least now I will be away from your snoring.'

'It's not my snoring, it's you. You snore so loud you wake yourself up.'

It was an ongoing lighthearted argument; neither man snored and anyone who did would soon be wakened by a jab in the ribs from an alarmed comrade, desperate to maintain the security of their position.

'Be careful, Jan.' Gabčík was serious now. 'Don't let your guard down. Not even for a moment.'

'I won't.' And Jan rewarded his friend's concern with a warm smile. He would miss their comradeship, if not the cold.

As Kubiš walked off towards the choir loft, Opálka and Bublík followed on behind. Jan was glad to be heading away from the crypt. The place made him feel like a dead man already.

At first Čurda's story was treated with some suspicion. He appeared to be yet another in a relatively long line of lunatics, would be collaborators or terror struck family men who had visited the Petschek Palace in the past week. All were eager to either claim the reward money or the amnesty and avoid the arbitrary punishments of the assassination's aftermath; men whose stories of possessing information on the killing were soon exposed as the desperate fantasies of often unhinged individuals, some with petty grievances against neighbours they were only too keen to link to the plot.

All of that changed when Čurda was able, unaided, to pick out the briefcase Gabčík left at the scene of the attack, despite its presence among twenty similar ones. This successful ID parade afforded Čurda an exalted status and the Gestapo began to beat him with enthusiasm.

During the course of long hours of questioning, Čurda would eventually admit to being a parachutist himself but would repeatedly state he had done nothing wrong and in fact wholeheartedly disagreed with the assassination. Furthermore he did not support Beneš' exiled government which had so treacherously persuaded him to return to Prague for the sole purpose of relaying messages back to London on the state of affairs in the Protectorate. On arrival he had immediately abandoned this plan and sought to keep himself to himself, accepting the status quo of the occupation and staying out of trouble. In many ways he even approved of the German presence, he said. It had brought order and ensured no possibility of colonisation from the hated communists of the east.

This rambling diatribe proved insufficient to satisfy Čurda's accusers. They merely continued to beat him, in time with their demand for the whereabouts of the men who had killed their leader in such a cowardly and underhand fashion.

'I watched the last man we had down here scratching the floor, trying to pick up his broken teeth with smashed hands,' a smiling interrogator assured him.

Čurda, realising he was now in a situation entirely beyond his control, finally cracked and abandoned all sense of a partial, limited treachery. He began to betray with a relish that impressed even his interrogators. They stopped beating him and began writing; names, addresses, aliases, of parachutists, resistance workers and the owners of safe houses across the city. By the middle of the afternoon, Pannwitz held a piece of paper exposing entire networks and all from the mouth of just one terrified man.

Every scrap of the confession would be used – the networks rolled up, agents tortured for further intelligence then hanged, but all of that could wait for now. Pannwitz possessed one piece of information he would act upon immediately; for Čurda had finally supplied the names of the two suspected assassins. According to him, Josef Gabčík and his closest friend Jan Kubiš had killed Heydrich. Only a single crucial, undisclosed fact remained; the current whereabouts of the two men. No, Čurda did not actually know where they were right now but he was convinced they were still in Prague and might even be hiding in one of the city's churches, though he did not know which one. He assured the Gestapo he was keen to help in any way he could. In fact, he thought he knew someone who might very well be aware of the men's present location. With no further urging, Čurda gave up Aunt Marie's address.

39

'The Victor will never be asked if he told the truth'

Adolf Hitler

As young Ata Moravec was dragged out through the wrecked front door of his home he banged his head sharply against the solid piece of wood, which now hung at an angle, suspended from a single hinge near its base.

As the SS ransacked her home and two soldiers frogmarched her son from the building, Aunt Marie reached for the capsule of poison in her pocket. She did not hesitate for a second, knowing time was short before she would be led away. Surely a less idiotic soldier would never have allowed her the opportunity to visit her own bathroom before she was arrested. Perhaps her stout middle-aged figure and gentle, defeated countenance made the dimwitted private think of his own mother for an instant. Whatever the reason, his permission had been a tiny mercy and at least now she would die in her own home and not some cold, damp cell and maybe they would be happy then and let her son go.

As a woman she was a realist, holding no illusions that her life could continue beyond this day. There would be no reason for the Gestapo to keep her alive after interrogation. All Marie had to look forward to was torture and the certain realisation that she would eventually be forced to betray resistance workers all over Prague. For their sake, she knew too much to allow herself the luxury of a moment longer in this life. Aunt Marie said a silent prayer for the soul of her imperilled son and bit down into the capsule.

Ata was already secured in the back of the truck when a *Scharführer* discovered the scene in the bathroom. Aunt Marie was curled up on the floor in front of him as lifeless as any gunshot victim. The sergeant cursed, promised the foolish private under his command a swift posting to the thick of the fighting on the outskirts of Kharkov on the Russian front, then ordered the rest of his men to throw the body into a separate truck and immediately transport it and Ata to the Petschek Palace, adding quickly, 'Don't let him see her body or tell him his mother's dead. The Gestapo may want to use that little piece of information when it suits them.'

Drink and beatings, the level of which he would not have thought possible to survive, had stupefied Ata. One of his eyes was completely closed and that, together with broken bones on the same side of his face, gave him a lopsided look.

The vodka they forced him to consume made the young man repeatedly sick and he had soiled himself more than once during the agonies of torture. He tried not to look at his fingers, for he knew they had been turned to bloody stumps following the enthusiastic attention of a Gestapo thug, who had punctuated his use of the pliers with repeated vengeful reminders that, '*This* is for Heydrich'.

The interrogation had been as simple as it was horrifyingly brutal. And it always came back to one question, 'Where are the parachutists?'

'Tell us, Ata, and all this will end,' urged the young officer who led the part of the interrogation not dominated by physical torture. 'If you don't tell me I can't protect you from him.' He nodded at the burly inquisitor who had worked on Ata so resolutely; his only concession to the stifling heat of the cell being to remove his tunic and attack the boy in shirtsleeves.

'I can see you are a reasonable young man. You want to do what is right, I can tell that,' reassured the officer in a soothing, empathetic tone, 'so tell us, please. We will find out anyway soon enough and all of this will have been for nothing. You must see that surely?'

But Ata could not see, and he resisted all attempts to confess the whereabouts of Kubiš, the bright and glamorous hero who had befriended this young man and made him feel less insignificant as a result. Kubiš was everything Ata wanted to be. And so he blotted out all thoughts of the crypt and continued to deny any knowledge of parachutists until the young officer had tired of his lack of cooperation and ordered yet another beating, followed by a near drowning from the vodka bottle.

Then they left him for a while to wallow in the excruciating pain and alcoholic haze. He had no idea how long he had been alone but it must have been some time. Eventually the door was kicked open and his chief tormentor returned with two henchmen. They quickly freed Ata from the restraints in his chair and lifted him to his feet, causing a wave of nausea and intense pain to burn through his body. The young man was dragged upright along a corridor, feet trailing behind him, his bare toes scraping across the cold concrete. Then the door of another cell was flung open and he was thrown in, landing heavily, face first on the ground.

It took a while before the pain ebbed away sufficiently for him to peel his face from the cold stone floor and look about him. Ata's eyes instinctively went to a large, dark shape at the end of the room – it appeared to be a fish tank filled with water, an anachronistic presence in the bare walls of the Petscheck

Palace, where every item had a purpose. Mindful of this, Ata peered at the dark water. After a moment he was able to make out the message the Gestapo had sent him.

Through the glass he could clearly see his mother's severed head resting on the bottom of the tank – its opened eyes staring sightlessly back at him. Ata would never know, as he descended into a form of lunacy, whether his piercing screams were delivered aloud or merely confined to his fevered brain.

40

*'I do not see why man should not be
just as cruel as nature'*

Adolf Hitler

A handful of gurgled words from a crazed and desolate
Ata, who had been assured his father's head would join
his mother's if he did not cooperate, was all it took to
mobilise seven hundred Waffen SS Soldiers in full battle order.
Through his sobs and moans of despair the young man finally
gave up the church of St Cyril and St Methodius and that was
all the Gestapo needed. At four o'clock in the morning the
order was given to begin a seemingly endless procession of
lorries, which transported men from the handful of barracks
that encircled the capital. The night air was filled with the
growls and rumbles of engines as the trucks navigated the
myriad bends of the city streets.

Pannwitz and Frank arrived at the scene early, intent on
controlling this most vital of operations and ensuring nothing
could be allowed to go wrong. Ata and Čurda were forced to
attend as witnesses. There were no civilians on the streets at
this hour and residents of overlooking buildings were forcibly
evacuated by troops who ran up and down cradling rifles and
machine pistols under the direction of an SS Captain. When
they were finally in position, Frank was assured every door,

window, rooftop and manhole cover, within a twenty-street radius, had a German gun trained on it.

'Thank you, Captain,' said Frank. 'I will, of course, hold you personally responsible if any of them is allowed to escape.'

The captain saluted his understanding and returned to the task in hand.

It didn't take long for Valčík to work out what was happening. He'd been hoisted up to the vent in the crypt by Gabčík and Hrubý as soon as the men were disturbed by the rumble of the lorries. The sight that greeted him was chilling; seemingly hundreds of soldiers were dropping from the tailgates of those lorries then being ordered into the streets around the church, blocking their escape. Someone had betrayed them.

They could tell from Valčík's face as soon as they lowered him to the ground that their situation was hopeless. 'We're surrounded,' he told them and each man experienced a deep sense of terror. Their worst fears had been realised. The crypt that had been their sanctuary would now become a trap with no prospect of escape.

'How many?' asked Gabčík and when Valčík's eyes met his, the other man looked despairing.

'Hundreds,' he said.

'Jesus… could they be… do you think…?' Švarc was desperately hoping the Germans might not know where they were. 'Are you sure they realise…?'

'They know we are here,' Valčík assured him. 'It's over.'

Twenty men made the first incursion into the church. The nervous janitor of the St Cyril and St Methodius had been roused from his sleep to admit them. Pannwitz led the column of Waffen SS soldiers into the church himself. He was still a policeman and wanted to be in on the arrest. They had been told to move quietly but the men's jackboots signalled their arrival, footsteps echoing against the ancient flagstones as they fanned out between the pews, creating an effect not unlike the ripple of polite applause at a concert.

Realising their presence was already betrayed Pannwitz ordered the janitor to illuminate the building and the church was soon partially revealed. More than once the Germans gave nervous glances towards intruders present only in their imaginations.

The head of the anti-sabotage division watched as his men searched under every seat, peered behind the lectern, lifted cloth from the altar and found nothing. Then a voice came from out of a dark corner of the room.

'It's locked, sir.'

Pannwitz walked over to a solid metal grille and pulled on it. Sure enough, it was fixed firmly in place. He ordered the janitor be brought forward and the man stood before him trembling like a cornered rabbit.

'What's in here?'

'It goes right up into the old choir loft but it's never used, so far as I know.'

'Open it.'

'I don't have that key. I'm not sure where it is. Like I say it's never really used. No, not really.'

'Private, point your rifle at this man's head.'

The chosen soldier drew the bolt of his rifle, took a step back, shouldered the gun and aimed it directly at the janitor's head. The flinching fellow tried to move out of harm's way but only succeeded in pressing himself back against the stone wall. The other soldiers quickly moved out of the range of possible ricochet.

'Take the key out of your pocket and open the grille. If you do not I will order him to shoot you here and I will simply have it blown open with explosive.'

'Yes, yes,' mumbled the quaking janitor and he instantly

forgot his evasions. The bunch of keys was produced once more and, despite quivering hands, the correct one selected. The lock turned easily and the grille swung open in front of them.

A loud knock made the soldiers start, then a second, which was followed swiftly by another, each one preceded by a rolling sound. It took Pannwitz another two knocks, closer together this time, to realise what was happening. A heavy metal object was rolling down the stairs towards them, thumping against each one in turn as it descended.

'Grenade!' he screamed and threw himself behind a bench. The soldiers who reacted slower than the Gestapo man actually witnessed the hand grenade landing at their feet before it exploded in their faces, sending a flurry of mutilated men flailing in all directions.

Before the noise of the blast diminished, Kubiš was on his feet, firing short machine gun bursts from the choir loft into the backs of fleeing soldiers, pitching them over like skittles where the bullets found their marks. From their positions either side of him, Bublík and Opálka fired too, creating a lethal crossfire, which had the Germans diving for cover. The less disciplined ran in a blind panic before they were inevitably picked off by the murderous hail. Kubiš had a moment to hope God would understand and forgive the sacrilegious devastation of his church.

Return fire was sporadic at first and confused by the conflicting shouts of shocked troops yet to fully comprehend where their enemy was or how many they faced. Pannwitz crawled desperately for the door, using the heavy wooden seats as cover, for he had retained the presence of mind to work out where the firing was coming from. The parachutists were strung out at three separate points of the choir loft and, by edging his way along the blind side of the seats, he was able to escape the worst of the crossfire. Just as he had crawled to within a few yards of the door all hell broke loose around him. Startled troops outside opened up on the church with everything they possessed, sending massive bursts of machine gun fire raking through the windows, decimating everything in its path; furniture, finery and their own men.

As Pannwitz ducked his head and ran hell for leather out of the door, someone was screaming, 'Hold your fire!'

It may even have been him.

Good, let the Germans do my job for me, cutting down their own soldiers, thought Kubiš as he ducked while the huge church windows exploded in a shower of crystal. No sooner had he dropped to the floor than machine gun fire sailed over his head, shattering the plaster on the wall behind him, which broke into pieces and floated to the ground like snowflakes.

Kubiš ducked to keep the debris from his eyes and, cradling the Sten on his forearms, crawled away from danger. The Germans continued to fire at the spot he had occupied. He evaded them simply by moving a few yards to the left or right before popping up above the lip of the choir loft again and sending some more of them to hell. He would repeat this process and kill as many as possible before they could regroup and attempt a more organised assault on his position.

How had they found him? It didn't really matter. He had known there would be no way to avoid this fight as soon as he heard the lorries outside and picked up the sounds of the troops disembarking. Jan was certain he had despatched a good number of the SS men already but, as he crawled the length of the choir loft, he realised grimly it was now just a question of numbers and time. There was no other exit from the choir loft so they were completely trapped. How many could he kill before they came to take him? How long could he hold out? Jan already knew this was going to be a last stand.

41

*'Even the brood in the cradle must be
crushed like a puffed up toad.
We are living in an iron time and have
to sweep with iron brooms'*

SS Reichsführer Heinrich Himmler

Gabčík hefted the Sten gun on one shoulder and threw
the bag of spare magazines and grenades on the other.
Valčík intercepted him.

'What are you doing, for Christ's sake?'

'What do you think I am doing? I'm going to help them.'
Even as he spoke another burst of machine gun fire was
discharged above them.

'Josef, no, you can't – you won't get five feet before they cut
you down. If you go out through the hatch you will come up
among them.'

'Good. They'll get the shock of their short lives. Let's see how
many we can get before they work out what's hitting them.'

'No, it's suicide.' Valčík seized his arm hard now. 'You will
get us all killed and for nothing. You can't help them.'

'What would you have me do? Stay here hiding like a
coward while they kill my friends? I'm not leaving Jan out
there alone.'

This time it was Hrubý who persuaded him. 'Valčík's right,

Josef, we can't help them. Listen to that firepower, there must be a battalion up there. We won't even be able to get to them and even if we could, what then? There is no way out of the choir loft – you know that. We would all be killed.'

Gabčík stopped in his tracks, realising the futility of his actions but hating the irrefutable logic they presented to him nonetheless.

'I can't just stay here while they die.'

'You have to. There is nothing else you can do,' reasoned Hrubý desperately. 'The Germans don't know we are down here. We can hide out here until they leave. That is what Jan would want you to do, Josef, not sacrifice yourself for no reason.'

'Do you really believe that?'

'Either way we have a much better chance if we stay down here. You know I am right, Josef.'

'But what about Jan and the others?' pleaded Gabčík.

Valčík gripped his arm once again; this time it was an attempt to calm him. 'Listen to me, Josef, listen to me, they are already dead and you know it.'

Outside Pannwitz was still shaken, unable to countenance how close he had just come to death. His uniform was coated with dust and splinters. Frank was unsympathetic. 'What the hell is happening in there? How many men do we face?'

'It's hard to tell,' he answered breathlessly. 'Could be three, could be six. It might be more.'

'Right, it's simple. We send in more men to deal with it and flush them out properly. It shouldn't take more than ten minutes.'

'But we need them alive. They must be fit enough for interrogation.'

'Alive it is then,' confirmed Frank and he sent the SS captain to deal with the matter.

The firing was mostly one sided. When Kubiš was able to fire at all, it had to be done in one swift movement. He would pop up above the stonework, aim at a blur of dark blue tunic and let off some rounds, immediately dropping to the ground before the answering burst of machine gun fire that always followed. His ability to halt the progress of the second wave of troops was limited by the sheer ferocity of the firepower they possessed. Kubiš knew it could not be long now.

For almost two hours Kubiš, Bublík and Opálka had held hundreds of elite SS men at bay with the judicious use of their limited ammunition and the occasional devastating deployment of a hand grenade. They had certainly acquitted themselves way beyond the expectations of any professional soldier but now the game was almost at an end. Jan could hear German voices at the foot of the staircase. He had no grenades left to roll down and, even if he had, was unable to get close enough. The Germans had managed to set up a heavy machine gun at the foot of the staircase and were now slowly demolishing the area around the stairs with bursts of fire – undoubtedly the prelude to a final assault. The MG 34 stopped firing for a moment to reload and Kubiš called out.

'Bublík, Opálka… are you with me?'

The answering silence filled him with a sense of absolute loneliness. He had to assume they were both dead; killed by the grenades periodically lobbed into the choir loft or hit by accompanying fire.

There was a third possibility; that struck by the sheer hopelessness of their cause they had elected to take their own lives, and avoid the brutal certainty of hours of torture followed by execution. This was the one thing they all feared more than a death in combat, which would hopefully be quick and certainly more befitting a soldier.

Kubiš reached inside his pocket for the cyanide that had

not left him since he set out from England six months earlier. He held the capsule in the palm of his hand. He had known the risk. He was a soldier and the possibility of death was with him constantly but it still felt so unreal somehow. That it should come down to this when there was so much to live for, with his mission complete, his obligation to his country fulfilled and Anna awaiting him. It was this simple cruelty that hurt him most.

Kubiš knew he had no choice. He had merely been buying enough time to resolve himself. The alternative, being captured alive by the Gestapo, was too terrible to imagine. He had hoped for some miracle yet known there was no way out. Kubiš realised his last act on this earth would be to somehow find the strength to take his own life.

'Forgive me, Anna. I tried.'

He placed the capsule of fast acting poison in his mouth. As he did so an SS corporal reached the top of the staircase and fired a burst from his machine pistol. It tore down the long narrow corridor of the choir loft and more than one of the bullets caught Jan in the torso, wounding him. There was a moment of searing pain before he collapsed into unconsciousness. The cyanide capsule, still unbitten, lolled uselessly in his mouth.

42

*'I believe today that my conduct is in accordance
with the will of the Almighty Creator'*

Adolf Hitler

It took a while before full order was established. Three men were found – two of them apparently dead from a combination of wounds and self-inflicted poisoning once their ammunition had run out. The third, however, was still breathing and the order was quickly given to take Kubiš from the church and get him to a hospital. Here the best surgeons in Prague would treat his wounds, in an effort to keep him alive and make him fit enough to face interrogation.

'Then we'll prove the British are behind this whole thing,' sneered Frank as he witnessed Kubiš being lifted on a stretcher into the back of an ambulance. 'Make sure you keep him alive. Alive!' he ordered as the doors were closed on the unconscious figure and the vehicle driven off at speed.

Pannwitz approached Frank. 'I don't think it's over.'

'What do you mean?'

The Gestapo man indicated Čurda who was standing to one side of the ambulance 'He says that none of these men is Gabčík.'

'Then where is he?' demanded Frank.

'It's definitely over,' announced Valčík in a whisper, the absence of firing causing a return to quieter communication.

'God rest them,' said Hrubý finally.

'What do we do now?' asked Jaroslav Švarc.

'We do nothing. They do not know we are down here and there is no reason to look,' answered Hrubý. 'They have three men and no idea how many of us have been hiding out. Only the priests, Zelenka and Aunt Marie know that.'

'What if we have been betrayed?'

'No, I don't think so. I refuse to believe it. Who would do such a thing and what would they have to gain in return? A reward they could not spend anywhere with half of Prague after them. No, if we stay quiet we will probably be alright. Agreed?'

Valčík and Švarc muttered their agreement. Gabčík, sitting on his pack, continued to stare silently down at his boots in desolation at the loss of his friend.

Vladimír Petřek's bravery was never in doubt. The priest had not wavered for a moment when he was entrusted with the safe keeping of the parachutists, and he had remained steadfast during the weeks of random executions. But now he faced disaster. The Gestapo dragged him from his home, bundled him into the back of a truck and drove him down to the St Cyril and St Methodius church to show him the aftermath of the gun battle. Opálka and Bublík were already dead, their bodies lying uncovered on the path outside the church. A third man had been rushed to hospital with serious injuries and the Nazis knew there were more parachutists hiding in his church. How they were aware of this he could not tell but the sight of a Czech with bruises on his face standing next to a disfigured young man under armed guard gave Petřek all of the clues he needed. The presence of his brave young charges had been cruelly betrayed. Pannwitz came straight to the point.

'We want Gabčík. We know he is in the building somewhere and we will level it brick by brick if we have to. I have field guns and will turn them on your house of God. I'll consign it to rubble and bury you under it if that is what you want. You can't help Gabčík. He will be ours before the end of the morning. You know it. If you tell us where he is and he surrenders it will be better for him.'

Petřek remained entirely unconvinced of that but realised he was left with little room to manoeuvre. The Nazi became more emphatic as his rage grew.

'Tell us where he is hiding, priest, or we will burn him out of there.' Again Petřek said nothing. 'You have ten seconds to tell me where he is or I swear I will round up one thousand men, women and children and execute them today in your name and we will still smoke Gabčík out. Think of it, one thousand people will die at your hands and for what? For nothing, because a stupid priest chose to protect an assassin who died anyway.'

Petřek took a deep breath before answering. 'No, they will die at your hands and be certain your maker is watching you. Know this Nazi, when you die, as all men must, He will be waiting to punish you for this and every other vile deed you have committed.' He challenged the Gestapo man defiantly. 'But if I have to give up one man to save a thousand then so be it. The hero you seek is hiding in the crypt.'

'Show us,' demanded Pannwitz. The priest reluctantly pointed out the air vent on the exterior wall of the church, then he took Pannwitz inside and showed him the western entrance to the crypt, barricaded from within, and the old blocked up entry way, no longer in use, at the other end of the catacomb's thin corridor.

'Now we are getting somewhere,' Pannwitz reported to Frank when he returned to a street still filled with angry, vengeful soldiers.

The four men sat on the stone floor of the crypt staring at the thin gap in the wall that gave them their only hint of a world outside. The air vent was ten feet above them, covered by a heavy metal grille and not even wide enough for a man to place his head through but it transfixed all of them. Minutes had passed since the firing upstairs ceased. Now Gabčík and Valčík, Hrubý and Švarc waited, in a silence filled with trepidation, for the German soldiers to either disperse or come crashing through the hatch. They held their weapons close to hand and kept the spare ammunition within reach. Each had sworn to the others he would not surrender and promised to take as many Germans with him as possible. They had Sten guns, Colt automatics and hand grenades and they could at least fight and die like soldiers if it came to it.

But perhaps there would be no need for such heroic gestures after all. Maybe Hrubý was right. If the Germans thought they had caught Heydrich's assassins they might be content and leave them in peace. Sure it would be many days before anyone would be able to run the risk of visiting them down in the catacombs but they had food and water enough till then. Sitting in silence in the dark crypt would be unpleasant but not such a huge price to pay to survive this ordeal. After all, it was a choice denied to Opálka, Bublík and Kubiš.

And so they listened together as the sound of soldiers running by the vent and lorries reversing and accelerating along the street drifted down to them. Eventually all was entirely quiet and the silence that reached them became so absolute they found they instinctively held their breaths for fear of disturbing it. The four men exchanged tense glances, straining their ears to hear any sound from outside.

Finally, as the tension became unbearable the calm was shattered by the harsh grating crackle of a megaphone.

'Parachutists! We know you are in there. Come out and surrender!'

The harsh guttural sound of a German voice butchering the Czech language cut through the air.

'Jesus Christ,' mumbled Hrubý in terror.

'You down there in the crypt. We know where you are hiding. Come out now and you will not be killed.'

'They know we are here,' said Valčík uselessly.

'We have been betrayed,' whispered Gabčík.

'Gab-chik! Jo-Zef Gab-Chik!' barked the German voice. 'Surrender now and you will be treated with mercy!... a Prisoner of War... and you will not die like your friends!'

At the mention of his name Gabčík rose to his feet to call back. Hrubý instinctively tugged at his shirtsleeve to stop him. Before he could say a word Gabčík asked him, 'What difference does it make now?' and Hrubý relented, releasing the grip on his comrade's arm.

Gabčík walked up to the vent and stood before it. He tilted his head upwards, the better to address his Nazi tormentors through the gap in the brickwork, and when he called out his words echoed round the stone walls of the crypt with a power that startled them all.

'Never!! We are patriots and soldiers of the Free Czech army, loyal to Beneš, Masaryk and Czechoslovakia! We do not recognise Nazi scum, except as enemies, and will never surrender! Come down here and get us and see how many of you lose your lives on free Czech soil! Down with Adolf Hitler and down with Germany!!'

'There's your answer, Pannwitz. I told you they would not respond to a German voice,' said Frank.

Pannwitz hauled Ata to his feet. 'You, call out to your friends down there and tell them to give themselves up. Tell them it will be alright if they do.'

'Alright?' and Ata let out a bitter little laugh at the thought. When Ata refused, the SS Captain drew his Luger and pointed it at the boy's head. Ata did not flinch.

'Do it then – I know you are going to do it anyway.'

Frank shook his head and the officer holstered his weapon. 'Yes, we are,' the Brigadeführer assured Ata, 'but we will do it when we choose. You have no say in the matter.'

Frank gestured towards Čurda. 'Use him instead. He does what he is told.'

Pannwitz nodded. 'You know what to do,' he told Čurda. 'Go and persuade them to give up.'

Obediently but very reluctantly Čurda took a step towards the church, treading as if he was heading for the gallows.

'Traitor,' hissed Ata as Čurda walked towards the vent. Frank did not care enough about Čurda's state of mind to even have the boy beaten for his insolence.

43

*'The independence of Czechoslovakia was
not crushed; it continues, it lives, it exists'*

President Beneš

'Well said, Josef,' Hrubý told Gabčík weakly. 'I don't think I could have done that, not the way you...' And the rest of his words faded.

'What do we do now?' asked Švarc desperately.

'We dig,' answered Valčík.

'What?' asked Švarc as if he had suggested they make wings and fly out of the crypt.

'We dig. Here, through the walls and into the sewers. If we make it through the wall we can get away. What difference does it make if we create noise? They know we are down here anyhow. Two of us can dig while the other two hold the place. Then we swap over.'

Švarc thought for a while. 'I think it could work,' he said eventually.

'I'd say it is better than just sitting here waiting for the end,' confirmed Gabčík, grateful for the distraction. 'Get the shovels and the climbing axes from the packs.'

The area around the vent had been deliberately cleared of men and machines to allow the negotiations to take place.

The majority of the troops had retired to side streets, leaving a contingent covering the church from vantage points on the ground and high up in surrounding buildings. Another group covered the two entrances to the crypt from within the church. Consequently, Čurda found himself walking across an almost empty and silent street, his eyes fixed on the gap in the wall from which Gabčík's familiar voice had resounded so clearly a moment earlier. He had no idea what he would say to his former comrades in response to such fervour but knew he had to try. Events were now moving at a pace entirely of their own making and Čurda was caught up in them. Shame burned his face as he trudged towards the vent and prepared to call out to the doomed men in the crypt. Sweat poured from his torso and he had to spit on the ground before he was capable of speaking at all.

'Lads, it's alright, it's alright. It's Čurda, boys. Everything will be fine if you just give yourselves up.'

'Čurda? Is that really you?' asked Valčík unsurely, wary of some Gestapo trick.

'Yes, it's me. I've been well treated and so could you be if you just give up this hopelessness and come out.'

'Well treated?' asked Hrubý quietly to himself, as he contemplated the implications of that phrase.

'Oh my God, what have you done, Čurda?' Valčík called in frustration when the realisation dawned on him.

'What I had to do, Valčík. This is the only way to survive and you must surrender too. It will be okay if you do.'

'You led them here.' This was not a question but a bitter accusation from Valčík and it was the final word as far as Gabčík was concerned.

'Murdering, treacherous bastard!' he screamed in fury and before anyone could say another word he grabbed the Sten, pulled it up to his shoulder and aimed a burst of fire through the vent. The bullets tore through the hole in the wall and sailed above the panicked figure of Čurda who turned on his heel and ran back the way he had come, expecting at any moment to be cut down. SS men on the other side of the road returned fire at the vent and Čurda found himself fleeing in terror across an open stretch of road transformed into a killing ground. He ran with the fear of a man who knew just one stray bullet could end his life. As he flew at full pelt back towards Frank and Pannwitz he noticed they were actually laughing at him.

'Looks like your friends are not so happy with you, eh, Čurda?' called Pannwitz.

Frank became impatient as soon as the firing ceased.

'Let's stop this nonsense now. Get the fire brigade down here.'

Valčík swung the short handled axe into the brickwork and a sizeable lump of masonry fell to the floor. Encouraged, he hefted the axe repeatedly at the stones while Hrubý stabbed at the emerging hole with the blade from his shovel.

'How far do you think it is?'

'I don't know,' he called to his comrade. 'Just keep digging.'

At that exact point a press-ganged fireman was climbing warily up a ladder outside to bring him within touching distance of the vent. With one hard swing of a large axe he knocked the metal grille clean out and it tumbled down inside the catacomb, narrowly missing Valčík's head in the process. Gabčík grabbed the Sten once more and shot out at the fleeing fireman. Covering the vent with the Sten he called to Valčík.

'Keep digging!'

Before his comrade could answer the first hose appeared in the vent above them; another closely followed it. Gabčík was about to fire but could see no target. A second later the hoses twitched into life. Gabčík and Švarc were instantly soaked from the force of the water, which cannoned off the walls behind them and rebounded in an icy spray.

'They're flooding the place!' shouted Gabčík and he sent a couple of bullets out through the vent, which carried harmlessly through the air beyond.

The hoses were too high for them to reach and they continued to relentlessly pump water at a rate of over six hundred gallons a minute. Before too long the men in the crypt were standing in puddles of freezing water. Valčík and Hrubý began attacking the masonry with a new urgency. Bricks were loosened and smashed with axe and shovel but the progress was slow. They were able to move only slivers of brick with each assault and it was some time before deep scars began to form in the ancient walls.

A German soldier appeared at the vent. He held a grenade and Gabčík, using the automatic he now preferred to the Sten, shot him in the face.

'Grenade!' he shouted and everyone ducked to avoid the effects of the blast that reverberated outside. There was pandemonium in the street and Gabčík hoped the explosion had taken some more Germans.

Hrubý held a knife in his hands and shouted above the din. 'Help me cut those hoses!'

Valčík stopped what he was doing and linked his hands together to form a foothold for Hrubý to step into, so he could grab for one of the hoses. At the second attempt he reached it and swung the knife into the rubber, ducking under the force of the water. After sawing for moments Hrubý managed to slice off the end and he pushed the remainder of the hose back into the street – an act that triggered a hail of machine gun bullets that ricocheted above his head and sent him tumbling backwards from Valčík's grip. He landed heavily but his fall was partly cushioned by the rising water level, which now reached the men's knees.

Outside, Frank surveyed the scene as small groups of SS men rushed the hatch. Some attempted to reattach the damaged hose that was now pumping water harmlessly out onto the road, others fired bursts from Schmeisser machine pistols or scaled the ladder in an attempt to send grenades down into the crypt. Invariably they were forced back by well-aimed volleys of fire from within.

'Get some tear gas down there!' Frank commanded the leader of the assault team and two men were sent to carry out the Brigadeführer's request.

'Swap with me, Švarc!' shouted Valčík, exhausted from his digging.

His hands were cut and bleeding and he handed over the axe. As Švarc took his place at the hole, which now went back two feet into the masonry, a grenade was dropped into the crypt from above, closely followed by another. Again the cry went out from Gabčík and he fired a shot to keep German heads down. Sticking the automatic in his belt, he scurried forwards and scooped up both grenades from the water. Valčík once again cupped his hands together, Gabčík stepped into them, was hoisted aloft and in one movement he pushed the grenades back through the vent. They exploded on the street simultaneously.

'Hrubý, cover the vent with a Sten!' Gabčík screamed. 'They almost had us!'

The heavy machine gun was in place and the burst commenced on an officer's signal. The firing chipped away at the masonry around the grille and sent the four men inside stumbling for the cover of the near wall. As soon as the covering fire ceased, two volunteers ran forwards to the grille and lobbed three tear gas grenades through the vent. Hampered by the deepening water, the prospect of further covering fire and the impossibility of instantly returning so many grenades, Gabčík gave the order.

'Fall back!'

The four men waded, waist-deep now, away from the hole in the wall, turning to their right into the larger section of the L-shaped crypt, just as the grenades exploded sending clouds of tear gas billowing after them.

'The gas is not working, Herr Brigadeführer,' reported the commander of the assault team moments later. 'There are too many gaps in that old brickwork. It is seeping out into the church and affecting my men. For the same reason the water is not flooding the crypt quickly enough. At this rate it will take half a day to get to a sufficient level to force a surrender.'

'We can't tolerate that,' insisted Frank. 'All of Prague woke this morning to the sound of gunfire and explosions. What sort of message does it send to the population? That Germans cannot control their own city? It took three hours to remove three parachutists from the church loft and now we take hours more to drive a handful of men out of a crypt without success. It is simply not good enough.'

The SS commander bridled. 'That is because our friends in the Gestapo will not allow us to do the job properly. We are soldiers, an assault group. We are not meant to negotiate or bring people out alive. Our way is to take the target and that means nothing less than a full frontal assault.'

Pannwitz had listened to every word and replied with astonishment, 'And how will that achieve our goal? We need these men alive. If we had wanted them dead we could have accomplished it hours ago. They must confess their crimes and be put on display before the world. It is the only way to prove they were sent by the British and not the product of some mythical, heroic home resistance force.'

'But you will kill them anyway,' retorted the captain.

'I agree. This farce has gone on long enough,' said Frank. 'They are making us a complete laughing stock and the longer it takes the more those assassins become an example

to misguided nationalists everywhere. Do what you have to
do to end this.'

'No, you cannot…,' began Pannwitz.

'Cannot? I am acting Reichsprotektor, until Reichsführer
Himmler advises otherwise. I think I know his will in this
matter better than you, Pannwitz. He would want us to end this
intolerable situation now even if we have to kill every last man
down there. We have one prisoner who may yet recover and
you are welcome to him but I will not allow the Czechs to laugh
at us in our own backyard. Is that understood, Pannwitz?'

'Completely, Herr Brigadeführer,' replied the Gestapo man
sullenly but he resisted no more.

Valčík and Gabčík were just above the water level, lying
horizontally on their bellies in an empty catacomb each.
Hrubý and Švarc were opposite, adopting a similar position,
as the freezing water gradually rose towards chest height and
showed no sign of abating.

'I don't think we could have made it through the wall even
if… we only got three feet in all that time,' said Valčík.

'What matters is you tried,' Gabčík consoled him.

'Up till now,' said Hrubý, 'I had always assumed we would
somehow get away. Now I realise there is no hope for us. Oh
God, I don't want to die down here, like this.'

'It is not over yet, Hrubý. Myself, I want to kill more
Germans before this day is over,' answered Gabčík.

'Me too,' Švarc assured them all, 'and if I am going to die,
what better place to do it than a church. At least here we are
close to God.'

'Let them come for us then,' Gabčík announced, 'and we
will be ready.'

The explosive took the hatch off the entrance to the crypt as
if it was the top off a beer bottle. As soon as the smoke died, a

volunteer inched his way onto the first of the stone stairs that led down into the crypt. He placed a rag to his mouth with one hand, to protect himself from any last residue of the tear gas, and in the other held a borrowed Luger. Four more men followed behind him.

Subdued light came from the air vent on his left but this was some yards away and around a corner so he was unable to make out his surroundings in the gloom. He cursed the fact he had been standing in daylight a few moments ago and could now see little ahead of him as a consequence. His boot made contact with another step and it disappeared under the water. He made a slight splashing sound as the second boot went deeper and he began to wade cautiously forward, the gun pointed ahead of him ready for any movement. As he touched the bottom step the water level reached his chest and he was forced to hold the Luger high and at an unnatural angle out in front of him. He took more steps and could hear the slight splosh as each man entered the water behind him and was reassured by their presence. The sergeant's eyes began to adjust to the darkness and he noticed a shape stir to his left but he was too late to prevent what happened next. The man behind him saw the flash from the barrel of the Colt but the sergeant did not, as the bullet from Gabčík's pistol had already passed through his forehead. There was a cry of alarm from one of the Germans and they began to fire at the shadows around them. As the sergeant fell backwards into the water, dead before he hit it, Valčík fired at the next man and was gratified to hear a cry of pain and distress. Hrubý and Švarc opened up too and the four men of the assault team beat a hasty retreat through the water, crying out in pain as they took wounds from well-aimed pistol fire.

With the attack successfully repelled, the crypt fell momentarily silent.

'They will come again and there will be more next time,' said Hrubý and nobody disputed it. 'I don't have much ammunition left, just two or three bullets. There's no hope anymore. None.' Then he concluded firmly, 'I don't want to be taken alive.'

There was a long pause. Finally, Gabčík answered him. 'It's alright, Hrubý.'

There was another devastating silence, which went on for seconds that felt like minutes, until it was broken by the clearly discernible snick of a pistol being cocked. When the shot finally came, it echoed around the crypt.

Gabčík and Valčík did not look over at the space in the catacomb now occupied by Hrubý's body but they could tell that, close by, Švarc was praying; his mumbled message to God barely audible above the noise of the free-flowing water still gushing through the vent, almost at shoulder height now. Then Švarc suddenly stopped and Gabčík turned his head away until he heard the shot.

Valčík climbed down into the water then and Gabčík followed him. The level reached almost to their chins in the centre of the crypt and they had to hold the pistols above their heads to keep them dry. The water was paralysingly cold. They were shivering and their breath was visible. They instinctively waded away from the bodies of their comrades and back to the open area beneath the vent, taking care to avoid the gushing water. Then they stopped and Valčík turned around to face his friend. Gabčík could see he was tearful and when Valčík spoke his voice was weak.

'I don't want to be last, Josef.'

'That's good because I do.'

Valčík's eyes showed his gratitude. 'I'll see you in heaven or hell, Josef, whichever will take us.'

Valčík cocked his pistol and slowly raised it to the side of his head. He held out the other arm until it reached his comrade's shoulder and gripped onto it tightly, needing human contact to help him complete the act. Valčík screwed up his eyes and Gabčík, motionless now, closed his. Even though he knew it was coming, the crack from the pistol still made Josef start. Valčík's hand went limp on his friend's shoulder and he fell sideways from the force of the shot then his body toppled over and dropped into the water. Gabčík stepped backwards from the body of his friend. He was entirely alone now.

The crypt seemed darker somehow, and the sound of the water as it cascaded onto the flooded floor filled his senses. It seemed to be urging Josef on.

There was no point crying for Liběna. It was not in his nature, would do no good anyway and he told himself he had been lucky to have her at all. Their brief weeks together were as good a time as he had ever known. He prayed he had used up all of their bad luck and she would somehow find the strength to carry on without him.

There was a commotion from above, prompted by the shots. Orders were shouted in haste and activity seemed to centre on the area around the sealed hatch that was the crypt's second entrance. At the same time he could hear footsteps close to the already exposed western entrance. They were going to come at him from both sides this time and he realised he had seconds left before explosives blew the sealed entrance.

Gabčík should have realised it could never have turned out any other way. He was not the sort for wife and family and happy endings belonged in children's stories. Any ideas he once had to the contrary were just vanity. It had never entered his mind to use the cyanide capsule and he now realised his life was always destined to end with a bullet. *Good then, it's fitting.*

He cocked the Colt and aimed it at the side of his head, then immediately altered the pistol's position so the end of the barrel was now pressed tightly against his temple. Gabčík would not be carried from here half dead. He needed to be sure.

As the commotion above him grew louder and the shouts of his pursuers ever more urgent, as the men from the second wave inched down the steps into the crypt to get him, Josef closed his eyes for the last time and squeezed the trigger.

44

'Where once the Swastika flies, there it will fly forever'

SS Brigadeführer Karl Frank,
State Secretary of Bohemia and Moravia

The SS corporal had been gone less than a minute. The fearless man volunteered to lead the group and investigate the three shots they had heard from within. Stripped to his vest, he had entered the catacombs armed with only a pistol. As he descended the stone steps, a fourth shot made him freeze and aim his gun towards it. It was a moment before he could be sure it was not directed at him and he inched forwards to examine the site. Emerging moments later, his grimy head appeared, water dripping from his hair and face onto the smashed stonework below.

'Finished,' he told them.

Outside the church a motorcycle despatch rider drove up to the edge of the building, dismounted and saluted Frank.

'Professor Hollbaum sends his compliments, Herr Brigadeführer, but he regrets to inform you the parachutist died shortly after arriving at the hospital.'

'Damn him,' cursed Pannwitz as he realised Kubiš had cheated them all.

'He's luckier than he thinks,' muttered Frank resentfully,

robbed of the one live prisoner within his grasp. There would be no way of proving the British were behind this now, no show trials or staged confessions, no public execution of the assassin.

'Pannwitz,' continued Frank, 'I want everyone on that list of yours arrested, interrogated then shot. Is that understood?'

'It's already in hand,' answered the Gestapo man with an all-consuming weariness. 'What shall we do with the priests?' he asked eventually.

'Execute them. Execute them all,' answered Frank.

'Without trial?'

'Hold a trial if you like then execute them.'

'And Bishop Gorazd?'

'Him too, especially him,' and Frank gave a look that brooked no argument.

'And this creature?' He indicated Čurda, a lone seemingly shocked figure who appeared to be trying to blend back into his surroundings.

'Oh yes, our little Judas Iscariot.' Čurda became fearful the Nazis might conveniently forget their bargain now. 'Give him his thirty pieces of silver.'

'Do we let him go?' Pannwitz spoke as if the turncoat was not within earshot.

'Oh no,' Frank was emphatic, immovable. 'Čurda works for us now. There will be many more operations against the partisans before this war is over and he will prove very useful.' Čurda realised he was trapped then. There would be no way out for him. 'What's wrong, Čurda? Lost your taste for betrayal so soon. Don't worry, you'll soon regain it.'

Frank walked away from the traitor then. The stress of the morning left him craving a cigarette, which he lit on the move in an effort to gain a few moments of solitary reflection.

At least it was over. The assassins were all dead, which was something he could use in his favour while making a claim to be confirmed as Reichsprotektor and the embarrassment caused by a long drawn-out siege in the middle of a Reich-controlled city was over. As he surveyed the scene around the church, the line of dead bodies by its walls, the pools of rippling water from the silenced fire hoses, the anxious toing and froing of ambulance men tending to injured German soldiers, Frank told himself he could not have handled matters any differently.

A young private marched up to him, saluted and handed him a telegram. Frank took a long drag from his cigarette and passed it to the bemused soldier.

'Hold that for me,' he commanded and the private clicked his heels before accepting the Brigadeführer's cigarette gingerly as if it were a fragile piece of jewellery.

Frank opened the telegram and began to read. On closer inspection it revealed itself to be an urgent message from Himmler. The Reichsführer had heard of the siege from his own sources and wished to take a personal interest in proceedings.

The telegram read, *'All means should be employed to capture the men alive.'*

Frank knew instantly that he had lost.

Anna had been waiting for the knock on the door and when it came she made no effort to escape. For three weeks she had lived in a despairing uncertainty; knowing neither Jan's whereabouts nor the state of his wellbeing. Now all this was at an end, the news of his death far worse than the dreadful anguish she perpetually carried when she worried he might somehow come to harm. Her worst fears had been confirmed. Now she knew she would never see her Jan or hear his sweet voice again, and it was the end of all hope. Anna was simply unable to comprehend a life without him. Dumbly she rose to her feet to admit them. Let the Germans come then and her agony would soon be over.

Zelenka sat down on the edge of the bed just as the timber of the front door first splintered then shattered as it gave way. The resistance man had already dismissed the possibility of fleeing from his would-be captors. There were too many, they had blocked every exit and, most crucially, they knew where to look and who for.

Was every safe house in Prague compromised? It seemed so. Čurda had betrayed everything – the fool. It would do him no good in the long run. No pact with the devil ever led a man to anything but damnation.

Others would deal with Čurda. Zelenka now concentrated on a different form of escape. As the jackboots thundered up the staircase towards him, he bit down hard on the capsule in his mouth, tilting his head back to hasten the effect of the poison and his salvation from these barbarians. His lifeless body was still twitching involuntarily when the Nazis burst in.

It took a week for all of the facts to reach London.

'An entire village?' Beneš asked in disbelief. Moravec nodded. 'You're certain?' And when the lieutenant colonel gave no answer Beneš climbed to his feet. 'Murderous bastards,' he hissed. 'How many others?'

'It's impossible to tell at this stage. It's too early and most of our sources of information have gone, Bartoš included. Reports are unclear but we think many hundreds have been executed.'

As he was wont to do in times of stress, Beneš walked over to the windows of his study and stared out at the surrounding fields. 'Gabčík and Kubiš?'

'Killed in the church it seems – we also lost Hrubý, Opálka, Bublík, Švarc and Valčík.'

Beneš' back was to him so Moravec could not tell the effect

his report was having on his President but he clearly heard him say, 'God rest them.'

There were no more questions for the time being and neither man spoke for a while. The President merely continued to stare out of his window. Moravec found he could clearly remember the faces of the men his deputy had selected more than six months before and he tried hard not to think of the fate they had shared.

'So, did they give the top job to Frank?' asked Beneš finally, half turning from the window.

'No, Daluege.'

'Who?'

'General Kurt Daluege, head of the ORPO, the uniformed police. It seems an appointment made in haste,' said Moravec. 'He is a senior SS man and already posted in Prague but I have heard even his fellow Nazis regard him with derision.'

'Really?'

'Yes, they call him "Dumi" apparently,' and when Beneš raised an eyebrow quizzically he added, 'it means "The Idiot".'

'Better an idiot in charge than a hangman.' The President turned back to face his secret service head then.

'We would have lost more in a battle, wouldn't we?' Beneš appealed. 'If we had fought them when they marched over our border?'

At first, Moravec did not answer his President.

'How many, František? Five, ten thousand maybe?'

'More.'

'Yes, more. And think of the lives we have saved in the long run.' Beneš was warming to his theme. 'The country has paid a heavy price but history will prove it was worth it to preserve the existence of our nation.'

Beneš walked back to his desk and sat down. 'It falls to men like us to make these decisions,' he said, sadly. 'Few will ever understand our burden.'

There was a short pause while he tried to find his words. 'I think… I think we can be proud of our actions, František. I'd say, on the whole, that it was a highly successful operation.'

EPILOGUE

'Most of you men know what it is like to see one hundred corpses side by side, or five hundred or one thousand. To have stood fast through this and – except for cases of human weakness – to have stayed decent, that has made us hard'

SS Reichsführer Heinrich Himmler

The young girl walked unhurriedly along the riverbank, keeping the road between her and a passing cluster of German soldiers.

Don't rush. Suspicious people rush, innocent people plod their way home or go about their business calmly.

A late evening breeze chilled the back of her neck and she turned the collar of her raincoat upwards, pulling it tightly forward against the bare skin until it flattened the base of her short-cropped hair.

She crossed the road briskly, avoiding a troop lorry that accelerated towards her. It growled like an animal as the driver changed gear and drove swiftly by, slicing through a deep, muddy puddle of rain, sending its contents rolling after her in undulating.

She took the few yards to the St Cyril and St Methodius church slowly, unsure how she would feel when this cold stone edifice came in sight. Disconcerted German soldiers still routinely policed the church, as if the building itself somehow held the power to summon a rebellion and they were eager to keep everyone away from its mysterious, shrine-like powers.

Oh my poor Josef, what did they do to you here?

Don't think about that now, Liběna. Keep going.

She had barely registered the pockmarked stones and the harsh white scarring from the machine gun bullets that chipped away the centuries-old grey walls when the sentry approached her.

'And where are we going this cold night, *Maminko*?'

Why was this idiot calling her mother? Did he think the word was Czech for *Fräulein*? The sentry was a tall and strapping soldier, his pale complexion heightened by the chill of the evening, and Liběna realised he was taking his time examining her. Her hair may have been cut away as short as fashion would allow, but she was still far from boyish in appearance. The curve of her hips was only slightly masked by the unbuttoned raincoat, leaving an obvious gap through which the sentry could admire her figure. It was a cold night with little to commend it and the soldier, in his evident boredom, saw no reason to disguise the fact he was enjoying her.

Use your looks if you have to. All men become idiots when they see a pretty face.

'The railway station,' she answered quietly.

'Are you meeting someone or going somewhere? Ah, I see you are going somewhere, your case.' He seemed embarrassed to have asked the question now the answer was so obvious.

'Žilina, to work in my uncle's munitions factory.'

Remember, you have nothing to hide so don't give too much information. Tell them the life history of your 'uncle' and it will sound as if you learnt it this morning.

Next the question she knew he would ask but dreaded just the same.

'Good, then you will, of course, have all of the necessary papers.'

It does not matter if you look uneasy when he asks for them. Everyone feels that way.

'Of course.'

She set down her case and began a slow and measured retrieval of each document. Her first reaction was to pull all of the papers from her bag and throw them at the soldier, the better to end the charade quickly, but she managed to keep her composure, handing him first the identity card then her train pass and authority to travel and finally the ration book with its little yellow vouchers. She even made a play of absent mindedly checking the wrong pocket for her identity card, as if it was of no consequence and must be somewhere on her person.

The sentry took the papers together in his left hand then passed them one at a time to his right, opening each, and squinting to examine them in the half-light. He took so long to make a pronouncement that she realised the forged papers could never have been good enough to pass even this cursory examination. What had it been – her hastily taken photograph? Some out of date watermark, the careless misspelling of a German word by the renowned forger Gabčík had entrusted with her life? Or did she just not resemble a Hana Kovály?

'Fine,' he said eventually. And she realised he had merely been dragging out the process, for he was starved of human contact on a street so studiously avoided by the law-abiding folk of Prague.

The sentry returned the clutch of papers and she took them in her right palm, picking up the suitcase at her side with the same hand so she could leave as swiftly as possible without arousing suspicion. Liběna walked on without another word, almost shaking with relief. Her breathing instantly eased, becoming more regular.

'*Maminko!*' the soldier barked after her and Liběna understood at once the deceit was over.

All the time he had merely waited till her back was turned so he could remove the rifle from his shoulder and level it. She knew when she turned back it would be pointing straight at her – that his cruel and mirthless face would be the last thing she would see before the bullet slammed into her, ending her life. Liběna prayed it would at least be quick and clean and she would not be left to bleed slowly to death in the gutter.

She pretended not to hear his call. Why assist him? He would be forced to shoot a woman in the back and that might just be enough to send his soul to hell if it were not destined there already. She had barely gone a handful of steps before he called again, this time with an irresistible authority.

'*Maminko*, stop!!'

The volume of his call was impossible to ignore and Liběna reluctantly turned to face her death. It was all she could do to prevent herself from closing her eyes.

But, instead of a gun, the sentry was holding what seemed to be a piece of card. She could not understand why he waved it at her so animatedly.

'Your ration book?' the soldier called after her incredulously, with apparent amusement, as if to add *of course if you don't want it*. And she realised, in her clumsy struggle with the papers and suitcase, she had allowed the precious document to slip from her fingers and had not even noticed.

Liběna walked like a ghost to collect the ration book, hating the look of smug superiority in the soldier's eyes. When he smiled at her flirtatiously, as it was handed back, she felt an inner defiance that made her want to lash out and hurt this foreigner. Who did he think he was, embarrassing her in the street like this? How dare he?

'Thank you, I am not myself today.' She spoke it quietly with a slight undercurrent of shame, before adding, 'You understand?'

The sentry flushed – the change in his complexion more noticeable because of the contrast to his frozen pallor. He had turned nothing less than the colour of scarlet. Certainly he wished he had not drawn so much attention to her clumsiness, when it seemed now to be derived from some mysterious, and to him excruciating, hormonal lightheadedness.

'Of course,' he mumbled quietly and looked away as Liběna collected the ration book from his hand. As she walked the road towards the station she could almost hear Josef's laughter.

Liběna told herself she had been strong – even as she had passed the cold, lifeless crypt where they had taken her love from her. How many times had she felt the pointlessness of her existence since that day? How often had she actually welcomed the prospect of her own merciful death at the hands of the Nazis? And then, when she heard the Gestapo was rounding up all those associated with the fallen resistance men, she had somehow found the strength to move, telling herself she had promised to survive.

First, she took down the suitcase from the top of her wardrobe, already packed with clothes, and added a few necessities and enough food to cover the length of her journey. Then she took up the floorboard in her bedroom, just as Gabčík had shown her, and removed the tightly bound package containing the precious forged papers he insisted on arranging in case anything were ever to happen to him. He had ignored her protestation that this would surely bring them bad luck. *Worse luck to have no papers, Liběna.*

Next, she had gone to the crumbling house of Hlinka the forger, who welcomed her like a gentleman then left her alone in his draughty bathroom as she cut her hair as short as the custom would permit and dyed it. The surplus colour ran through her fingers like blood as it poured into the cracked porcelain sink.

Hlinka took her photograph and she waited patiently while he disappeared into a room at the top of the house before eventually returning with a miraculously aged likeness, officially stamped and fixed to the well-worn identity card she already possessed. Liběna kissed the forger gratefully on the cheek and immediately set out for the railway station just as dusk began to fall.

With each step she felt certain she would break down, releasing more of the tears that had fallen almost unceasingly since the news of Gabčík's death reached her. Whenever she felt she could not go on and doubt began to cloud her judgement, she would remember the words Josef had spoken to her so often during those last days together. Liběna could hear his urging voice in her head now as she walked and it soothed her, allowing her to act as he would act.

Maybe a Nazi on the train will stop me and they will take me off to a concentration camp like poor wretched Anna Malinová.

Maybe we will live to be a hundred and maybe we will not.

What if I get to your uncle's house and he does not want me there?

Don't be foolish, my uncle will love you. The first thing he will say is how did plain old Josef Gabčík land a beauty like you, eh?

Maybe I will make it to Žilina and die there anyway of a broken heart.

Maybe you will love me forever, or maybe you will run off with the baker's son. Maybe we will grow old and have a dozen children and too many grandchildren to count.

Maybe I am carrying your child already, Josef.

It was too early to tell for sure and she lacked the certain instinct some women claimed to possess. All she knew was it could at least be a possibility. She would just have to wait and see; as she had once waited for Josef to complete his mission and return to her. After the death of her lover, Liběna could accept whatever the fates delivered her.

She bought the train ticket with a minimum of fuss and no conversation.

Remember, the ticket seller may be a Czech but that does not make him your friend.

There were two further document checks before boarding the train. Liběna still refused to believe she could be free, even after finding an empty compartment, stowing luggage in the rack above her, and taking a seat by the window to gaze out at a near empty platform. The lateness of the hour and restrictions on travel meant few would be joining this train and the solitude was a comfort to her.

She endured a seemingly endless wait, fully anticipating the bitterness of her arrest at this final hurdle, then, to her absolute amazement, the train finally began to roll gently forward. Liběna peered out of the window, watching the last light corner of the sky begin to darken above her as the train picked up speed. It was going to be another bitterly cold Prague night and, for the first time in her young life, she would not be there to feel it. Liběna was leaving her city, unsure if she would ever be able to return.

By morning she would find herself in Slovakia, a territory proclaimed loyal to Germans, which meant, ironically, that it was entirely free of them. Liběna could visualise nothing beyond her arrival at the house of Josef's uncle, but resolved that, whatever happened, she would prevail, with or without his child to care for. As the train pulled inexorably away from the darkening city, she whispered his mantra quietly to herself, alone in the cold and empty carriage:

'Each day in turn, Liběna, each day in turn.'

THE END

RECKONING

'*Pravda Vitezi*' – '*Truth Shall Prevail*'
Czech National Motto

Three days after the siege at the St Cyril and St Methodius Church, Captain Alfréd Bartoš was wounded during a Gestapo attempt to arrest him. He died the next day.

Ladislav Vaněk was also arrested and immediately offered to cooperate with the Gestapo. He betrayed agents from his own Jindra group and was spared as a reward for his treachery. He survived the war.

On 24 June the Nazis targeted another village for destruction. This time the entire adult population of Ležáky was rounded up and killed. They joined the many thousands of victims of the terror instigated in reprisal for the death of Reinhard Heydrich.

Bishop Gorazd was eventually executed on 4 September 1942. Father Vladimír Petřek followed him before a firing squad the next day.

After the war, the village of Lidice was rebuilt and the anniversary of the tragedy that befell it is still remembered. Max Rostock, the man who oversaw its destruction, was finally arrested in 1948 and sentenced to death, eventually commuted to life imprisonment. He served just eleven years in a Czech prison before being released and allowed to return to West Germany, on the condition that he worked there as a spy for the Czech authorities under the cover name 'Fritz'. He died in 1986.

President Beneš returned from exile in triumph. Thousands turned out to welcome him home but his victory was short lived. He was outmanoeuvred by the communists and resigned in June 1948. He died a broken man just three months later. Beneš always denied any involvement in Operation Anthropoid.

Anton Svoboda, the man meant to go on the mission instead of Jan Kubiš, survived the war and lived to be an old man.

Walter Schellenberg was arrested in 1945 and sentenced to six years imprisonment for war crimes. Released in 1951, he completed a fascinating memoir, which confirmed the perilous existence of a life working for Heydrich. This autobiography, The Labyrinth, published in 1956, includes the use of his wife's racial impurity against him by his own superior. Schellenberg died of liver disease, aged just forty one.

Paul Thümmel, the double Agent 54, was kept in Theresienstadt for three years under a false name to avoid scandal. The Gestapo murdered him days before the end of the war.

Adolf Eichmann fled to Argentina but was kidnapped by Mossad agents and taken to Israel to stand trial for his crimes. He was hanged in 1962 aged fifty-six.

Martin Bormann committed suicide in Berlin during the final Russian assault.

Heinrich Himmler was captured by the allies in 1945 and killed himself with a cyanide capsule.

Karel Čurda never got to enjoy the rewards of his treachery. He was arrested at the end of the war trying to smuggle himself and his money across the border. Condemned by a Czech court, he was hanged as a traitor.

Karl Frank finally achieved his ambition to be the most

important man in Prague on 22 May 1946 – when more than five thousand Czechs, including survivors from Lidice, made the journey to Pankrác prison to see him publicly hanged. It is not recorded if he appreciated this irony.

Poor Anna Malinová died in Mauthausen concentration camp, one of the six million victims of the Holocaust. However, I could find no record of the fate of Liběna Fafek. It is not inconceivable that Gabčík would have tried to get her out of the Protectorate following the assassination. Slovakia was a logical destination as he had many relatives there – all of whom were spared Nazi retribution to continue the façade of supposed neutrality. By contrast, twelve of Kubiš' relatives were executed in the reprisals and thirteen of Valčík's. So, when Liběna boards the train at the end of the book, it could very well have happened this way and I like to think that it did.

Reinhard Heydrich was responsible for the deaths of millions. His part in the implementation of the Holocaust came to light when a single copy of the minutes of his Wannsee Conference was discovered in the archives of the German Foreign Office after the war. Left there by Martin Luther, it was the only evidence the meeting ever took place, and remains the sole document confirming that senior German officers discussed the systematic annihilation of the Jews. Heydrich really did worry he might have Jewish blood and shot his reflection in the mirror in a fit of self-loathing when drunk.

Heydrich was the most senior Nazi figure to be assassinated by the allies in World War Two. His relatively early demise meant he avoided the scrutiny other leading Nazis received during the postwar Nuremberg trials. As a result he is not as widely known a figure as he might have been and his name subsequently avoided the infamy it thoroughly deserved as the true architect of the Holocaust.

An enormous thank you to my loving wife Alison, who lived with the research and writing of this book, as well as the countless rewrites. She came with me to Prague to visit the locations where the story unfolded. She knows how much it means to me to have *Hunting the Hangman* published and her support has been unflagging.

My amazing daughter Erin is a constant source of inspiration and makes the hard work worthwhile. The best thing about being an author is being at home with you Erin. Love you always.

About Us

In addition to No Exit Press, Oldcastle Books has a number of
other imprints, including Kamera Books, Creative Essentials,
Pulp! The Classics, Pocket Essentials and High Stakes Publishing >
oldcastlebooks.co.uk

For more information about Crime Books go to
> crimetime.co.uk

Check out the kamera film salon for independent, arthouse and
world cinema > kamera.co.uk

For more information, media enquiries and review copies please
contact marketing > marketing@oldcastlebooks.co.uk